WEAVER'S FOLLY

WEAVER'S FOLLY

THE SHADOWSPINNER CHRONICLES BOOK ONE

SARAH MADSEN

Charlotte, NC

FALSTAFF
BOOKS

WWW.FALSTAFFBOOKS.COM

For Logan

I pocketed my keys as I walked up the sidewalk to Manny's Pub, my boot heels clacking against the pavement. A cold breeze ruffled my hair and wound its frigid fingers under the collar of my leather coat, and I glanced over my shoulder at the city street as a shiver skated across my skin. Nothing was there, of course—only the usual pedestrians heading to and from dinner or work, and a few electric cars idling at the red light—but a little healthy paranoia never hurt anyone.

Inside the pub, the scent of exhaust, ozone, and wet asphalt gave way to the aroma of roasted meat and lingering wood smoke, with an undercurrent of good beer. My shoulders relaxed as the warmth wrapped around me. Manny's Pub always made me feel like I'd stepped into some sort of fantasy novel or really expensive medieval reenactment. Shadows hugged the corners, heavy, high-backed wooden benches lined booths along the walls, and a fire flickered in a large hearth at the far end of the room. The illusion was spoiled, though, by the hum of the city outside and the pair of retropunks whispering to each other as I passed their table.

Jeremiah sat in the darkest booth at the back of the pub, strategically tucked in the corner so he had a view of the entire room. He saw me coming and smiled, raising his glass in my direction. A few unruly curls of dark hair peeked from beneath the hood of a navy blue sweatshirt with a Miskatonic University logo emblazoned on it. I recognized the shirt. Jeremiah was a good customer of mine, and what he didn't purchase from me honestly I gave him as payment for…favors rendered.

I pulled the most recent gift from the breast pocket of my jacket, slid into the empty bench in his booth, and tossed the slender bottle to him. He tilted it in the dim light to read the label, making an approving sound.

"Gold Reserve. Nice," he said in a deep voice, then regarded me over his wire-rimmed glasses, tucking the bottle away in the pocket of his hoodie. "You must have something special for me tonight. You only bring out the good stuff for the important ones."

I reached into my back pocket and pulled out a small paper the size of an old-fashioned credit card. "I had an offer come in today that sent up some red flags. I was wondering if you could give me any insight into this one."

"The job sound too good to be true?"

"See for yourself," I said, laying the paper on the table in front of him.

He rubbed his hands together in anticipation, then reached out and took the paper. A small smile pulled at his lips. "Still making them write it all out by hand?"

"Only the ones I don't like." I grinned back, but the smile slid off my face a moment later. "The suit who gave me the details showed up *in my shop* and asked for Lysistrata."

He raised his eyebrows at that. "How'd he know where to find you?"

"No idea, but I'll be looking into it. *Mr. Steven Reed,*" I said the name slowly, my tone emphasizing my doubt that the name was genuine, "seems like he's new at this. He wanted my Neurocomm number."

Jeremiah snorted, then scanned the tight scrawl on the paper and made a surprised sound low in his throat. "That's a nice little sum."

"Yeah." I leaned back in my seat and waved at Manny where he stood behind the bar, getting his attention before signaling for a beer. "The job itself seems simple enough. Break into an office building, steal a statue, start a fire in the office and get the hell out. Easy as heat-and-serve pie."

"But?"

"The deadline." I gestured at the paper in his hand and slouched in my seat. "There's no prep time. I'd basically be going in blind."

"No wonder you don't like the guy." He closed his eyes, the paper held lightly between two fingers, and inhaled deeply. I sat quietly and watched him focus. After a few slow breaths, he shook his head and opened his eyes. A frown pulled at his lips. "Why take the job if it has you concerned?"

"As you said, that's a nice little sum. It could just be that Reed doesn't know the etiquette yet. No point in turning down a perfectly good job because the guy lacks manners." I ran a hand through my hair and sighed. "Besides, I figured you're my best bet to find out if this is going be the run that gets me caught."

"I'll see what I can do for you." He pulled a small tin of dried crushed leaves from his pocket and placed a small line of them on the paper, then rolled the paper around the leaves methodically. "How's the store?"

"Slow," I answered. "No one seems to be in the market for gently used MP3 players and vintage Converse lately."

With an amused grunt, he licked the edge of the paper, pinched off the ends, put the resulting cigarette to his lips, and produced a lighter from the pocket of his hoodie. The lighter sparked to life and he lit the end of the cigarette, inhaling a deep lungful of smoke and leaning back in his seat. I watched silently as he tilted his head back, making smoke rings in the air. After a few more drags, he looked back at me with an unfocused gaze, and the pupils of his brown eyes were white.

A shiver went up my spine. It always creeped me out when he did this.

"You don't get caught." His voice was low and monotonous, the vision unfolding somewhere only he could see. "No, you won't get

3

caught this time. But…things don't go exactly as planned." He laughed once, loudly, startling me before taking another pull of his cigarette. "Oh, no, they don't go as planned at all. And, man, are you gonna be *pissed*."

He laughed again and I fought not to sigh in exasperation. Jeremiah was clairvoyant. He could see visions and read people's intentions by coming into contact with them—or with something they'd touched. I hadn't made this *Mr. Reed* write out the run details on a tiny sheet of cigarette paper because I was spiteful—though the sight of the smooth businessman grumbling as he hunched over my desk had been amusing—it was the easiest way for Jer to get a solid read on the situation without me delivering Reed himself.

Jeremiah took several more drags, and when he was almost to the end of the cigarette, his expression changed. All the amusement drained away, and his eyebrows pulled together in a mix of confusion and concern. "This job will open a door. One that should remain closed, one that…" he trailed off, shuddering as the last puff of smoke curled from the tip of the cigarette. The red glow reflected off his glasses, making his eyes look like smoldering coals in the shadows of his hoodie.

Then the ember on the end of the cigarette went out, and when he looked up at me, his eyes were normal again.

I gave him a moment to come down from the vision, my foot bouncing impatiently. "So? What sort of door will this job open?"

He furrowed his eyebrows again, stubbing out the already extinguished cigarette in the ashtray by his elbow. "I don't know. The—" He stopped as Manny stepped up to the table with a frosted mug of brown ale.

"Here you go, Alyssa." Manny placed the beer in front of me, then wiped his hands on the rag that hung from his waist. "You two aren't getting into any trouble, are you?"

"Oh, you know." I grinned. "Nothing out of the ordinary."

He laughed. "Just watch what you say," he added in a quiet voice. "You've got an audience." He tilted his head toward the retropunks across the room.

I glanced at them over my shoulder, taking quick stock of their appearance. They both wore the tight, bright clothing classic to their subculture: the girl sported various shades of green and blue, and the guy's bright yellow jeans matched the leather tie in his hair. His long magenta ponytail showed off the pointed tips of his ears—a little too short and angular, obviously implants. He needed a better mod surgeon. They both cast furtive glances in my direction and murmured to each other.

I sighed heavily. "I wouldn't worry about them." When Manny raised his eyebrows at me, I waved a dismissive hand. "It's the ears." Probably wondering who *my* mod surgeon was.

He nodded and looked at Jeremiah. "Anything else for you?"

Jeremiah shook his head and Manny headed back to his spot behind the bar. I watched him go, taking a long, appreciative sip of my beer.

"So, why am I going to be pissed?" I asked.

"Oh no, sweetheart, you'll have to find *that* one out on your own." A shadow of his earlier amusement flickered across his face, quickly replaced by a frown. He picked up his glass, studied the dregs of his drink, and set it back down on the table before pulling the small bottle of whiskey from his sweatshirt pocket.

"Thanks a lot, Jer," I sighed.

"You gonna take the job?" The cap to the whiskey bottle popped open with a twist, and he took a long swig.

"Did you see me blown up or arrested?"

"No, but…"

"*No but* nothing, Jeremiah. I need this job. If I don't do something soon, I won't make rent." The beer was suddenly bitter, and I set it aside.

"Rose can't cover you this month?"

"Rose has her own payments to worry about. I'm not going to ask her to carry me again." As my best friend and fellow runner, she would probably smack me on the back of the head for not coming to her if this job got me in trouble, but according to Jeremiah it wouldn't.

I slid out of the booth, pulling my keys from my pocket.

"I dunno, Lys," he grumbled. "I have a bad feeling about this one."

"Well, when 'bad feeling' turns into 'bad premonition,' call me. Otherwise, I've got some work to do, and not a lot of time to do it." I rubbed the bridge of my nose. This was going to be a tight one, but if Jer wasn't prophesying doom, I had to at least try.

"Call you? You still tech free?"

I nodded, and he chuckled.

"That's my good little greeny. All organic, huh?"

"You know that's not why, Jer," I gave him a look, and he regarded me silently, his face sobering.

"Yeah, I know."

"I'll see you around." I turned and made my way across the bar. On impulse, I stopped at the retropunks' booth and grinned down at them. They both stared at me, the guy, at least, having the grace to blush as he realized they'd been caught eyeing me up.

"They're real," I whispered. Then, with a wink, I walked out of the bar.

I had just finished changing when the door to my apartment slammed shut. A moment later, I heard the *thud* of a duffel bag hitting linoleum.

"Alyssa?" Rose's voice echoed in from the kitchen. "You home?"

"In here," I called back, slipping my leather jacket on over my matching leather pants and black tee. I slid my pistol into the holster at the small of my back, glanced once at myself in the mirror to make sure I wouldn't accidentally flash it at a stop light, then tucked my black knit hat into my belt and headed out to the living room.

Rose stood at the counter, popping an instant coffee pod into the machine, still in her rumpled paramedic uniform. She looked me over and raised an eyebrow before hitting the "brew" button. "You got a run?"

"If you can call it that." I grabbed my phone off the coffee table and zipped it into a jacket pocket.

"What do *you* call it?"

I sat on the arm of the couch and pulled on my soft-soled boots as the scent of coffee filled the small apartment. "A client who is ignorant, inconsiderate, or wants me dead." I kept my voice light, and tempered the comment with a smile. A dagger went into the sheath in my left boot, and I wiggled my foot to make sure it was comfortable.

She paused with her mug halfway to her mouth, blinking. "*...what?*"

"I was offered the job today. I need to complete it tonight." Peering past her to the coffee, I added, "Make me a cup, will you?"

She pulled the spent pod from the maker and popped in a fresh one. "The job needs to be done *tonight?*"

"Yup."

She watched the mug fill. "Yeah. 'Inconsiderate' at best. Any other reasons to be worried?"

I shook my head. "Honestly, I think it's 'ignorant.' He seemed new at this. And the pay makes up for the short notice. I've got all the blueprints and everything already, though, thanks to the permit office's crappy website security. Besides," I said as she continued to look dubious, "I went to Jeremiah. He said I won't get caught. Or killed." I added as she opened her mouth to argue. I conveniently left out the part about the job "opening a door."

"You want my help?"

I paused and considered, but shook my head. "No. With so little time to plan, it'll be easiest if I don't have anyone else to worry about."

"You know I can handle myself, Lys." She handed me the mug of coffee and I cringed at the hint of hurt in her voice. Rose was a top-notch runner, but she had a tendency to use a lot of tech in her work, even for a human. Tech and I didn't get along very well. If worse came to worse, I'd have to choose whether to use my full arsenal of abilities and risk harming her, or chance getting caught or killed.

"I know you can, and you know why it would be easier for me to go solo."

She studied me for a long moment and I could see her deciding on whether or not to argue. Then she sighed and lowered herself onto

7

the couch. "Yeah, it's probably for the best anyway. I'm *exhausted*." She pulled the band from her hair. It tumbled around her shoulders in brown and pink waves.

"Rough day at work?" I sipped my coffee. *Mmm, vanilla.*

She grunted in response, stretching her back.

"That bad?"

"We didn't lose anyone," she shrugged. "Could have been worse. We *did* hire a new tech, thank God, so I have the next few days off."

I nodded.

She chewed on her lip as I pulled my bright-red hair into a tight bun at the back of my head. "You sure about this?" she asked.

"Oh my god, you and Jeremiah need to get over it. It's just a simple run."

There was silence from the armchair, and I realized what I'd said. *Crap.*

"You told me he said you won't get caught." Her voice turned from anxious to accusatory, and I could tell she was ready to argue this time.

"He did. He's just worried about future consequences of *something something something*." I waved a hand in the air. "You know how seers can be."

"Yes, but I thought you'd have sense enough to listen to one."

"You ever heard of self-fulfilling prophecies? Sometimes actively working to change your future is what propels you straight into it. Do you really want me to be that girl?"

"Lys—"

"Look, it's fine, okay?" I downed the rest of my coffee, put the mug in the sink, and crossed the room to where she sat. "If I thought it would be a problem, I wouldn't go." I bent down, kissed the top of her head, and walked to the front door, grabbing my keys from the counter as I went. "I'll let you know as soon as I'm done, promise."

She opened her mouth again, but I shut the door on her protests.

Even though it was after two in the morning, the streets in the Fifth District were still crawling with people. Clumps of partiers huddled together for warmth in their impractical club wear, the denim and bright colors of the retropunks clashing with the black and white vinyl and glowing EL wire of the Neos. Once out of the Fifth District and into the business areas north of the city, the streets quieted.

By the time I neared my target, the roads were all but empty, save for me and a lone car of teenagers looking for a quiet place to get stoned. The driver and I regarded each other through his window, and I could see myself reflected in the glass, a figure in black with features hidden by a helmet with a full visor. Then he turned down a side street between the office buildings of the business park, heading in the opposite direction. Neither of us were looking for company tonight.

The low speed limit made it easy for me to make a slow pass of my building without looking overly conspicuous. The building itself was a typical older brick building—square, symmetrical, and utilitarian—set back from the road, with a small parking lot in front and a larger one out back. Both lots sat empty, and the windows were dark, aside from the dim security lights inside. Only one obvious camera aimed at the entrance. A tall fence enclosed the three-story building, with another camera at the gate next to an RFID tag reader. I passed the building, made a quick U-turn several parking lots down, and went by it again. My second pass yielded nothing new, so I pulled into the parking lot of the building next door, parked my bike behind their dumpster, and removed my helmet. I adjusted the edges of my knit hat, making sure no stray pieces of hair had pulled free. My extreme shade of red wasn't too unusual, thanks to the retropunks' and elf poseurs' love of hair dye, but the hat also hid my pointed ears. I wanted to cut down on as many descriptors as possible.

I approached the fence at the back corner, away from any security cameras and the view of the road. Made of black wrought iron, the bars were set too close together for me to fit through and too tall for the average person to reach the top.

Good thing I wasn't the average person.

A tree grew from the soft grass on my side of the fence, its branches carefully trimmed so none hung within reach to give any would-be thieves an easy entrance. I smiled to myself. Perfect.

I backed up several paces from the fence, eyeing up my trajectory, and crouched low. In a burst of movement, I surged forward and, seconds before I slammed into the iron bars, I leapt, my foot hitting with a muffled clang. With several quick jumps, my momentum took me up the space between the tree and the fence before I caught the top with my gloved hands, pushed my weight up and over, and hovered in a brief handstand before shifting and continuing to the other side.

My feet hit the pavement with a soft thud, knees bending to absorb the impact. I froze, listening, but no alarms wailed. One obstacle down, who knows how many to go.

A quick sprint got me to the side of the building, and I hugged the shadows along the wall as I approached the back service entrance. As expected, there was yet another security camera aimed at this door. The camera would have a little LED that would either be glowing or blinking to show that it was on and actively recording.

The LED was dark.

Puzzled, I approached cautiously, making a wide path around the camera just in case it *was* on and the light was just not working. But as I got close to the camera and listened, I knew it was off. There was no telltale high-pitched whine, no hum of electricity. The wires were still connected, everything looked fine.

The camera was just…off.

My skin prickled with unease, but I approached the door and sized up the key card lock.

It was disengaged.

I hesitated. This wasn't right. Some companies would install fancy security cameras for insurance purposes and then never use them, but there was no reason to leave the doors unlocked after hours. I had to be missing something. Maybe there was still an employee here? It was after two in the morning, though, and all the lights in the building were off. If anyone was working overtime, the hall lights would at least be on.

I reached out and pulled on the handle. The door opened easily.

No alarms blared. I stood, racking my brain for the obvious answer I was missing, but it swam just out of grasp.

Jeremiah said I wouldn't get caught.

The thought emboldened me, and I took the first step into the building. I eased the door shut behind me and made my way down the hallway, pausing occasionally to listen for any other signs of activity. All was quiet except for the sound of my breathing and the soft hush of my boots on the bland carpeting.

The sterile smell of industrial-strength disinfectant and lemon air freshener tickled my nose as I made my way to the staircase. The office I was looking for was on the top floor.

I emerged into the carpeted hallway on the third floor. The hallway and offices on either side were all dark. Four other doorways flanked the corridor between me and my target at the end of the hall.

My senses on alert, I crouched low and ran quietly to my goal.

The office door stood open.

What the—

The answer clicked into place, and I straightened up out of my crouch. Stepping into the office, I crossed my arms over my chest and looked at the other runner standing in front of the display case. He had his back to me and seemed so far unaware of my presence, focused on his work.

"What the hell do you think you're doing?"

2

The runner froze, then slowly turned toward me. I could tell by the build that he was a man, although slender, wide in the shoulders but thin at the waist. He was dressed much the same way I was—black hat, black jacket, black pants with lots of pockets, black boots—though his clothes tended toward a thick utility fabric rather than leather. His eyes were wide, though he visibly relaxed when he saw that I was another thief and not some security guard or hapless employee.

He gave me a once-over and then turned back to the case.

"What does it look like I'm doing?"

I bared my teeth at his back. "It *looks* like you're in my way."

"Oh, I don't think so. I got here first, babe."

"Excuse me?"

"You heard me. Took your time getting in here, didn't you? And I even left the door open." He *tsked*, fiddling with the lock on the display case. I stepped up to his side and glanced down at it. It was a classic key lock, and seemed far too simple for a case like this, unless the owner really didn't care about the net worth of the contents.

The statue I needed to steal stood about two feet tall, made of white marble. The shape itself was some abstract thing, all twisting forms, looking like a person or a tree or who-knows-what depending on how you wanted to interpret it. I wrinkled my nose, and looked back down at the runner's attempts to pick the lock.

"Not used to classic locks, huh?" I sniped. "You want me to help you out with that, or should I just wait 'til you give up?"

He cast a scathing look in my direction and, after a few more seconds of trying feebly to pick the lock, dropped his hands to his sides with a sigh. Then he pulled a gloved fist back, aimed toward the cabinet door.

"No, don't—"

He smashed his fist through the glass, grabbing the statue and pulling it free of the shards still hanging from the top of the door. I heard a soft click, and cursed.

"You stupid *glitch*. You just set off a silent alarm!"

He shrugged, looking unconcerned, and hefted the statue in his hands. "No problem, babe. I'll be gone before security can get here. Will you?"

Jeremiah said I wouldn't get caught.

He took a few slow steps backwards toward the door, the statue in his left hand. He lifted his right hand in a wave, a push-button detonator held in his fingers. With an apologetic smile, he put his thumb down on the switch.

Son of a—

The file cabinet next to the desk burst into flames, and I jumped, startled. A trail of fire circled the perimeter of the room, and I glanced back to the doorway to see the runner's back disappearing into the darkness.

"Damn it!" I ran toward the door, hesitating as the trail of flame continued its course and cut off my exit. With a deep breath, I took two big steps and jumped the fire, landing in a rolling crouch on the carpeting of the hallway. I sprang to my feet and reached the stairwell door just as it slammed shut.

I wrenched it open and paused at the landing. My competition's footsteps headed *up* instead of down. Grasping the railing with my right hand, I yanked myself into motion around the curve of the stairs and raced upwards.

His rubber-soled boots pounded on the steps, echoing through the stairwell in sharp contrast to my quiet, soft soles. Their tone changed as he pushed open the door at the top and went from the tile of the stairs to the gravel of the roof. The door slammed shut as I reached it, and this time I kicked it open and tucked into a roll. His fist cut through the air where my chest should have been and my foot flashed out, sweeping his legs out from under him. He yelped in surprise and landed hard on his back, his arms wrapping the statue tight against his chest to protect it.

"Hey! What the hell are you trying to do, break the prize? Take it easy there, babe."

I stood and reached under my jacket to pull out my gun in one fluid motion. Standing with my feet apart, I leveled the barrel at his chest with both hands. "Give me the statue. And don't call me 'babe.'"

"Okay, okay, relax b—I mean, relax, okay?" He held one hand up in front of him harmlessly while the other still gripped the statue, then he placed his empty hand on the ground and pushed himself slowly to his feet. I kept the pistol trained on his chest and switched the gun from a two-handed grip to my right hand, holding my left hand out for the statue. He held it out for me, his turquoise eyes on mine. Just as my fingers touched the cool marble, there was a flash of victory in his eyes, and he dropped the statue.

I lunged for it, knowing as I did that it was exactly what he wanted me to do. As I reached forward and grabbed the statue, he grabbed my right wrist, pulling my arm and gun past him and rendering both useless. In the same swift motion he pulled me tight against him, pinning the statue between us, and pressed something with two sharp points against the small of my back, under the edge of my jacket.

"Sorry," he whispered, his breath hot against my ear.

My body spasmed, every muscle contracting violently as he pulled the trigger on the taser against my spine. My teeth clenched together and I struggled to move, breathe, *anything*, but the wave of electricity pulsing through my body kept me rigid. The gun slipped from my fingers and clattered to the rooftop.

Then the pain stopped and the sudden cessation was almost as painful as the shock itself. He stepped back, releasing me and scooping the statue from my hand before I could drop it. My knees gave out and I gasped violently. I managed not to fall on my face, but my palms hit the gravel rooftop hard enough to bruise.

Paralyzed, I retaught my body how to breathe. I took several ragged breaths, vaguely aware of him picking up my gun before his footsteps retreated quickly across the roof.

He disappeared over the ledge as I staggered to my feet and lurched after him, stumbling to my knees at the edge of the roof in time to see his feet touch the ground three stories below me. A small grappling hook I hadn't noticed released itself from the wall next to me and retracted back into his belt. He hefted the statue in one hand, winked at me, and took off across the parking lot.

I fumbled with my own hook, about to go after him, when blue lights flashed in the distance. If I followed him, I would be heading in the opposite direction of my bike and my escape. I would most likely be left running from the authorities on foot while he took off in whatever vehicle he had, not to mention that the cops would most likely find and impound my bike. Uttering a string of profanities, I turned and ran to the back corner of the building, pulling my hook free from my belt and rappelling down to the pavement below.

My feet hit the asphalt hard, jarring my teeth, and I tasted blood. The blue lights bounced off the buildings out of the corner of my eye as the sirens got closer. I took aim at the tree as I ran, shooting the hook over the top of the fence, the rope pulling taught as it caught on one of the branches. I used it to pull myself up and over the fence, and ducked behind the tree just as the cop car reached the building, its headlights making stark shadows leap into existence and fall again as the light passed.

A searchlight on the side of the car flipped on and moved across the front of the building. I needed get to my bike without getting caught. I could probably make it if I timed it right and kept to the shadows, but my knees still shook from the taser shock. If I tripped, I was done.

Time to use my secret weapon.

I closed my eyes, took a deep breath, and reached out with my senses. There, hovering like a thousand-thousand glowing silver threads of gossamer, were the strands of creation and possibility. Magic.

The Eldergloom.

This was the reason I didn't have a Neurocomm, why I avoided tech and didn't want Rose with me on this run.

I reached out with my mind and tugged on one of those threads. A warm breeze that had nothing to do with the weather tickled across my skin, bringing with it the soft scent of freshly turned earth, of honeyed milk and jasmine, of petrichor. I spun the thread into shadow and wrapped the it around myself like a blanket. When the last of the magic settled around my shoulders, I opened my eyes and knew I'd be invisible to anyone whose gaze might pass over me.

Hey, being an elf has its perks.

I walked calmly from my hiding spot, confident I was well and truly hidden. I let the Eldergloom dissipate once I was behind the building next door, my fingers going from semi-transparent to solid as they wrapped around the handles of my bike. I popped open a covered panel and flipped a switch. The engine turned over without its typical growl, and I shoved my helmet on and revved the bike silently. Thank God for electric engines.

I drove slowly, headlight off, and made my way through the maze of small access roads until I was far enough away from the crime scene as to not accidentally run into a cop. I pulled out onto a main road and picked up speed, making my way to the highway as quickly as possible.

That stupid son of a glitch! What the hell just happened? Why was another runner there? Someone else could have had hired him to steal it, but little details nagged at me. That fire he'd set in the office, it was exactly what I would have done. Exactly what I'd been *hired* to do. Almost as if he…

Cursing, I pushed a small button on my handle bar and listened through the wireless headset in my helmet as the line rang.

After a few rings, a groggy voice answered.

"Yes?"

"You have a hell of a lot of explaining to do, Mr. Reed," I growled.

"Ms. Lysistrata, is that you?" He sounded suddenly much more awake and interested. "Am I to assume that you were *not* the one who acquired the statue?" When I didn't reply, he went on. "That's rather surprising. I'd heard such good things about you. Oh well, it doesn't matter. If Grendel was the one who won this little competition, he's the one we want."

"*Competition?*" My voice was indignant. "What *competition*, Mr. Reed? There was no mention of this in the details I was given."

"No, of course not." His smooth voice was polite and matter of fact. "Why would we inform you of it? We wanted to gauge your abilities as a runner, especially in unexpected circumstances. Telling you about this would only have poisoned the results."

I clenched my teeth together to keep from cursing again. "Well, I hope you got the results you wanted, Mr. Reed, because I will never work for you or your *employer* again. Have a good night."

I hung up and let loose another string of profanity.

Well, now I knew what Jeremiah meant when he said I'd be pissed. I was definitely going to pay *him* a little visit tomorrow night. A beer on his tab wouldn't make up for this, but it would be a good start… since I failed at obtaining the statue, I wouldn't get paid. *Grendel* got the prize, so he got the check.

I should have listened to Rose and just stayed home.

After I parked my bike in the parking deck of my apartment building, I took the stairs to my floor, too full of pent-up anger to wait for the elevator. I took the steps two at a time, pushing myself to keep up a fast pace, panting with exertion by the time I reached my apartment on the ninth floor.

Rose was curled up on the couch with an eReader and raised her head when I stormed in. I shut the door behind me and dropped my helmet in the corner, breathing heavily.

"Are you okay?" She got quickly to her feet and started looking me over for injuries.

I shrugged her off, pulling my boots off my feet. "I'm fine. I just took the stairs."

"The stairs?" She stepped back and regarded me. "Elevator not working?"

"I don't know. I didn't have the patience to wait for it."

She crossed her arms over her chest and frowned. "Guess the run didn't go well."

I gave her a scathing look, but she just regarded me mildly, one eyebrow raised. "You could say that. Apparently it was some sort of contest between me and another runner. Only I had no idea." I clenched my hands into fists, looking for something to hit but seeing nothing in the kitchen that would be satisfying enough to break—or that Rose wouldn't kill me for breaking. "You ever heard of a runner called Grendel?"

Her eyebrows pinched together. "Grendel? No...doesn't sound familiar. Was he your competition?"

"Yeah," I muttered, and stripped my clothes off layer by layer as I walked to my room. I pulled the lock pick set out of my coat pocket before throwing my jacket across the back of the armchair, and unsnapping the empty holster from inside my pants.

"Where's your gun?"

"*Grendel* took it." My voice was full of venom.

"I'll ask around this week, see if any of my contacts have heard of him." She followed me and stood in the door to my room as I pulled the rest of my equipment from my body and threw everything back in my trunk.

"Don't bother," I said grumpily. "It's over." I shoved the chest back into my closet and threw the pile of clothes on top of it again.

"He at least owes you a gun, Lys."

"Really. It's fine. I'll just get another one. It's not like I have another run any time soon, so I shouldn't need it for a while." Crap, how the hell was I going to make rent this month? "Besides, I don't know anything about him. How would I know any gun he gave me wasn't rigged or stolen?"

"Good point."

I turned away from her and pulled off my shirt, glancing around for my pajamas. She took a sharp breath.

"Oh, Lys, what happened?"

"Huh?" I replied, confused. She took a few steps into my room and gently touched the small of my back. I hissed in pain and she jerked her fingers away.

"Sorry."

I stepped to my mirror, facing away from it and looking over my shoulder.

On the small of my back were two round burn marks, about an inch apart, each about the size of a dime. They were red and angry looking, and I could see blisters forming already.

"He *tazed* me," I said through clenched teeth. The burns hadn't hurt until I noticed them, and now it felt like they were on fire. "Son of a—"

"I'll get something for that. Hang on." She walked out of the room to rummage around in the kitchen.

I carefully slipped out of my leather work pants and into a pair of cotton pajama bottoms that hung low on my hips. Coupled with a sports bra instead of my normal night shirt, they minimized the chance of accidentally brushing the burns in my sleep.

Rose walked back in with a box of second skin, some disinfectant wipes, and a snap-activated ice pack. "Lie down."

The sheets felt smooth and cool against the bare skin of my stomach. Cellophane crinkled, and I hissed again at the sting of disinfectant. Then, setting the wipes aside, Rose carefully laid the second skin on top of the burns. Tension fled from my shoulders as the cool, moist bandage helped relieve some of the pain.

"Thanks." I smiled at her.

"No problem." She twisted the ice pack in her hand until there was a soft crack, then she shook it and laid it gently on top of the second skin. "Go to sleep. I'll come back in and take the ice pack off it in about twenty."

"M'kay." I snuggled deeper into my pillow.

She picked up the scraps of wrapper and the wipes and walked out of my door, flipping the light off as she went and pulling my door halfway shut behind her. The lights in the kitchen went off, but I could see the soft glow from the living room lamp. The couch cushions sighed as Rose settled back into her place.

The adrenaline from the night finally washed away, leaving exhaustion in its wake. My body suddenly felt heavy and my eyelids drifted shut as I tried not to think about the night's events—I had all day tomorrow to be pissed. Instead, images of all the things I would do to Grendel if I saw him again danced through my head as sleep rose up to claim me.

I had surprisingly pleasant dreams.

3

The sound of Rose moving around the kitchen woke me. We ate our bowls of cereal in silence and spent the day binge-watching shows from the couches, too exhausted to do much else.

We were halfway through a dinner of delivery pizza when a soft chime echoed from my room. I raised my head from the plate balanced on my knees, listening. The chime sounded again, similar in tone to a Tibetan singing bowl being struck by a cotton mallet. I set my plate aside and stood, wiping the crumbs from my fingers as I walked to my room.

A shallow silver bowl sat on my dresser between two candle stubs. I tugged on the Eldergloom just enough to set a spark to the wicks, and the candles flared to life. My reflection stared back at me from the surface of the water, then I waved a hand over the dish, and the image wavered as if touched.

When the water stilled, a new face stared up at me. It was another elf, with moss-colored hair pulled back in intricate braids and a simple diadem at her brow.

"Lorelei," I said with a smile. "*Am'fialte.*"

"*Am'fialte,* Alyssa." Her voice was high and light, and she returned my smile with one of her own, the corners of her eyes crinkling. "How does the evening find you?"

"I spent the day in my pajamas, so can't complain." I laughed softly, pushing away any lingering annoyance at the night before. I could talk to Lorelei about it, but now wasn't the time. Besides, if she was calling me, it was for some reason other than a friendly chat. "What's up?"

"I was curious if you could make a short visit to Arcadia. I have something I need to discuss with you."

My smile faltered.

"Nothing too urgent, but probably something you should hear sooner rather than later."

"Sure," I said. "I can come now, actually."

She visibly relaxed, her shoulders slumping. "As long as you're not busy. Don't let this pull you away from anything important."

"I think Rose can handle the rest of the pizza without me."

"Very well. I shall see you when you arrive."

I nodded in agreement, then waved a hand above the dish. Her image wavered and disappeared, her emerald eyes fading into the reflection of my gold ones.

I dressed hurriedly, throwing a pair of high-heeled boots on over jeans and a black sweater.

"I'm going out, Rose," I said as I walked out of my room.

"But we're almost done with season five!"

"I know. I'm sorry. Go ahead and watch it without me if you want. I need to go to Arcadia." I gathered my things and threw on my jacket.

She sat up straight. "Everything okay?"

"Lorelei needs to talk to me about something. Maybe I accidentally pissed off the Order or something." The Order of the White Hart was the ruling council of elves, and if you stepped on their toes, they were quick to get grouchy. I'd been keeping clear of them, but if I wasn't in trouble, I had no idea why Lorelei would summon me like this. Her tone had been rather dire, no matter how she'd tried to hide it behind a smile.

"Well, just don't get grounded. We need to have drinks before I get stuck at the hospital for another month of shifts."

"I'll do my best," I answered with a laugh, and stepped out of our apartment.

I loved the city at night, especially later when most people were in their beds. The quiet streets and bright lights against the dark sky were calming, a sharp contrast to the bright shiny crowds that dominated the city during the day. Despite my growing concern over Lorelei's call, I made a large circuit through the Fifth District, cutting back and forth under the highways.

Much of the Fifth District was dotted with parks, but there was a higher concentration of them toward the west side. You couldn't go two blocks without coming across one, and they were large, with wide open spaces of green and small clusters of trees. Nestled against the southeast corner of the biggest of these parks was The Grove, an old stone building with wide arched doorways and large, deep-set windows.

I parked my bike in one of the small spots reserved for motorcycles, pulled off my helmet, and shook out my hair as I made my way to the front. "The Grove" was written in green flowing lettering above the door. I hefted my helmet in one hand and pushed the door open with the other.

Inside, the coffeehouse was dimly lit, and the smell of espresso warmed me to my toes. Apparently, it was open mic night. A cluster of people sat around a small stage in the far corner around a man with an acoustic guitar singing soulfully into an old-fashioned microphone. I counted only four sets of human ears...the crowd was mostly elves and elf poseurs. The Grove was fairly well-known as an elven sanctuary, so it drew in groupies who wanted to come and ogle us. A few heads turned in my direction and eyed me as I applauded with the rest, but I continued toward the back before they could do much more than look.

The back half of the coffeehouse was divided into smaller sections with couches, tables, and small cushioned chairs arranged in more intimate groups. The entryway to this room was a large stone arch, much like every other doorway in the place, but this one had etchings in the stone. A curving, flowing script was carved above the entry, and gleamed in the dim light as if inlaid with silver.

It said "Speak Friend and Enter" in Elvish script. Thanks to a famous writer from the mid-1900s almost everyone knew the answer to this riddle, but like most works of fiction there were only a few grains of truth hidden among the misinformation. He got this part right, but he got a lot more wrong, including that whole immortality thing. A long-lived elf might see three centuries, but that was rare. He also completely glitched up our language, but even if he *had* gotten it right, the password only allowed you entry if you were of actual Elven blood. Anyone else who tried to pass through this doorway would find themselves in the back room of the coffeehouse and nothing more. Most humans didn't even give it a second glance, thinking it purely decorative.

I stepped to the edge of the archway and muttered *"a'chara"* low under my breath. The engravings flashed silver, and I glanced sideways at a girl with short dark hair and modded ears who was watching me, giving her a wink as I stepped through the doorway. I had a brief second of seeing her eyes widen in shock as I disappeared, and then I was in Arcadia, the home of my people.

Overhead, the half-moon shone brightly, the myriad of stars scattered across the sky like a shimmering dust. The night air was cool on my face. I took a deep breath and inhaled the scent of fresh earth and greenery, and the tension instantly seeped out of me. There were no city sounds here, no constant buzz of electronics, no distant hum of cars on the street. There were only crickets and night birds, the sound of a brook, and voices pitched low in quiet conversation.

Old trees that had never been cut with a blade or touched by human hands towered over the clearing. Within their branches sat buildings, woven out of the very wood itself, each branch slowly and gently coaxed to grow into intricate patterns of floors or walls or rooftops. The white wood glowed in the moonlight, each green leaf dark in the shadows. More buildings nestled at the base of the trees, built and carved from stone and dead-fall collected from the forest.

Behind me stood a stone arch, identical to the one I just stepped through, except this one stood on its own without walls or supports, and I could see the coffeehouse through it. The young elf poseur stood in front of the arch, peering through with wide eyes, no doubt looking for me. Then she stepped toward me and disappeared from my vision, having passed into the back room of the coffee shop. A moment later the shop disappeared, leaving nothing but night on the other side. The doorway would remain quiet until it was used again.

A woman's voice calling my name got my attention, and I turned to see Lorelei walking toward me. She wore a long flowing gown and soft-soled slippers made of crushed velvet the color of new leaves.

"Am'fialte, Lorelei," I said, stepping up to greet her.

"Am'fialte, Alyssa." She embraced me, placing a soft kiss on each of my cheeks. "I'm glad you could come so soon." She glanced down at my attire, looking askance at the helmet still held in my hand. "Could I get you some more comfortable clothes?"

I smiled again. "No, these are fine. Thanks."

She nodded. "How's Atlanta?"

I shrugged. "Being dragged kicking and screaming into winter. It's putting up a good fight, though."

"I still don't understand how you live there," she said, and nodded in an invitation to walk with her back toward the buildings. "All that metal. The smoke and noise. And the humans...how can you stand to be around such banality?"

"It's not so bad once you're used to it," I said. "And not all humans are so terrible."

She made a noise that said she didn't quite believe me, but didn't argue.

We walked in silence, passing several other elves, some faces familiar and some not, but they all looked me over with interest. Many of my kind still lived in groves such as this, separate from the rest of the world, and some of them did not see modern clothing except once every few decades. There were groves all over the world, pockets of Arcadia that touched the human world but didn't really exist within it. The gates provided easy access but weren't completely necessary. You could be out hiking in a remote part of the Catskill

Mountains, for instance, and accidentally stumble across the borders and find yourself in another land. The distances were different here, too…you could walk through the Atlanta gate, travel an hour by horseback to the Colloquiate, and then step out of Arcadia somewhere in Ireland.

This particular grove was called the Arcanum. It housed the Hall of Relics, a storage facility for all of our artifacts, both ancient and new. It was also a place of peace, of healing, and of learning. All of the arches in the mundane world lead here, and one could then step through other arches into distant parts of Arcadia. Lorelei was the Keeper of Relics, in charge of maintaining the archways, the Halls, and the Acolytes that worked and studied here.

She was also my friend, and was looking at me with a hint of worry in her eyes as we passed through a short hallway and into a garden.

"So, what's this all about?" I asked.

She didn't answer, and I glanced sideways at her to see her deep in thought.

Panic rose in my chest, and I let out a shaky laugh. "You're sort of freaking me out here. What is it? Are my parents okay?"

"Yes, they're fine." She gestured to a stone bench tucked beside a flowering bush, and we sat. She took a deep breath as if to steel herself, then raised her eyes to mine. "Tristan has been here looking for you."

My stomach dropped with the sensation of the earth falling out from beneath me and I froze, unsure if I'd heard her correctly. "…*what?*"

"He was here at the half-moon, asking if anyone had seen you or knew where you were."

The now-full moon shined like a silver disk in the sky. Fifteen days ago, more or less.

"He came through the Chicago doorway. I didn't call you right away because I was unsure if you'd want to know. However, I thought it best to tell you so you could be prepared if he *did* find you."

Something akin to dread settled in my stomach, making it hard to breathe. "What did he want?"

"He didn't say." She shrugged elegantly. "If anyone can guess, it's you."

"How should I know? I haven't seen him in five years."

"Yes, I remember," she mused, her eyes full of pity. "That mess with the human girl."

"You mean *girls*," I said bitterly.

She studied me for a long moment. "Indeed."

Why was Tristan looking for me? It had been years since I'd walked out on him. His infidelity on its own wouldn't have been a deal-breaker—elves aren't strictly monogamous by habit—but a girl can only handle so many broken promises. If he'd been open and honest with me, it might have been a different story...but he hadn't.

Old doubts and insecurities began to resurface at the idea of having to face him now, memories of me grasping for something solid to believe in as everything I'd trusted turned out to be false. Panic spread through my chest and I gasped as it squeezed my ribs and made it hard to breathe.

Lorelei took my hand in hers and I held on tight. "Now you see why I wished to tell you in person."

I nodded.

"Do you need some time alone, or do you wish me to stay?"

"I..." I struggled to speak past the drowning sensation. "I think I need to take a walk."

"Of course. I'll be waiting here when you're done."

I nodded again, and she squeezed my hands reassuringly before letting me go. I walked through one of the larger stone buildings, half in a daze, and stopped at the back door. A wooden shelf stood beside the doorway. Folded pieces of heavy fabric were stacked on the shelf and I grabbed one before stepping out into the moonlight.

Taking slow, deliberate breaths, I walked across the soft green grass in my wildly inappropriate high-heeled boots, following the sound of running water. Down a small hill a stream came into view, large but not quite big enough to be called a river. It ran deep, though, and its dark waters bubbled over rocks hidden below the surface, almost singing. I rounded a stand of trees and came upon the bathing pool.

The pool was almost a perfect circle, naturally formed from the rock of the stream bed. Its surface shone smooth and silver in the moonlight, rippling only slightly as the stream emptied into it by way of a small waterfall. I smiled and put my helmet on the ground, sitting on a large stone to remove my boots and socks. Standing in the cool grass in my bare feet, I flexed my toes, feeling each blade under my soles. The rest of my clothes quickly followed my boots in a heap in the grass, and I slipped into the water.

Goosebumps prickled up my legs and across my arms, and I dove all the way under the surface in one swift motion. I came up dripping and lay on my back in the cool water, my hair spreading out behind me in a scarlet fan. The moon hovered above, and I let myself float, staring up at the stars.

Panic began to overtake me again, but I took several deep breaths, pushing all thoughts of Tristan from my mind. I wouldn't fall back into that. Whatever he wanted, he wouldn't get it—and if he did manage to find me I would kick him back out on the street as quickly as he walked in the door. Simple as that. I wouldn't think about it again.

Easy. Right.

I let myself float, drifting in circles around the deep pool, and let my thoughts go. Breathing slowly and deeply, I concentrated on the feel of the water in my hair, the sensation of it flowing between my fingers. The light touch of a breeze on my face, cool where my damp skin broke the surface of the water. The sounds of the night, muffled by the water rushing around my ears. The full, bright moon, framed by the branches of the grove; the black canvas of the sky sprinkled with stars.

Voices and the sound of approaching feet pulled me out of my meditation. Two elves rounded the corner with their own towels in hand. They nodded in greeting when they saw me and began to undress. I held back a sigh of irritation. They had as much a right to the pool as I did, but their presence had shattered the tranquility of the night.

It was just as well. I needed a drink.

Stepping reluctantly from the water, I dried myself with the soft cloth. I squeezed my hair out, toweling it off and then pulling it back in a loose braid that brushed the base of my spine. I realized that my burns hadn't hurt, and put my hand to the small of my back. The bandage was still in place, cool from the water of the pool. Maybe the burns weren't as bad as I'd thought.

I dressed myself in my street clothes, but carried my boots, socks, and helmet in my hands, savoring the sensation of the grass on my feet. I padded back toward the buildings, watching as small lamp lights traveled up and down the stairs woven into the tree trunks, carried by Arcadians going about their business. I hung my damp cloth on a hook by the door and made my way back through the stone building and toward the archway.

Lorelei stood waiting for me. She smiled softly, taking in my damp hair and bare feet, and held out her hands. I leaned toward her and she put her hands on my upper arms, kissing both my cheeks again.

"You sure you don't want to stay, Alyssa? This was your home, once."

"It may be my home again one day, Lorelei, but the time is not right for me." I sat on the grass and slipped my socks and boots back on my feet.

She watched as I finished, and then helped me rise. "I hope that time comes soon. You are missed."

"As are you. Goodbye, Lorelei."

"Farewell, Alyssa. Don't wait so long to return next time."

I smiled, and turned to the arch. Whispering *"a'chara,"* I stepped through the doorway and back into the world of humans.

Stepping back into the coffeehouse was like a slap in the face after the serenity of the grove. The sudden noise, the crowd, even the light seemed harsher here. I tucked my helmet under my arm and began to make my way out of the shop. The short-haired poseur murmured to her friends as I walked by, taking in my now-wet hair with wide eyes, but I avoided their gaze and kept walking.

Once outside, I pulled my helmet on and hopped on my bike, starting it up and merging with traffic, heading to Manny's Pub for a beer—and a well-deserved word with Jeremiah.

4

I parked my bike in my usual spot in the side alley and pulled open the heavy door. I stopped short halfway to Jeremiah's table when I realized he wasn't sitting at his booth. There was no ashtray full of half-smoked butts, no empty glass of whiskey to show that he'd been there at all. The table sat clean and unused.

Frustration furrowed my brow as I turned and walked to the bar. Manny nodded a greeting as I approached. He was in his late forties, but still looked like he could hold his own in a bar fight, with short brown hair that was greying at the sides and a strong square jaw. He wore his typical outfit of black pants and a white shirt, and had a bar towel slung over his shoulder.

"Hey, Manny. Have you seen Jer?"

"Nope, he hasn't been in tonight."

My stomach twisted with unease, but Manny went on.

"He did, however, leave something for you yesterday." He popped open the till, lifted the cash tray, and pulled out a small folded piece of paper. *Alyssa* was written in black ink on the front. "What, are you guys in middle school or something?" Walking back to my side of the bar, he held it out for me, but pulled it away from my fingers when I reached for it. "I'll give it to you, but you better tell me if you just 'like' him or if you 'like like' him."

"Very funny, Manny."

He grinned and held out the paper, and I took it with a shake of my head. I unfolded the note and quickly read it.

Lys,

    Yeah, right. You think I'm crazy enough to hang around while you're still all riled up about last night? I'm psychic, not stupid.

    ~ Jer

I sighed, irritated, and shoved the note in my pocket. Manny leaned on the bar and raised an eyebrow.

"When you see Jeremiah, tell him that I'm sorry but I don't like him like that."

"Poor guy. He'll be heartbroken."

"I'm sure," I snorted.

"Maybe this will help, then. A beer comes with the note. You want it now?"

"Gods, yes." I slid onto a bar stool and watched as he filled a frosted glass. He set the beer in front of me with a smile.

"Bad night?"

"I think 'bad night' might just be the understatement of the century, Manny."

He chuckled. "Well, you…have your health? You *do* have your health, don't you?"

"At the moment." I raised my glass in a cheers motion, then downed half the beer in several gulps. "Let's see what we can do about that, though. Better get another one of these ready. And put it on Jeremiah's tab."

He laughed and poured me another beer.

Manny was easily the best bartender in Atlanta.

T he next day I was at the shop early for a delivery. I crouched behind the counter, unpacking and tagging a box of shoes when the bells on the front door chimed.

"Welcome to D'Yaragen's Imports," I said without looking up. "I'll be with you in just a moment." I affixed the bar code to the last pair of shoes and stood, my gaze meeting a pair of turquoise eyes.

A *very familiar* pair of turquoise eyes.

"*You.*" I didn't try to keep the venom out of my voice as I glared across the counter at Grendel.

He grinned at me, piercings that hadn't been there when I'd last seen him glinting in his lower lip and eyebrow. Earrings adorned his ears—large gauge blue silicon plugs in his lower lobes and silver hoops on the top. Long blond hair trailed down his back, the top dyed dark cobalt blue and cut shorter, sticking out in all directions. A streak of blond peeked out of all that blue and hung in his eyes. He was young, too, probably in his early-twenties.

"What are *you* doing here?" I hissed through my teeth, glancing around to make sure the store was empty of any other customers. He leaned on the counter, his hair falling forward over his shoulder. His shirt was black with a glowing blue design stitched into it, with geometric spirals on his shoulders and lines that followed the seams. I sensed a color scheme in the making.

"I was curious. I wanted to meet the runner who gave me a run for my money the other night." He gave me a once-over, eyebrows rising slightly when he saw my pointed ears.

I crossed my arms and glared down at him. "How did you find me?"

"I told Reed that I wouldn't give him the statue until he gave me your contact information. He said I was to come here and ask for a Ms. Alyssa, and she'd put me in touch with you. I didn't expect to see you here."

It was my turn to raise my eyebrows. "You risked your payoff to get in touch with me?"

He shrugged. "There wasn't much at risk. I had the prize, he wanted it. And he wants me for another run, a bigger one. Couldn't risk losing me over something as small as giving out another runner's info."

My face flushed hot with irritation. "Mr. Reed has a lot to learn about runner etiquette," I grumbled.

"That he does," he chuckled. "But, he pays well, so I can overlook it."

"Yeah, hope you're enjoying that paycheck," I said bitterly. "Now that you've met me, you can leave and let me get back to slaving away at my honest job so I *cannot* make enough to pay rent this month." I turned my back on him and began putting the tagged shoes back in their box.

"Actually, I think I can help with that. The money thing, I mean," he added as turned to stare at him incredulously. "This other run Reed hired me for…I'm going to need help on it, and I've been given the go ahead to bring on other runners if necessary. You want in?"

I stared at him in silence, and he cocked a crooked smile at me. "You don't even *know* me," I said finally. "You trust me to have your back on a run?"

"I saw your work the other night, it was good—even if I was better."

I opened my mouth but he spoke before I could say anything, and I bit my lip against my insult.

"Sorry again about your back. I didn't want to have to do that." He looked apologetic. "Besides that, if you were the other runner Reed hired, I figure you must be good."

I crossed my arms over my chest again. "And *I* should trust *you* on a run because…?"

"Because I'm not like Reed," he said, straightening up with an offended expression. "If you go on a run with me, I make sure you come out. I'm not going to hang you out to dry."

I just stared at him and must have looked unconvinced, because he went on. "You don't have to believe me, but I figured I'd offer you the job. It's the least I could do after the other night. Which reminds me…" He reached under his shirt and pulled out my gun, laying it on the counter. "I figured you'd want that back. Just don't shoot me with it, okay?"

He turned to leave, and I picked up the gun and tucked it in into the waistband of my pants. It dug into my stomach, but it was better than just leaving it under the counter. Just before he reached the door I called to him. "Meet me at Manny's tonight, around ten. We'll discuss the details."

He stopped, then glanced over his shoulder and gave me another crooked smile. "Sure thing."

"You never told me your name."

He turned around a little further, his expression sobering and his eyes lingering on mine. Exchanging real names was a leap of faith, a bigger act of trust than handing me a gun and turning his back. He had the high ground right now...he knew where to find me and what my name was. If he wanted me to do this, *really* do this, he'd give me his name and level the playing field.

Finally, he answered. "Logan Turner."

"I'm Alyssa D'Yaragen. Nice to meet you."

He flashed a smile once more and pulled open the door. "See you tonight."

As soon as he was gone I walked to my office, tossed my gun inside the side desk drawer, and slammed it shut.

One thing was for sure, tonight would be very interesting.

⸺⸺⸺⸺

It was quarter until ten when I walked into Manny's. The bar was only moderately crowded, several patrons sitting at the bar itself, a few groups at tables and booths. It was dim as usual, and I glanced at Jeremiah's table, surprised when I saw him sitting in his usual spot under a cloud of smoke. I raised my eyebrows at him, and he took a drag from his cigarette and grinned as I walked toward him.

"I thought you were psychic, not stupid." My helmet clattered into the booth seat across from him and I slid in after it.

He exhaled a long cloud of smoke and eyed me over his glasses. "I did not lie. You're much less pissed today. I'm guessing that run opened some doors."

"I thought you said the door should stay shut."

"I said it would open *a* door that should stay shut," he mused, "not that *all* of them should stay shut."

I ground my teeth together and did my best to glare at him. "I've got another job offer."

A low laugh followed the smoke across the table. "I should probably test the details, just to be sure. You got anything for me?"

I shook my head. "Not this time. But someone is meeting me here to discuss it. You could see what you can get from him."

"Sure thing."

I slid out of the seat and picked up my helmet. "Oh, and Jer?" I leaned down, close enough that I could smell the whiskey and smoke on his breath, and spoke quietly. "I'm still pissed. Just how pissed will depend on how this run goes."

"Everyone blames the seer," he sighed, affecting a martyred expression. "You ever heard the phrase 'don't shoot the messenger'?"

"I won't *shoot* you." I said it like a threat, but grinned as I stood up. I took a few steps, slid into the booth in front of him so I could see the door, and waited.

At five minutes after ten, Logan walked in, wearing the same long black shirt with blue lines as earlier, the slightly glowing design standing out even more in the low light of the bar. He had his hands tucked into the pockets of his blue pants, eyes scanning the room leisurely. His gaze finally settled on me and he made his way across the bar to my booth.

I gestured for him to sit as he reached the table, and he slid into the bench across from me. A perky waitress bounced over to our table, her brown curls bobbing, and asked us if we wanted to order anything. I was momentarily taken aback, as the staff tended to ignore me when I came here to see Jeremiah. Logan and I both ordered beers. She bounced off again to give our orders to Manny behind the bar, and I waved my fingers at him as he looked over at our table. He flicked his gaze between me and Logan, raising an eyebrow, and then glanced at Jeremiah and smirked at something the seer did. I rolled my eyes. I didn't even want to know.

"So," I said to Logan. "What's the run?"

"Straight to business, huh?"

"It's why we're here." I spread my hands and then leaned back in my chair.

He regarded me for a long moment, then leaned back, mirroring me. "Okay, then. You know Americorp?"

I blinked. "Americorp? Like, *the* Americorp?"

He nodded, smiling slowly. "Yep. That one."

"Are you serious?" Americorp was one of the biggest corporations in the States. They manufactured everything from toilet paper to tech implants, and had the security to match. They even had their own army of security guards. Getting in—and, more importantly, getting out—of any of their facilities was going to be far from easy. Their main office and factory was in Atlanta, but I couldn't remember what it was this particular facility made.

"I'm totally serious. And so is Reed. This job pays four times as much as the last one."

My eyes widened. *Four times* as much? "What does he want?"

"He—" he broke off as the curly haired waitress returned with our drinks, grinning and making sure we were set before skipping off to her other tables. Logan watched her go appreciatively, and I rolled my eyes.

"Ogle the chicks on your own time, techie."

He smiled sheepishly. "Sorry. He wants a design, or formula, or something." He took a sip of his beer and went on. "I don't know what it is exactly, but it's a data file. Code maybe? I dunno. I have the file name, but it's just a bunch of numbers and letters so it doesn't tell us anything about what's in it. We'd have to hack into their network to access the files and download it. Unfortunately, I think that getting into their system from the outside is going to be next to impossible. We need a computer with high enough clearance to be able to reach the file anyway, or we'd have to hack our way through a million pass-words and firewalls."

"*Please* tell me this job has a longer deadline than the last one."

He tossed his head, flipping the blond streak out of his eyes. "Two weeks."

"Huh." I leaned my chin in my hand, staring at the table in thought. This wouldn't be an easy job, but if we could do it, the payoff was well worth the risk. I might think differently if we got caught and I was looking at the decision from an Americorp security cell. Hindsight is twenty/twenty and all. "You really think we could pull it off?"

"I may need to pick up a new piece of tech or two, upgrade some software, but between the two of us, I bet we can get it done."

"You have an awful lot of confidence in someone you've never been on a run with."

"Like I said, I know talent when I see it."

We studied each other for the span of a few heartbeats, then I shook my head. "I just hope that confidence doesn't get us both caught. Or killed."

He grinned. "So you're in?"

I sighed. This was so dumb. "Yeah. I'm in."

His grin got even bigger, if that was possible, and made him seem years younger. I wondered how old he really was, then I pulled my phone from my pocket, sliding my finger over the touch screen to unlock it.

"You want to give me your information?" I asked.

He stared down at my hand in blank disbelief. "What is *that?*"

I held up my phone, waving it in the air. "A phone? I know it's old fashioned, but I'm not the only one with one of these things. Just give me your Neurocomm number and I can connect to you the same way as everyone else."

"You don't have a Neurocomm?" His eyes widened in panic and his gaze darted from my phone to my face and back again, as if he thought he had made a mistake about me.

"No. I don't."

"Are you a greeny?"

"No."

"Is it—" he lowered his voice, his eyes flicking nervously. "Is it an *elf* thing?"

"No." I tried to keep the exasperation out of my voice, and took a long drink of my beer.

"Then…why…" His eyebrows pulled down in confusion, making the piercing in his left eyebrow skew sideways.

"Look, it's a personal choice, okay? I am not required by law to have a Neurocomm, and I don't want some machine plugged into my brain where anyone can get to me whenever they want to."

He still looked doubtful. "How will we communicate on the run?"

I sighed. "You know, it wasn't that long ago that *no one* had Neurocomms. They managed to communicate just fine." He raised his eyebrows incredulously. "Don't worry, techie, I have what we need."

His tone still skeptical, he told me his number and I programmed it into my phone. I attached a voice tag to it and then called him so his Neurocomm could store my number for later. We sat together in silence for a few minutes, each of us lost in our drinks and our own thoughts.

When the silence got uncomfortable, he began to squirm and then downed his beer in one swift motion.

"Well, I should get going," he said, and waved the waitress over for the bill. She brought the check pad and he glanced at the small screen.

I reached into my pocket for my money but he raised a hand.

"I got it. No worries. It's the least I could do after the other night." I shrugged and he waved his hand over the check. The tablet beeped as it registered the debichip just under the skin of his wrist, and he pressed his thumb to the print reader to approve the purchase.

He stood in one smooth motion and grinned down at me. "See ya 'round, Alyssa."

"Bye." I watched as he crossed the tavern.

I heard a snort of laughter from behind me and rolled my eyes. It sounded as if Jeremiah had some colorful commentary for me. As soon as Logan walked out the door, I picked up my helmet and my beer, slid out of my booth and turned to Jeremiah.

"Well?"

"The only thing Blondie there wants is expensive toys...and maybe a tumble in the sheets with that waitress."

"Oh, please. Be serious, Jer."

"I am. You've got nothing to worry about from that one except a case of excess hormones and a surplus of overconfidence. How old is he, anyway?"

I dropped into the seat across from him. "What about the run, Jeremiah?"

He shrugged. "Not sure. Blondie only knows what's been told to him. He's being honest, but I have no idea if Reed is. He doesn't have a good track record with that thus far, but I can't get any impressions from *him* unless you can get me something of his to read, or if I can get close to him."

"Fat chance *that's* going to happen," I muttered.

"Until then, I can't really help you with this one. Sorry, Lys."

"It's ok," I slumped in my seat. "This run's not going be easy, Jer. I'm nervous."

He snorted again. "Good. When you stop being nervous is when you start making mistakes. You rush things, get sloppy. Stay nervous, it's a survival instinct."

"Yes, oh wise sage."

"Don't be a smart ass. It's not an attractive trait."

"Says the smart ass," I said wryly.

"Yeah, but I make it work. It's part of the seer package. Roguish charm, devilish good looks, visions of doom and destruction..."

"Roguish charm, huh?"

"You wouldn't have me any other way. Admit it."

Laughter bubbled up in my chest. He was right, though. I downed the last of my beer, set the empty glass down on the table, and stood. "Night, Jer."

"Night Lys."

R ose was at our small kitchen table when I got home, sitting cross-legged in one of the two chairs. The thin strip of her holoprojection computer was on the table in front of her, and she tapped away at the projected keyboard, fingers making soft pattering noises against the smooth surface of the table. She was looking at something I couldn't see, the holoprojection only visible from her side.

She glanced up when I walked in. "Hey, there you are. I made dinner." She gestured at a pot simmering on the stove, and I walked over, lifting the lid. The smell of chicken soup wafted out, and I inhaled gratefully. My stomach rumbled, and the remnants of the beer from earlier churned, reminding me that I hadn't eaten since…when *had* I eaten last?

I grabbed two bowls from the cabinet and ladled out a generous portion of soup for both of us, placing them on the table before going back for spoons. I tossed one to her and she caught it one-handed without looking up from her screen. Sitting across from her, I lifted a spoonful of soup to my mouth, making a noise of appreciation.

"Mmm. Good. You made this?"

"Opened the can all by myself and everything."

I chuckled and went back to my dinner. We ate in silence for a few moments until I looked up. "So…I've got another run."

She glanced up from her screen. "Already? That was fast."

"Yeah," I paused, not wanting to tell her the rest, and took another spoonful of soup.

She eyed me suspiciously. "And?"

I avoided her gaze, chasing a noodle around the bottom of my bowl. "It's a job from Reed. I'm working on it with Grendel."

She blinked. "You're kidding, right?"

"Nope." I kept staring at my soup as if I could divine the future from the noodles and cubed chicken.

"I'm really starting to doubt your sanity these past few days, you know that?"

"Yeah, well—"

"Seriously, Lys. You're taking a job from a guy who's already proven he's not an honest employer, and you're teaming up with a runner you don't even know, who had no qualms about tazing you to win last time? Does this sound like a good idea to you?"

I sighed. "Look, I know it sounds dumb, but I've got a good feeling about this. Logan came into the store this morning, returned my gun, apologized for tazing me, and offered me the job."

"Logan?"

"Grendel, Logan, whatever." I waved my hand in the air.

"He came into the *store*? How'd he know where to find you?"

I sighed again. "Reed told him."

She threw her hands in the air. "I rest my case. This is the most ridiculous thing you've ever done." When I just shrugged, she sighed. "What's the job?"

"Data file theft."

She nodded, taking a bite of soup. "That's simple enough anyway. What company?"

I tried—and failed—to suppress sly grin. "It's, uh, Americorp."

She stared at me in stunned silence. "Americorp."

"Yep."

"You're going to steal data files from Americorp."

"That's the plan."

"That's it, I'm having you institutionalized."

"I know what I'm doing, Rose, okay?" I wasn't about to admit my doubts to her, not when she was being overprotective like this. "What are you, my mother now?"

"No, I'm not," her voice went quiet. "I'm your best friend, Lys. That should count for something."

"It does. It's just…I need to do this."

"Why? I know Grendel got one up on you on the last run, but wounded pride is a dumb reason to risk your life."

I ignored her barb, refusing to acknowledge how close to home it had hit. "No, it's not that. I just…" *I'm a good runner. I can handle this. I don't have to be a burden.* "I just *want* to, okay?"

She gave me a long searching look, then sighed. "Okay. If you're sure."

I smiled with reassurance I didn't quite feel. "I am."

She nodded and we went back to our soup, the silence settling back to comfortable. I ate the last few vegetables from the bottom of my bowl and looked up at her again.

"So," I said nonchalantly. "Tristan is looking for me."

She laid her forehead on the table and laughed. And laughed. And laughed. Finally, she lifted her head and wiped her eyes. "Man, you are just full of good news today."

"Tell me about it," I muttered, running my hands through my hair.

"What's he want?"

I shrugged. "No idea. Lorelei didn't know either, just that he'd been to the Arcanum and had been asking about me."

"What are you going to do?"

"Nothing. I'm certainly not contacting him. And if he does manage to find me, I'll make sure he knows just how badly I *don't* want to see him."

"Good." She gave me a hard look and went back to typing on her computer as if that settled the matter. I hadn't met Rose until after I'd left Tristan and moved to Atlanta, but she knew the whole sordid story inside and out. She probably hated Tristan more than I did.

After all, she'd never loved him.

5

Grendel and I stood on the sidewalk at the entrance to Americorp, looking up at the large chain link fence. Sunlight gleamed wickedly off the razor wire coils at the top, and a booth with an armed guard stood between us and the gate. Past the fence we could see a long stretch of parking lot, dotted with cars, and the factory looming over everything. Somewhere within that factory was an office with the computer we needed.

I turned and looked at Grendel, raising an eyebrow, and he grinned down at me. "You sure you're up for this?"

"Nope," I said, looking back at the gleaming razor wire. "Are there any other entrances? It's a pretty huge complex to have only one way in or out."

"Let's look," he said, and his gaze unfocused as if he were looking through me. Then we were moving—or rather we were standing still and everything else was moving—as the virtual mapping program shifted around us. The fence rushed past, the sidewalk moved under our feet, and we paused briefly at the end of the block before everything pivoted and we were following the fence line again.

I closed my eyes, disoriented and dizzy. "Let me know when we stop."

He chuckled, and a few moments later said "Okay, you're good."

I opened my eyes. In front of me stood another gate, this one double-wide and rolled open to the sides to allow large trucks through. A service entrance. An *unguarded* service entrance. I grinned.

"Looks like the biggest challenge is going to be the computer itself," Grendel said, sounding pleased.

"What do you mean?

"Well, this all seems pretty standard," he waved a hand at the gate. "RFID tags for entrance, cameras, armed guards…it might be top-of-the-line but it's all still basic stuff. We can get through that no problem. The computer security, on the other hand…that's a little harder to anticipate."

"So, we plan for everything. What's wrong with that?"

"Nothing, except they may have some security measures in place that I can't just hack my way through. Passwords, ID scanners, key codes—those are all gravy. But seeing how big this company is…" he trailed off, looking out over the parking lot. "They may have biolocks."

I cursed. In all honesty, I should have expected it—a company this profitable would invest some serious money in keeping their secrets safe. But if they had biolocks, that presented a whole new problem. Codes could be cracked, but we couldn't get through a DNA reader or a retina scanner without the person required. Hair we could get, but an eye…

I wrinkled my nose at the thought and studied Grendel. I couldn't tell what he was thinking, but his gaze was distant as he regarded our target.

"I'm closing out," I said. "We can come back if we need to look at the fence again." I put my hands to my head and pulled off the Neuro-helm, disconnecting from the program.

I looked across my desk in the back office, watching Logan as he disconnected and pulled off his Neurospecs—a pair of glasses that projected images from his Neurocomm. I needed the full helmet since I lacked a Neurocomm implant. I placed the sleek, visored contraption back in its box and slid it under my desk.

He folded his specs, putting them in a small case and slipping them into one of the many pockets of his black pants. I wondered what else he had stashed in all those pockets, and then he spoke, distracting me from my train of thought.

"We need a plan." He leaned forward, elbows on knees, and ran a hand through his hair.

"That is possibly the understatement of the century." I sat back in my chair and crossed my legs.

He paused, his eyes narrowing in thought. "What we need is access to Thomas Lucca."

I let out a loud laugh. "The Americorp CEO? You don't do things by halves, do you?"

He grinned up at me through his cobalt hair, the streak of blond making his blue eyes look even brighter. "Nope."

I stood up and stretched. "Well, when you can tell me how we can get access to Lucca and his DNA, I'm all ears. Otherwise, we need a different plan."

He rested his chin in his hand, staring blankly at my desk, and I could almost see him weighing our options.

"We need to find out what biolocks they have, if any." I said, pulling my hair up into a rough bun and shoving a pen through it to hold it in place. "You have any contacts that might know?"

He shook his head. "None I can think of off-hand. I'll have to give it some thought. With a little creative hacking I may be able to dig up the records from whatever company installed their security system."

"Well, you get on that. I'll do some digging on my own, just in case your superior skills fall through." I didn't fully trust him yet, either, so it wouldn't hurt to double check in case he decided to be less than forthcoming with me.

He stood, giving me a look that said he clearly didn't think his skills were in question, and walked out of the office.

I followed and stopped at the main counter in the middle of the store as he continued to the front door. He looked over his shoulder and gave me a small smile before he walked out onto the street. I smiled back and watched the door close behind him.

Cinda, my only employee, walked up beside me. Her blond curls fell into her eyes as she peered past me, trying to catch a glimpse of Logan as he walked past the storefront. "Who was that?"

"What? Oh. That's Logan." I turned and followed her gaze in time to see him cross the street and disappear around the side of the building. "Why?"

"Just curious," she said.

When I mentioned it to Rose that night she just laughed. "What's so funny?"

"You."

"Gee, thanks," I drawled.

"You're welcome."

We were sitting in a corner booth at Café 1337, a small cybercafé with a heavy pro-tech atmosphere. I'd passed the place a million times but never stopped here...the techie scene wasn't really my thing.

I wanted to go to The Grove for coffee but Rose shot that idea down right away. She thought being at the most likely place Tristan would look for me was a stupid idea. I sort of wanted to confront him and get it out of the way so I could go back to forgetting about him, but she was adamant.

So instead of normal coffee, I was drinking some doctored-up version of a latte and I was not happy about it. I wasn't even sure it *was* a latte—it was bright green and served in a clear mug—but that's what they called it and I wasn't going to argue so long as it was hot and caffeinated.

Glowing lights lined everything inside the place, the contrasting darks and brights creating a completely different atmosphere from the calm, well-lit rooms of The Grove. Music with a relentless beat piped through a sound system, and most likely into the customers' Neurocomms as well. The barista had looked at me like I was insane when I paid with cash; most people used debichips, and the customers here looked like they had at least two each and had never handled cash in their life. The tables were all a clear high-density polyresin with LEDs inlaid underneath. The resulting effect was that the glowing table top in front of me gradually and constantly changed color. It was pretty but mildly disconcerting.

Tristan would never look for me here.

I sipped my drink and made a face across the table at Rose. The light from the table reflected off her hair and made her pink bangs change colors. One moment purple, then red, then brown...the constant shifting was almost as dizzying as the table. I wondered what the light was doing to my so-red hair.

A loud shout came from the far end of the shop and I glanced up sharply, but it was just a group of kids hooked up to a Virtu-sensory game. They all wore Neurospecs, and their game was displayed on a screen on the back wall of their booth. I knew their experience would be much more intense than what was on the screen—linked to their Neurocomm, the game simulated not only the sounds and sights of being in battle, but the smell of smoke and gunpowder, the heat from the sun-baked metal and the feel of the wind against their skin. I spared a moment for envy, then sighed and sipped my drink.

I'd told Logan I didn't have a Neurocomm out of personal choice, but the truth was I didn't have a one because it was too dangerous for me.

I was a Weaver.

Most Elves could do small magic—manipulate the Eldergloom to help plants grow, nurture a small spring into a deep pool, perhaps even control an existing element such as a small flame. Others had the gift of healing, and could stitch bones and muscle back together with the touch of their fingers.

My skill was in manipulating reality. The Eldergloom ran like an undercurrent to our existence, the energy of life and death, creation and destruction. The essence of existence. I could twist the possibilities around me and become invisible. I could gather and intensify them into a ball of potent and explosive energy...the possibilities were as endless as my imagination—and my stamina. It helped make me an excellent runner.

The downside was the Eldergloom didn't agree with tech. The

more advanced the tech, the more violent the disagreement. I could twist reality while holding a simple gun, and the worst thing that would happen was a jam if I was really unlucky. If I tried my tricks with a Neurocomm implant, though…let's just say the idea of a crispy brain didn't appeal to me. I don't know if it would fry someone *else's* Neurocomm, but I didn't really want to find out. I liked to avoid killing people if I could—which is why I hadn't used my powers on Logan when he stole my run.

Also, while I was *technically* able to bend the Eldergloom in front of others, it would mean revealing what I was, which was severely frowned upon by the Order. Rumors of Weavers had surfaced when the Elves had first come out, and those rumors were met with awe, fear, and in a few cases, a strong desire to *use.* I'd be a powerful asset—or weapon—for any company or government agency that could get their hands on me.

A Weaver's power could do amazing things, but left unchecked in the wrong hands, the results could be devastating. My people told stories of a Weaver born before me, who'd fallen prey to temptation. They'd banished her from Arcadia, but not before the other Weavers dredged up an ancient ritual and locked her powers away from her.

I wondered how long she'd lasted.

I never wanted to look down that road, let alone travel it. I'd made my home among the humans, but to never be allowed back into Arcadia, never again walk the halls of the Arcanum…I shuddered at the thought, and pushed it away with a long sip of my drink, turning back to Rose.

She was watching me, quietly sipping her own bright blue drink. She smiled as I turned my gaze back to her.

"Where'd you go there, Lys? You were far away for a minute."

I smiled softly. "Yeah, just thinking about what could have been, and what will never be."

She raised her eyebrows at that. "That's awful cryptic of you. Want to be a little less poetic and a little more specific?"

I shrugged one shoulder, holding my mug up to my lips. "Being jealous of all the tech in here."

Her eyes lit with understanding, and she gave me a sympathetic smile. Rose knew, of course. I'd met her just after I'd left Tristan, and we'd been best friends ever since. There wasn't much about me she didn't know. She didn't quite share my aversion to tech, but she had so far steered clear of any Neuro implants purely from the desire to keep any unwanted visitors out of her brain.

We sipped our coffee in silence, listening to the music and the hum of the conversations around us.

"Don't you ever think about going back?" She asked quietly.

I looked at her. "To Arcadia?"

She nodded.

I shrugged one shoulder. "Yeah. I mean, of course I do. It's home." I turned my mug around in my hands. "It would solve the whole problem of having enough money to pay rent *and* eat." My voice was sarcastic and she stuck her tongue out at me. I grinned and then sobered. "But...this is my home, too. As long as the Order of the White Hart is stubborn and refuses to open Arcadia to humans, I'll be here." Truth was, I hadn't expected to love humanity as much as I did. I'd fled Arcadia in an immature attempt to hide from my problems and ended up starting a new life. Now I couldn't see myself anywhere else.

She nodded. "You think they'll ever allow it?"

"I don't know. They're just so...so..."

"Racist?" She quirked a half-smile to take the sting from the word, but I still winced.

"That's such a strong word. Insular? Purist?"

She raised an eyebrow at me.

"And yeah, okay, maybe kind of racist. Arrogant. Burdened with a massive superiority complex." I rolled my eyes.

She laughed low in her throat. "Well, at least no one can accuse them of breaking any stereotypes."

I chuckled, taking another sip of my drink. I leaned back in my seat and looked around the cybercafé. Maybe Rose and I should rent a Virtu-sensory booth and play a bit. I wouldn't be able to get the full immersion, but they'd probably have a Neurohelm we could use...

I lost my train of thought as Logan walked in the front door.

Rose noticed my sudden attention and looked around. "What is it? Tristan?"

I shook my head and waved at Logan as he noticed me. He showed surprise before a grin spread across his face and he weaved his way across the room.

"I didn't know you came here," he said as he pulled out a chair, turned it around, and sat backwards.

"Of course you can join us," I said dryly. "And I don't, not normally. I'm, uh…branching out."

"She's avoiding her jerk ex-boyfriend," Rose said with a smile. I could tell by her suddenly solicitous smile that she saw the perfect opportunity to distract me.

If she only knew.

I kicked her under the table and smiled pleasantly when she yelped. "This is Rose, my nosy roommate. Rose," I paused, and the silence was heavy, "this is Logan."

Her eyebrows shot up and she stopped rubbing her shin. "*You're* Logan?" She looked him over slowly as he nodded. "Well, then I owe you something."

"Oh?" he said, suddenly apprehensive. "What's that?"

"Taser burns," she grinned wolfishly.

He shrank back. "I apologized for that!"

She glanced across the table at me.

"He did," I shrugged.

She frowned. "Fine," she said, turning back to him with narrowed eyes. "She might trust you for some god-forsaken reason, but I don't. If you double-cross her, get her caught, hurt, or killed, you'll be answering to me, do you understand?"

He looked from her to me with wide eyes. "She knows?"

"Mostly. She's a runner, too."

"Oh!" He perked up. "You're both runners *and* roommates? That's seriously hot."

Rose and I leveled withering stares at him, and his grin slowly slid from his face as a blush surged up his neck and cheeks

Wow, he really *was* young.

"I, uh…" He cleared his throat and looked lost.

"You were going to promise me," Rose reminded him, "under pain of torture, that you weren't going to get Alyssa in trouble."

"Uh." He glanced from her to me and back again. "Yes, ma'am. I promise."

"Good. Now if you'll excuse me, I need to go powder my nose." She pushed up from the table, gave me a long, warning look, and made her way toward the back of the café.

We watched her go, then I sighed, taking a sip of my latte.

"Sorry about her," I said wryly. "She can be…overenthusiastic."

"No, it's fine." He turned his attention back to me. "I'm glad I ran into you, though. I got some intel on our job."

"Already? That was fast, techie. I'm impressed."

"Yeah, well, save it until after I tell you."

"Oh no," I sat back, putting my mug down heavy on the table.

He leaned forward after looking around to be sure no one else was listening in. It was busy and loud enough in here that no one would accidentally overhear our conversation, but I leaned forward anyway, allowing him to speak quietly. "The Americorp factory and office had their security done by Zeus Security Systems. Their setup includes RFID tags, cameras, motion detectors…and fingerprint ID scans on their computers."

"Bless it," I cursed. Everything else we could bypass, but the addition of the fingerprint scanners threw a wrench into everything. We'd need a fingerprint from someone with high enough clearance to access the document we needed, and that wasn't an easy task. "Okay," I said, pinching the bridge of my nose and closing my eyes. "What we need to do is get an employee list with the security clearance levels for each employee, and then we can—" I looked up and him and stopped. He was grinning at me. "What?"

He pulled a small projector from his pocket and ran his finger over the touch screen, then laid it on the table. With another touch, a projection of the local news appeared on the surface of the table. The headline stuck out in large bold print.

Thomas Lucca to Host Biggest Charity Event of the Year.

I stared at the picture of the smiling Americorp CEO, and reread the headline before looking up at Logan. His eyes were bright and eager. "I'm here to meet a friend of mine about that. I'm hoping to get a job as a server." He grinned even larger, looking far too pleased with himself.

"You've got to be kidding."

"Nope."

"You're seriously going to go after Thomas Lucca?" I hissed, glancing around. The crowd in the café was suddenly pressing, and there were far too many eyes and ears. "Isn't that taking a rather large and unnecessary risk?"

He swept the projector from the tabletop and returned it to a pocket. "He'd have the highest clearance. If we had his prints we wouldn't need to be concerned about what level the information is. It'd be an all-access pass to everything in Americorp's database!"

I chewed on my thumbnail and mulled it over. It *was* reckless, but I was beginning to get the feeling that was Logan's particular flavor. And the idea certainly had its appeal...*if* we could pull it off, it'd be sexy as hell.

"Fine," I said, leaning forward. "Get me a spot, too. I want to go in with you."

He blinked. "Uh."

"I'm serious."

"I'll see what I can do. I don't know if—" He broke off as a pair of slender, dark hands slid over his eyes.

I looked up to see a slim female elf standing behind him. She had dusky gray skin, elegantly arched eyebrows, and long raven hair that was shaved on one side of her head. It cascaded down her back and fell forward into her scarlet eyes. The one pointed ear I could see had several small studs along the tip and two large hoops on the lobe, and she wore a high-collared black jacket over tight jeans.

I tensed.

"Guess who," she drawled, the hint of a foreign accent on her tongue.

"Eyja." He grinned, and pulled her hands from his eyes. "I'm glad you're here, I was just talking about you."

"Good things, I hope." She let her hands fall to his shoulders and eyed me sidelong. "Who's your friend?"

"This is Alyssa." He gestured at me. "She was the one I was telling you about."

She gave me a long look. "You didn't tell me she was *Alfheimer.*"

I bristled. "Should it matter, *Talmorin?*" I spat.

She slid her hand down Logan's shoulders and stepped out from behind him, her stance relaxed yet holding a threatening tension just under the surface. "You tell me."

My hands balled into fists and I pushed up from my chair. "You picked the wrong night," I growled. If she wanted a fight, I'd give her one.

"Whoa," Logan stood, holding his hands up between the two of us. "Did I miss something?"

Eyja and I stared at each other. She stood as if she knew what she was doing, poised to defend herself if I made a move. The music thumped through my feet, but the hum of conversation had quieted and the customers at the tables near us watched with wide eyes.

I let my breath out and looked at Logan. "Remind me to give you an Elvish cultural lesson next time we talk." There was a gentle touch on my shoulder. Rose stepped up beside me with a questioning look.

"Everything okay?" She asked, her body tense but her face and voice pleasantly neutral.

"It will be. Sorry we need to cut this sort, Rose. You ready to go?"

"Wait, you're leaving?" Logan asked.

I glanced from him to Eyja and back. She had relaxed when I did, but her gaze was stony. "It's probably for the best. I'm not in the mood for a fight tonight." I downed the last of my coffee. "Or maybe I *am* in the mood. That's the problem."

"Uh, okay." His hands fell to his sides. "I'll come by tomorrow and we'll talk?"

"Sure." I breezed past him and Eyja and out into the night, with Rose on my heels.

6

"He was kind of cute."

Rose's voice startled me out of my thoughts. I was sprawled sideways across the armchair in our living room, staring at a water spot on the ceiling and trying to come down off the caffeine and outrage from earlier.

"What?" I pushed up on my elbows and looked at her through my hair. She was digging through the freezer and all I could see of her was blue leggings below the door.

"Logan. He was kind of cute, in a young and clueless sort of way. Do we have any more Rocky Road?"

"On the shelf on the door."

She made a happy sound. "Ah! There you are. Do you want Mint Cookies 'n' Cream or Pistachio?"

"Cookies 'n' Cream. What do you mean, he was kind of cute?"

"I mean, *he's kind of cute.* Nice eyes, lots of piercings. I wonder if there were any more we couldn't see…"

"Rose!"

"It's an honest question." She pulled two spoons out of a drawer and padded across the room. She handed me the pint of ice cream followed by a spoon, then flopped onto the couch. "Do you think he's with that Talmorin chick?"

"Eyja." My blood pressure rose just thinking of the dark elf. I pulled the lid off and threw it on the coffee table, shoving the spoon into the ice cream and scooping out a large hunk.

"Do you know her?"

I shook my head, my mouth full.

"It seemed like you did. You went from zero to pissed pretty quickly."

I sighed. I wouldn't let myself get worked up over this. "I know. I'm just in a mood. And she pushed my buttons."

"I could tell," she said wryly.

"I mean, what does it matter if I'm Arcadian?" The anger surged again and I stabbed at a chocolate chip. "What would that have to do with anything?"

"Is that what she called you? I didn't recognize the word."

"*Alfheimer*," I spat. "It's what they call us."

"And it's an insult?" She spooned some Rocky Road into her mouth and watched me.

"Not exactly. It's just their word for us. We're *Alfheimer*, they're *Dokkalfar*. Light elves and dark elves. For us it's Arcadians and Talmorins. It's just words." I shrugged a shoulder and tossed my hair behind my back, trying for calm and casual but failing miserably.

"Then why did it make you so mad?"

"I don't know," I huffed. "It was just her attitude, you know? Like it was important that I was Arcadian for some reason. Like I'd suck at my job because of it."

"You got all that from her attitude?"

"Yes." I said sharply, and took another bite of ice cream.

"Oh. Okay." Her voice was calm and matter-of-fact, and yet managed to get under my skin.

"What is that supposed to mean?" I shoved my spoon back in the ice cream and glared at her.

"It's not supposed to mean anything, Alyssa. I just said 'okay.'"

"You think I overreacted," I accused.

"I didn't say anything like that." She stared down at her ice cream, digging around with her spoon. "Why? Do *you* think you overreacted?"

"Oh for—" I turned and put my feet on the floor, slamming my cardboard pint on the coffee table with a *clack*. "Rose, if you think I overreacted, just say so!"

She raised an eyebrow at me over her spoon and my anger drained away.

"I'm doing it again, aren't I?"

She shrugged, but I could see a smile tugging at the corners of her lips.

"I'm sorry. I guess everything has been getting to me more than I thought."

"You don't say." Amusement tinted her voice.

I threw a pillow at her and she shrieked as it hit her knees.

"Hey!" She raised her carton above her head, laughing. "Watch the ice cream!"

I laughed and settled back into my chair, letting the comfortable silence settle over me. Rose was always good at keeping me grounded, even when I didn't make it easy for her. Which was most of the time, honestly. The woman had endless patience.

Sometimes I thought I was unworthy of such a good friend.

She looked up from her ice cream and met my gaze. She gave me a nervous smile. "What?"

"Nothing. Just…thanks."

She smiled gently and took a bite of ice cream.

"What about you? Any leads on any new runs?" I asked.

"One or two, but they were kind of crap jobs with crap pay. I'll let you know if I get anything good. I can toss it your way or bring you in if you want."

I shrugged. "Whatever works for you. I can always use the money, but if this Americorp run goes well, I won't have to stress about that for a bit."

This run *really* needed to go well. A lot of that depended on if Eyja would decide if I was worthy enough to get a job working the charity event. I trusted Logan to do his job, but I was more the hands-on type. I needed to be involved.

I didn't know if I could trust Eyja, though.

Humans had a difficult time understanding the bad blood between us and the Talmorin. Objectively, I understood that, but I hated looking like the bad guy. Rose wasn't really wrong when she'd accused the Arcadians of being racist... but the issue was a complex one, dating back centuries. It was hard to explain hundreds of years of feuds, both sides thinking they were right and neither side willing to admit when they were wrong.

The Talmorin dwelled in the underground, in the caves and caverns of Talimdor. They twisted the Eldergloom...instead of creation, their Weavers wrought death and spread decay. Some schools of thought maintained we were two halves of the same coin—light and dark, life and death, both necessary but neither innately good nor evil. Others viewed the Talmorin as the enemy, plain and simple. To those, there was no dealing with them, no reasoning with them; a Talmorin would strike down an Arcadian simply for being light, and the only protection we had was to strike first.

I'll let you guess which side of that argument my parents came down on.

I squashed any rising guilt with another spoonful of ice cream. Eyja could have been raised in the same sort of household as me, taught to hate us as we'd been taught to hate them. Her tone when she'd called me 'Alfheimer' had indicated that might be the case. She was in a perfect position to set me up for utter failure, or to rat me out to the authorities. Either way, it was out of my hands. All I could do now was wait.

I hoped Logan new what he was doing.

I was ringing up a purchase for an older woman when Logan came bursting into the store the next day, sending the string of bells jangling violently. He skidded to a stop when he saw I was with a customer and turned, pretending to browse my shelf of CD's. He kept casting furtive glances my way, and I could see him bouncing on his toes with impatience.

I wrapped up the woman's purchase, thanked her again, and watched her shuffle slowly out the door. As soon as the door shut all the way, he bounded across the store to the counter.

"I assume you got the spot?" I said dryly.

"I'm in. I pick up my uniform for the Gala tonight." He grinned.

"And my uniform, too, right?"

He grimaced. "I, uh, couldn't get you in."

I gave him a scathing look.

"I'm sorry, okay, but I used my one favor for my spot. There's no way I can get anyone else in. My credit's used up."

I cursed again. "It was Eyja, wasn't it?"

"What about her?"

"She's your contact. You're in. And she won't give me a spot."

"I don't think it was like that. She—"

"Forget it, it's not worth it," I said, dropping the subject of Eyja and turning back to the run. "I suppose we'd better start looking at other ways to get me in to the Gala, then."

"You could buy a ticket?" His voice was laced with doubt.

I eyed him suspiciously. "And how much do these tickets cost?"

"Three thousand a head." My expression must have said everything for me, because he winced. "You can get a table of ten for twenty. If there's any left, that is. That's only two K a piece."

"Oh, perfect," I drawled. "I'll just call nine of my closest friends and ask them for the money. I'm sure it'll be no problem." I turned away from him and began reorganizing a display of butane lighters. "Any other ideas, techie? Maybe some that are actually within the bounds of reality?"

He pulled a lighter from the stand and flipped it open and shut as the thought, turning it over and over in his fingers. *Flip-click. Flip-click.* "You could go as back-up. It's at the Botanical Gardens, so you could find a spot in the park outside the building and sit sentinel, watch the perimeter, that sort of thing. Just in case I need to get out fast."

"Hm," I said, more acknowledgment than agreement. I *hated* taking perimeter watch. Nine times out of ten it was worse than watching grass grow while all the action was happening inside. I recognized it as a necessary evil in certain situations, but this wasn't one of them. "The Botanical Gardens aren't exactly a high-security location. Should be pretty easy to get out. Next idea."

He frowned, his eyes distant. *Flip-click.* "You could...hm." *Flip-click.*

"Are you going to buy that, or just irritate me with it?"

The bells on the door chimed behind me, interrupting his answer. Logan and I turned toward the customer, and I put on my best smile.

My greeting froze on my lips.

Tristan stood in the doorway, cocked his head, and smiled at me.

"Hey, Alyssa. Long time, no see."

7

Logan's taser had hurt less than the sight of Tristan McCollough standing in my store, looking for all the world as if he belonged there. I fought to breathe as he strolled toward me and gave me a long once-over.

His blond hair was cut shorter than the last time I'd seen him, but that was the only noticeable change. Five years ago it had been all one length, the ends falling just below his shoulders in soft waves. It was much shorter now, the front falling in his eyes and the back just brushing the nape of his neck, showing off his pointed ears. I curled my fingers against my palms at the memory of running them through that hair. My face must have given something away, because his smile shifted to that sexy self-satisfied smirk that both infuriated me and made the blood rush to my cheeks all at the same time.

A pair of black jeans hung from his hips and a sleek black leather jacket barely covered a shirt made completely out of fishnet and bits of chainmail. My eyes involuntarily traveled to his barely clothed stomach, and I noted that he had the same beautiful abs before I caught myself and looked up. His smirk widened as he noticed my distraction, and I clenched my teeth together in embarrassment and annoyance.

I crossed my arms across my chest, trying to keep my eyes from wandering again as warring urges to either scream and cry or throw things at him rose past the pain in my chest. I clenched my fists and managed to do neither.

Go me.

His gaze flicked behind me and then back again, and I could see him mentally sizing up and then dismissing Logan in that one look. Apparently so could Logan, and the tension in the room rose in response to Tristan's disdain. I took a deep breath to calm the pounding in my chest and ears.

"Go away, Tristan," I said, my voice cold and empty.

"But I just got here." He sounded wounded and confident all at the same time.

"Yes, and now you're leaving."

"Ouch, Alyssa. I expected a better reception than that." He leaned an arm against the sales counter, much as Logan had earlier, looking up at me.

I laughed once, harshly. "The only thing you should have expected was a boot to the groin. *Goodbye*, Tristan."

"But I came to talk to you."

Logan's voice was hard, startling me. "She asked you to leave."

Tristan's gaze never left mine, and he went on without acknowledging the comment. "Is there somewhere we can talk in private?"

Logan bristled, his hands balling into fists as Tristan ignored him, and I held up a hand as the techie took a step forward.

"No," I said to Tristan.

"Oh, c'mon, Alyssa. Please? What do I need to do? Crawl on my hands and knees? Beg? Fine, I'll beg. Please, please will you talk to me? Let me take you out for dinner. Drinks. A walk. Five minutes of your time. That's all I ask. I'll do anything."

Ridiculous scenarios flitted across my mind: Tristan groveling at my feet as I leisurely ate from a bowl of grapes; Tristan scrubbing my apartment from top to bottom with a toothbrush; Tristan carrying my bags on a trek across Europe, all expenses paid—by him, of course. He could afford it—or, at least, he could five years ago. He'd been picked up by a tech start-up looking for a diversity hire, but he was actually good at his job, and his paycheck had proved it. I was pretty sure that he'd agree to whatever insane proposition I threw at him...even if I was wrong, and he *didn't* have the money, if he wanted to talk to me as badly as he said, he'd find a way.

One thing I could trust about Tristan: he would do anything in his power to get his way.

My face went cold as I realized, as much as I hated this, Tristan walking into my store might be the perfect opportunity.

I closed my eyes as an idea hit me.

A really, really stupid idea.

"Shit," I said. Silence surrounded me, and when I opened my eyes, both men were watching me. Logan looked confused, Tristan quietly self-assured.

"You'll do anything I want?" *Alyssa, this is so dumb.*

"*Anything*," he said, drawing the word out long, and a shiver went up my spine despite myself.

I stared at Tristan for a moment longer, then looked at Logan and raised an eyebrow.

Logan's eyes met mine, then widened when he followed my train of thought. His eyebrows pulled down and he shook his head. "No."

Ignoring him, I leaned an arm on the counter top, mirroring Tristan. "Okay, you want a chance to talk? Here's the deal. You get tickets to Thomas Lucca's Charity Gala on Thursday. I'll go with you then. And we can even *talk*."

Tristan grinned, and unease slithered through my stomach.

This was a really bad idea.

But I needed to go, to back up Logan, to make sure we got what we needed for this run. And there was no way I was getting in to this event without a job or a date, and without a favor I wasn't getting a job any time soon.

Logan's hand on my arm interrupted whatever Tristan was about to say. He pulled me gently away from Tristan, his voice quiet though earnest. "Lys, it's fine, I can handle it. You don't need to do this." He took a step forward so he was in my line of sight, looking at me imploringly.

"No, I want to," I said, trying to convince myself as much as Logan. "And this way, we all get what we want." I looked around his shoulder at Tristan. "And when the night is over, we're done, understand?"

Tristan straightened up and tossed his hair from his eyes with a grin. "Why don't we wait until the night is over before you make that decision? You never know how things may change between now and then."

I watched him for a long moment before answering in a low voice. "I'm pretty sure if things haven't changed in five years, they're not going to change over the course of one night."

He flinched, almost imperceptibly. If I hadn't known him as well as I did, I would never have noticed the slight tightening around his eyes. He searched my face and the grin slid away. "Well." He lowered his gaze. "See you Thursday night, then."

"Here. Eight o'clock."

"Right." He looked at me through his lashes, glanced once more at Logan, and walked out the door, sending the bells chiming.

I slumped forward, leaning my forearms on the counter and dropping my head. So much for throwing Tristan out on his ass.

Rose was going to kill me.

I waited for the tears to come, but instead they settled somewhere deep inside me. When it was clear they intended to stay there for the near future, I took a deep breath and stood to find Logan watching me.

He glanced once at the door, then back to me. "Are you okay?"

"I will be," I muttered.

"I assume that was the jerk ex-boyfriend Rose was talking about?"

I nodded.

"Then why'd you agree to go with him? I don't know what's between you two, but you seemed pretty sure that you wanted him gone the second he walked in the door. It should be an easy in-and-out job, I can do this solo."

"I can't let you do that." My voice sounded as tired as I felt, and I ran a hand through my hair. "What if you went in and didn't get the opportunity to get near Lucca? What if I could help get what we need? I can sacrifice my own happiness for one night to make sure we get this done."

"I wish you'd trust me."

"Trust is *earned*, Logan." I held up a hand to cut him off as he looked offended. "I trust you to get this job done to the best of your abilities, but you know as well as I do that you can't plan for every circumstance. Better to have options."

His shoulders slumped slightly. "Yeah, you're right. It'll be nice having you there just in case." He frowned at the door, his gaze thoughtful. "Just...you sure we can trust *him*?"

I followed his gaze to the door and sighed. "No. But I don't have much of a choice, do I?"

———

I was waist deep in my closet when Rose got home from work that night. I heard the door to the apartment shut and her footsteps clacked across the tile of the kitchen.

"Rose?" I called.

"Hey," She poked her head into my room and glanced at the dresses strewn across my bed. "What's going on?"

"I'm trying to figure out what dress to wear to Thomas Lucca's charity event on Thursday."

She was silent for a moment. "You're...what?"

"Logan got a job serving drinks at Lucca's event. He wants to try and get his prints so we have access to anything we need. I managed to wrangle myself a date who has tickets, so I'll be going in as backup."

She took a step into my room and leaned against the door frame. "I'll spare you the lecture about how stupid that is."

"Thanks." I leaned into my closet and reached into the back corner for my last dress. "I just hope I have something appropriate in here. I certainly don't have the money to buy anything new."

She pushed up off the door frame and came to look at the dresses, running her fingers over the beading on a short black dress. I surveyed my choices before picking up a deep emerald satin dress and walking to my bathroom, leaving the door open slightly so I could change in privacy but still talk to her.

"These things are usually black tie, right?" I called as I slipped the dress over my head, adjusting the fabric.

"I think so," she called back, and I walked out, twirling once so she could inspect me. She shrugged one shoulder noncommittally and I pulled the teal-blue dress off the bed before going back to the bathroom to change again. "Did your date not tell you the dress code?"

I cringed, happy she couldn't see my face. "We didn't exactly spend a lot of time chatting about it." I walked back out, tossing the green dress on the bed and spreading my arms, twirling again.

"Eh, the green one was better." She handed me the black beaded dress as I made a face at her. "Who is this date of yours? Do I know him?"

I paused as I slipped out of the blue dress, trying to figure out what to say.

"Well?" she called as I took too long to figure out an answer.

"I don't want to tell you." I slipped the black beaded dress over my head and pulled up the side zipper.

"What? Why not?"

"You're just going to yell at me." I stepped out into the room and she whistled, long and low.

"That's the one. Thomas Lucca would happily give you his spleen if you asked while wearing that."

I turned to look at myself in my full-length mirror. The dress was short enough to show off my legs but not too short, low cut to reveal *just enough* cleavage, and form fitted to emphasize my curves. The back dipped down low, meaning I couldn't wear a bra.

I sighed. "You had to pick the one dress that I can't hide anything in, didn't you?"

"What do you need to hide? You're not expecting a fight or anything, are you?"

"No."

"So you don't need any weapons—not that you'd be able to get in with them anyway. The less the better in this situation, I think."

I turned to the side, looking myself over again. "Maybe you're right."

"Of course I am. Just bring a small clutch for anything else, toss a lipstick in there, and you're set."

I pulled my hair up on top of my head, brainstorming possible hair styles, and glanced at Rose in the mirror as she picked up the other dresses and hung them back up in my closet. "Thanks, Mom," I said jokingly, and she made a face at me. I walked into the bathroom and changed back into my clothes. She was sitting patiently on the edge of my bed as I walked back out.

"So, who's your date?"

"Oh, no. I already told you, you'll just yell at me."

"I only yell at you when you deserve it."

"Well, can't I just admit that I deserve it this time and skip the whole thing?"

"The fact that you know you deserve it means you need it even more."

I walked to my dresser and opened my jewelry box, pretending to look through the various accessories to figure out which would work best with the dress. I already knew what I wanted to wear, but any excuse to avoid Rose's gaze right now was worth it. I stared down at a pair of silver hoops, steeling myself for her reaction. "I'm going with Tristan."

The silence from behind me was deafening.

I fought to keep my posture relaxed, pulling two necklaces out of the jewelry box and turning back toward her. "Understated yet elegant, or sparkly and attention-getting?" I held the necklaces up for her to consider, but she ignored them, crossing her arms over her chest and pressing her lips together disapprovingly. "I'm thinking understated yet elegant."

"Lys…"

"I know it's plain, but I feel like the rhinestones on the other one would clash with the beading on the dress."

"Lys—"

I turned toward the mirror and held both up to my neck. "Yeah, definitely the understated one."

"Alyssa!"

I sighed, dropping my arms and turning back to her. "I know, okay? Please spare me the lecture, Rose. I know."

"If you know, then why the hell are you doing it?"

"Logan got a gig at the dinner, and I didn't want him going in alone. Tristan showed up offering the moon, and it was just too good to pass up. It's not a date or anything, he's just a convenient way to the dinner party."

"Does he know that?"

"Yeah. He does," I sighed again, leaning back against my dresser.

"And he's okay with it?"

"Knowing Tristan, he's fully confident in his ability to sweep me off my feet with his charm and stunning good looks." My voice was dry, and Rose raised an eyebrow at me. "Oh, please, it's not going to work!"

"Right."

"It's not. Thanks, Rose, your confidence in me is staggering." I turned, placing both necklaces back in the jewelry box.

"I'm confident in you, hon, but I know you. You're a sucker for him. I'm just worried."

"I know, but it's different this time. I promise."

She stood, sighing, and gave me a long look before turning toward my door. "I hope so Lys. I really do."

8

I paced back and forth in front of my dark shop, pulling my long black duster tighter around me to ward off the cold. My strappy high heels made a sharp *clack clack clack* against the cement, and I huffed as I looked at my silver watch-style Wireless Media Accessory. The WMA would notify me of any incoming calls, text messages, emails, and the like, so I wouldn't have to pull my phone out of my clutch any time I wanted to check for notifications. The default display was the time.

8:45 p.m.

Tristan was late. Very late.

A flash of worry went through me. Maybe he couldn't get tickets after all and I was standing out here in the cold for nothing. I should have taken Logan's suggestion to sit sentinel. Getting into the gardens would have been easy. Or maybe I should have tried harder to get a server job. Eyja wasn't the only one with connections.

I shook my head and drowned the mounting anxiety with a wave of irritation. Tristan was probably just testing me, trying to see how much of his crap I was willing to put up with to get what I wanted.

Apparently, I was willing to put up with a lot.

A gust of wind wound its way through my sheer stockings and

short skirt, making me shiver and darkening my mood. I pulled the collar of my duster up against my bare neck and ran a gentle hand over my carefully-done hair, piled high in a messy-but-chic bun with a few curls hanging loose around my face. The low hum of an electric engine echoed of the buildings and my eyes widened as a sleek silver sports car rounded the corner and slowed to a stop at the curb. The tinted passenger-side window rolled down, and Tristan grinned at me from behind the wheel.

"You're late," I huffed.

"So get in or we'll be even more late," he quipped.

"You're not even going to open the door for me?"

"Would you have let me?"

I yanked the door open with a scowl and slid into the dark interior of the car. The smooth leather seat beneath me was heated.

I sat in sullen silence as he pulled away from the curb and headed toward the Botanical Gardens. I stared resolutely out the window, ignoring him and begrudgingly enjoying the warmth emanating from the leather. He must have turned on the seat warmer before I'd gotten into the car. It had been very…thoughtful of him. *It would have been even more thoughtful to show up on time.* I scowled. Still, it made me wonder what he was up to.

"Do you want to tell me what you're up to at this Gala?" he asked. "I know you didn't agree to go with me out of the kindness of your heart."

"I didn't, and no, I don't really want to talk about it."

"Don't you think I need to know at least the basics? I mean, I gather what you two are involved in isn't exactly legal, and I'd hate to misstep and cause your friend to get caught."

I flicked my gaze to him, unsure if he was being sincere or if there was a subtle threat under his words. "You're not concerned that I might be involved in something that 'isn't exactly legal'?"

"I'm not exactly in a position to tell you how to live your life, Lys."

"What about getting yourself involved? What if we *do* get caught, and they think you're in on it?"

"Good point," he said. "Better to be on a need-to-know basis. Less I know, less trouble I'll be in."

"Typical," I sneered. "Only worried about yourself."

"I didn't say that." He scowled over the steering wheel. "You want me to jump in front of a bullet for you, just say so. But I figured you're a big girl. You can handle yourself. But I said I was willing to do anything to talk to you, and I meant it. Tell me how to help, and I'll do it."

I gritted my teeth, weighing my options. Tristan's motives weren't clear, past his stated desire to "talk" with me. In all honestly, I wasn't really concerned with Tristan purposefully tanking our mission. He had been many things over the years, but spiteful was never one of them. It didn't make sense for him to blow our cover, either...if he was trying to get on my good side, sending my friend to jail was *not* a winning strategy. I could stay silent and let things play out, or I could have another person on our side in case things went wrong.

Need to know basis. Right.

I swallowed. "Logan or I need get close to Thomas Lucca."

"Okay," he said, drawing the word out long. He shifted in his seat and looked at me out of the corner of his eye. "Is this some sort of assassination attempt?"

"What? No!" I looked at him sharply. "What the hell do you think I'm involved in?"

"I have no idea, Alyssa. You haven't told me."

"Do I look like a fucking *assassin* to you?"

He didn't answer.

"No," I said again, clenching my fists around my clutch in my lap. He really thought I would kill someone. For money. "I'm not a killer, Tristan. We're going after prints. Thomas Lucca's."

He whistled, long and low. "Wow. I'll give Spikes some credit. That takes balls."

I glared at him, then looked back out the window. Beyond the glass, life continued, unconcerned with the tension inside the car.

"So, are you going to ignore me all night?" He asked. When I simply frowned out the window, he continued. "That wouldn't be very good for your cover. Need to keep up appearances and all that."

"You'd know a lot about 'keeping up appearances,' wouldn't you?"

"I apologized for that, Lys. Many times. I was young and stupid."

"You've got that last part right, at least."

"What more do you want from me?"

I ground my teeth together against my reply. "Look, I don't want to talk about it, Tristan. Tonight is not about us. It is not a chance at forgiveness. It is certainly not a date. I want to make that very clear."

"Crystal clear, babe."

"Don't call me that," I spat, finally looking at him. "You lost the right to call me that a long time ago."

"Fine," he sighed. "Crystal clear, *Alyssa*."

"Good." I looked back out the window at the passing lights.

The Botanical Gardens were snuggled up against the same park as The Grove, but on the north end instead of the south. Valets in black suits waved us to the side entrance, and Tristan cruised down the long, winding road. A parking deck stood to my left, partially hidden by mostly-bare trees, and a valet ran up to the car from my right as we pulled to a stop at the curb. He opened my door and I stepped out into the cold.

A brick building loomed in front of me, with large white marble columns guarding the front door and light glowing from every window. Echoes of music and conversation drifted on the air. Tristan's dress shoes scuffed on the cement as he stepped up beside me.

"Well." He cast a sideways glance at me and offered his arm. "Shall we?"

I steeled my resolve and wrapped my hand through the crook of his elbow, ignoring the little flip my heart did at the familiar feeling. He grinned down at me with a flash of teeth and led me to the open front doors of the building. Nostalgia spread through my chest, but I shoved it down. I'd be damned if I let my runaway emotions distract me from my job.

The music and conversation were louder and more distinct once we were inside, and we stopped to check our coats. I watched Tristan from the corner of my eye as he helped me out of my duster and then handed our jackets to a pretty young brunette. He smiled politely down at her but nothing more. I did notice, though, that she gave him a good once-over as he turned away, and I really saw him for the first time.

He did look good, but then, he always did. He wore a classic black tuxedo with a black bow tie and vest. It accented his thin waist and made his shoulders look broader than they were. His hair was combed back but still loose, so that it was back out of his eyes and showed off his pointed ears.

He looked at me and let out a low whistle. "Wow."

"Shut up." Heat rushed to my cheeks. I turned on my heel and walked toward the party, shoes clacking sharply on the tile.

"What?" He asked as he took a few long strides to catch up with me. "I can't even give you a compliment?"

"Nope."

"You're not going to make this easy for me, are you?"

"Nope."

He offered me his arm in silent surrender, and we stepped through open double doors and into the main room.

Large glass chandeliers bloomed from the ceiling, hanging high above the marble floor and mingling party-goers. Servers slid unobtrusively between the guests, pausing here and there to offer their round trays loaded with drinks or plates of hors d'oeuvres. I looked over the crowd for Logan, but couldn't find his blue-and-blond head in the sea of people. I raised my wrist, running a finger over the screen of my WMA, cuing up a text to Logan.

We're here.

Tristan led me into the throng, and I pulled my attention away from searching to take in the people around me. The women wore a rainbow of dresses, floor length and almost-too-short and everywhere in between. Some dresses were encrusted with jewels, some covered in glitter or sequins. Some even glowed ethereally, the fabric woven with luminescent fibers. A few were made out of simple silk or satin, though still managed to look expensive.

The men all wore tuxedos, though the styles varied almost as widely as the women's dresses. Some opted for the more current and trendy styles, made from biosynth fabric or woven with tastefully subtle EL-wire. Others went with a modern take on retro styles, with tails or ruffles. I even saw a top hat or two. Those with nothing to prove wore the classic black tux: simple, understated, and oozing with a confidence that was terribly sexy.

I flicked a sideways glance at Tristan, wondering why he chose the simple black tux. Either he knew it was my favorite or his ego was big enough that he thought he didn't need gimmicks to stand out. Or both. I guess it didn't matter. Whatever his motivations, he looked good.

I pushed my thoughts away from Tristan and back to the job at hand. I was here to back up Logan, not ogle my ex-boyfriend. Eyes narrowed, I scanned the crowd again as we moved through it, my frustration growing as I still failed to find him. Fine, if I couldn't find him, I at least needed to locate Thomas Lucca. I brushed my forearm under my breasts as I casually laid my other hand on Tristan's elbow, feeling the reassuring pressure of the fingerprint lifter taped snugly on the underside of my cleavage. I could do this.

"Do you want to go look at the auctions?" Tristan's breath was warm against my ear, startling me out of my thoughts. I glared up at him without answering. "Perhaps you can find Lucca and ask him for a dance."

"Fine," I said through gritted teeth. I was going to have a headache by the end of the night at this rate.

"You should smile. You look like you're going to stab the next person who gets in your way."

"I just want to stab *you*," I muttered, but I tossed a stray piece of hair out of my eyes and smiled as convincingly as I could.

We made our way past the string quartet playing something by Brahms to the far end of the room where more guests milled around the auction pieces lining the wall. Paintings were hung on the wall itself, and tables were set out in front of them, lined with sculptures and rare plants under glass domes. Each piece had a touch screen mounted next to it with a blurb about the person who donated it and a place to enter a bid. I looked at the going prices for some of the pieces and tried to calculate how many months of rent I could pay with that much money. I finally gave up and tried to enjoy the art.

I was making my way down the row when one picture in particular caught my attention. It was an oil painting of a clearing in the woods by moonlight. In the center of the clearing stood a circle of stone arches, and in the shadows you could just make out buildings woven into the branches of the trees, lantern lights winding their way up into the leaves.

The Arcanum.

"Well, that's certainly interesting." Tristan's voice was low and soft, pitched for my ears only.

I nodded ever so slightly. The screen said the title of the piece was *Home*. Artist and patron were both listed as Anonymous. It was curious, but not overly upsetting. Only the elves would recognize it as Arcadia.

Below the painting, a potted flower was nestled under glass, and the sight of it set my heart pounding and my cheeks flushed with anger. The broad, waxy leaves and long stems were a green so dark they were almost black. A single blossom perched at the end of each stem, and had seven long, delicate petals that were a vivid blue with speckles of white around the center. I knew that the blossoms would glow a soft violet at night, the intensity changing depending on the phase of the moon. It was a Sevenstar Orchid, and I'd never seen one outside of Arcadia.

"Even more interesting." I looked up at Tristan to see him casually scanning the crowd, his face neutral. I could feel the tension in his arm under my hand and knew he was noting every set of pointed ears. There were only a few elves here besides us, and I wondered if the donor had come tonight or if they had stayed safe at home.

It wasn't forbidden to talk about Arcadia to outsiders, but it was frowned upon. If the only thing here had been the painting, it wouldn't have mattered. But the Sevenstar Orchid was more condemning, and not something we could overlook. Bringing plants out of Arcadia for personal use was allowed, but selling them off, and to humans at that? It was an insult, plain and simple.

I stared at the screen next to the orchid, willing the word next to "patron" to change from "Anonymous" and give me a name.

"Wine, miss?" A waiter asked from behind me.

I shook my head and waved him off, my eyebrows pulling down in concentration. Maybe we should talk to the other elves here and see if they—

"You should really try the rosé. It's sweet but has a nice, dry finish."

Annoyed, I turned around. "I said n—Oh!"

Logan stood behind me, grinning and holding a tray laden with wine glasses. His hair was slicked back tight against his head and pulled into a low ponytail at the nape of his neck. His facial piercings and extra earrings were absent, and he had unobtrusive white plugs in his lobes. There was the faint metallic webbing of a Neurolense over the iris and pupil of his left eye. I blinked, feeling foolish, then composed myself, making sure my voice was politely neutral when I spoke. "Actually, yes, I'll have one."

He handed me a glass, bowing his head. "If you haven't yet, I'd suggest taking a stroll around the Parterre Garden just outside. It's a bit chilly, but it's quite lovely at night."

"Thank you. I might do that."

He bowed his head again and turned to Tristan. "Wine, sir?"

Tristan barely looked at him before taking a goblet of red and staring back over the crowd. A flicker of annoyance crossed Logan's face, but then he smiled pleasantly before turning away. I watched him melt into the crowd, then turned to Tristan.

"I need some air. You want to go chat up some of the other Arcadians and see what they know about this?"

He nodded absently and dropped his arm from mine before heading toward someone further in the room. I watched him go for the span of a few heart beats before turning on my heel and heading for the back doors.

Outside, the air was crisp and cold, snaking its way through my dress and straight to my bones. A large marble patio spread out in front of me, with wide steps leading down into the Parterre Garden—a twisting maze of hedges and stone pathways. In the center, a fountain topped with a twisting blue glass sculpture glowed in the darkness.

Heading down the stairs with my drink in hand, I wandered the path toward the fountain. The light notes of the string quartet floated out into the night and mingled with the sound of the water, creating its own melody and counterpoint. I sat down on a wooden bench, closing my eyes and enjoying the melodious cacophony of nature and man, resolutely ignoring the cold.

Footsteps on the stone walkway made me open my eyes. Logan was walking toward me, an empty server tray in one hand. I patted the space next to me and he dropped himself into the bench.

"I've only got a minute or two, but I wanted to bring you up to speed. Lucca hasn't been out yet."

"What? But the event started almost two hours ago. What's he waiting for?"

"I don't know. I've been told, though, that he'll make his entrance at ten and mingle for two hours. The bidding ends at midnight so he'll be announcing the winners of the auctions then. If I can position myself to be the one to take his wine glass when he's done with the opening toast, we're golden."

I nodded. "I'll see what I can do about positioning myself in case of a backup. I'm going to have to play this one by ear." I didn't like that I didn't have a plan, but I'd learned a long time ago that plans didn't always go as intended.

"All right." He bounced back up onto his feet. "I'm going back in. I can get text messages through my Neurolense, so send me one if something strange happens. I'll buzz you if anything changes on my end." Then he was off, walking quickly back toward the party.

I stayed in my seat for two more minutes, giving him plenty of time to mingle back in with the crowd before I started back toward the lights and sounds of the building.

Once inside, I wandered amidst the other guests, looking for Tristan and getting a better feel for the layout of the room. Besides the front door and the door out to the Parterre Garden, there were three doors marked "Emergency Exit Only—Alarm Will Sound" on either side of the room. There was also a door that I assumed led to the kitchen and prep area, as I'd seen only servers and employees going through it. I'd done some basic research on the layout of the gardens and buildings, but since I wasn't actually stealing anything of noticeable value I wasn't too concerned with having to make a quick getaway.

You never knew, though.

I finally ran into Tristan just as I started my second lap around the perimeter of the room. His head was bowed in conversation with a shorter Arcadian woman. She was thin and waifish, her long, white-blond hair tumbling in loose curls down her back. The front of her hair was pinned back, and at the tip of each pointed ear was a simple gold stud. Long diamond and gold earrings hung from her lobes to brush the tops of her bare shoulders. As she turned, I could see that the front of her long golden gown dipped low, and that her eyes were a molten gold just a shade lighter than my own.

I approached them, and Tristan raised his gaze to mine and smiled.

"Perfect, here she is now," he said, holding his hand out to me. I ignored it and stopped next to him.

"Tristan, you've made a new friend?" I didn't bother to hide the sardonic tone that seeped into my voice.

"This is Seraphina. Seraphina, this is Alyssa." He turned toward me. "We were just talking about you."

"Oh?"

"He was saying you had an interest in the Sevenstar Orchid that was up for auction." Her voice was much deeper than I expected, low and soft as velvet. I blinked in surprise, and she smiled pleasantly and held out a hand to me.

I reached out to take it, but as our fingers touched a jolt of static electricity snapped between us, causing me to yelp in surprise and pull my hand away. My cheeks flushed hot as several guests turned toward me with wide eyes, and Tristan stared at me as if I'd suddenly sprouted a second head.

"Sorry," I laughed self-consciously, curling my fingers against my palm. "Just...wasn't expecting that."

"Neither was I." Her voice was breathless, her eyes intent on mine.

Tristan cleared his throat and raised an eyebrow at me, one corner of his lips pulling up into a crooked smirk. I narrowed my eyes at him and then smiled at Seraphina.

"Um...so," I stammered. "You don't happen to know who provided the Sevenstar, do you?"

"No, I don't." She frowned, looking around the room much in the way that Tristan had earlier. "I don't know many of the others here, though."

"I'm not even sure who's here," I admitted. "I should walk around and..." I trailed off as the quartet stopped playing and the lights dimmed and then brightened three times. At the same time, my WMA buzzed. I shook my wrist and glanced down at the softly glowing screen.

Lucca's up.

I snapped my head up, then glanced back down as the message flicked off and the time reappeared. Ten o'clock.

Lucca walked out of a curtained doorway and up onto a raised platform a quarter of the way around the room for us, near the wall of auction pieces. He wore a classic black tux, and I could tell even from where I was standing that it was hand-tailored and fit like a glove. He had short salt-and-pepper hair, and he raised his hands in thanks as the crown broke into applause. Two men stood on either side and a bit behind him, obviously bodyguards. I made a mental note of them. Just in case.

A slender microphone was handed to him, and he smiled at the crowd and waited for everyone to quiet down.

"Thank you," he said into the microphone, his voice deep and friendly. "And welcome to the sixth annual Americorp Charity Gala." Applause exploded again, and he raised his hands for quiet. "Thank you. I hope everyone is having a wonderful time this evening. I'm so glad to see you all here tonight. This year's proceeds go to fund a brand new wing of the Botanical Gardens, the Arcadian Wing, to be added to the Fuqua Orchid Center."

With a gesture, the wall behind him lit up and displayed the floor plans for a half-circle-shaped building. Applause rose and fell.

"This wing," he continued, "will feature a mix of mundane and magical flora, provided by a very generous donor and with the blessings of the Arcadian Order of the White Hart." Murmurs rose with the applause this time, and I could feel human eyes on me, wondering. I glanced at Tristan and he simply raised an eyebrow at me, his face carefully neutral.

He hadn't heard of this either.

Why would the Order approve of this? It didn't make any sense. It could be that they were trying to reach out to humanity, educate them, to make elves less intimidating and more normal, but that really wasn't their way. The Order liked being mysterious. A whole table of our Elders wouldn't agree lightly to give up their perceived superiority over humanity. Perhaps it was a gesture of good will, a way of showing benevolence...that could be a little more believable, except neither Tristan nor I had heard of this. From the expressions of the other Arcadians in the crowd, none of us had.

Another round of applause snapped me out of my thoughts, and I realized Lucca was still speaking. "... and I'd like to raise a toast." Logan stepped up behind him with a tray of champagne, and Lucca took a glass. "To working together for a brighter future." He raised his glass to the crowd. I raised my glass back with the rest of the audience, if not a bit half-heartedly. Lucca took a sip of champagne. "Now go spend more money!"

The audience laughed with him, and Logan stepped up, tray in hand, ready to take the discarded glass.

Instead, Lucca stepped down into the crowd, glass still in hand, leaving Logan standing on the stage. The string quartet started up again in a waltz.

Logan's wide eyes met mine briefly, and I shook my head at him. He pretended not to see me and turned away.

I muttered a curse under my breath and looked for Lucca's head in the crowd, spotting him not far from the stage, surrounded by admirers. I looked at Tristan, and he met my gaze with a knowing smile and an almost-imperceptible nod.

"Seraphina," he said, turning to the fair-haired elf. "Would you care to dance?"

I took that as my cue and pushed into the sea of bodies, heading toward Thomas Lucca.

If you want something done right, you've got to do it yourself.

9

I gently but insistently pushed my way through the crowd, heading in the direction of the stage and where I'd last seen Thomas Lucca. I dodged several couples swirling in a waltz and dove back into the throng on the other side of the dance floor. There were only a few people between me and Lucca, now, and I hit the screen on my WMA, tapping out a quick message to Logan.

Back me up.

I hoped he got it. I counted silently to ten, straightened the hem of my dress, and wove through the crowd to Lucca.

He had his back to me, his broad shoulders shaking with laughter. I slowed down as I got closer, giving Logan another moment to make his way over here...and maybe to steel my courage. A tiny, round metallic dot shone behind Lucca's left ear, glinting just below the edge of his hair—the telltale sign of a Neurocomm implant. I gave him a good once over. Neurocomm: check. Expensive suit: check. I spared a moment to wonder if he was a Neurospecs guy or Neurolenses guy, then he turned toward me and his brown eyes met mine.

Neurolenses: check.

Okay, Alyssa. It's now or never.

I took a confident step forward, flashed my most charming smile, and held out my hand.

"Mr. Lucca? It's such a pleasure to meet you! I'm Alyssa D'Yaragen."

He took my hand and smiled in response. His handshake was firm and perfectly timed. His gaze flicked briefly to my ears before he dropped his hand and his smile grew.

"Welcome, Ms. D'Yaragen. Glad you could make it to our little event this evening." He took another sip of his champagne. "Find anything you like on the auction table?"

"Actually, yes, and I'd like to talk to you about it, if you don't mind."

"Sure thing," he smiled over my shoulder at someone and then turned his attention back to me. "Though I'm not sure how much help I'll be. I'm not a curator." He laughed, and I laughed with him.

"That's fine, I don't need a curator's eye, just yours." I cocked my hip in a way I hoped was flirty without being overly-obvious, and brushed a loose curl back over my shoulder. "While we discuss it, would you like to dance?"

He blinked once at me and glanced back at his security guards as they shadowed him through the crowd. "Of course."

"Excellent." I reached out and took his champagne glass from his hand and turned to find Logan standing beside me, tray ready.

I set my glass next to Lucca's on the black cloth-covered tray, winked at Logan, and took Lucca's hand. When we got through the crowd, he placed his hand on my waist and we began to twirl.

Logan, you better get those thrice-damned prints.

"Did you have an item in particular you wanted to talk about?" Lucca asked.

"Uh..." I tried to slow the spinning in my head and focus on the conversation. "Yes. The Sevenstar Orchid. What can you tell me about it?"

"Lovely, isn't it? Honestly, we're hoping whomever wins it this evening will allow us to display it in the new Arcadian Wing when construction is complete. That will be a few years down the line, obviously."

"Obviously. And the Order? How'd you get them to agree to the new wing?"

He laughed. "We worked through intermediaries. They seemed just as enthusiastic about the project as we did, to be honest. What better way to symbolize the integration of our two societies?"

I smiled brightly at him. "It sounds lovely." We lapsed into silence and I absently chewed my lip. That didn't sound like the Order at all.

A polite cough from behind me caught my attention and we turned.

"Mind if I cut in?" Seraphina smiled at me, her pale gold eyes glittering.

"Oh, uh, sure." I'd already gotten what I'd wanted—I hoped—so I dropped my hand from Lucca's shoulder and stepped back.

"Of course, Ms. Dubhan." Lucca bowed slightly toward her and held out his hand.

"Oh, no, I'm sorry. I should have been clearer," she said, and held out her hand to me. "I meant Alyssa."

"Oh…" I whispered as she slid her hand into mine. There was no shock this time, just a faint electric tingle. She wrapped her slender fingers around my waist and pulled me into a spin.

Energy hummed between us as we danced. It was as if the earth beneath our feet was singing, the low, deep notes flowing up through the soles of my feet and out of my fingertips to chime against her skin. We didn't speak and we barely looked away from each other. I was afraid if my gaze left hers it would break whatever spell had settled over us.

My WMA buzzed, pulling me out of the trance. I took a deep breath as the outside world came crashing back in. I felt like someone breaking the surface of the water—disoriented, overwhelmed with sensation.

My WMA buzzed again, and I reluctantly pulled my hand from Seraphina's. I shook my wrist and tilted my head as the text messages flashed across the display.

I got 'em. We're good to go.

"Business?" Seraphina's voice was low, her breath light against my neck and cheek. It sent my head whirling and it took me a moment to re-center myself.

"Yeah. I...I should go."

"All right," She slid her hands from me. "But before you go..." She raised her wrist and pushed a button on the side of her own WMA, a delicate gold band with a circular face. She lifted my WMA to hers, and a second later they buzzed in unison as she sent me her contact information. "Don't be a stranger."

Then she walked off the dance floor, giving Tristan a nod where he stood frowning at me over the heads of the guests, and disappeared into the crowd.

"A lyssa, are you okay?"

Tristan's voice cut through my daydreaming, and I raised my eyes from my coffee. "Hmm? Of course I'm okay. Why?"

"You've barely said two words since we left the gala. Did something go wrong?" He sat across from me in the little booth, his hands wrapped around his own mug, looking out of place in his tux among the all-nighters. His jacket was draped across the back of the bench and he had the sleeves of his dress shirt rolled back, showing off his forearms. He'd taken off his tie at some point, and his collar was unbuttoned.

"Sorry. No. Nothing went wrong. Logan got the prints. Sorry." Logan was supposed to be meeting us here when he finished up with his serving job. Better to close out the night than bail early and draw attention to himself. I glanced at my WMA. 11:15 p.m.

"Okay, now I *know* something is wrong." He reached over and wrapped his hands around mine.

"What? Why?"

"You just apologized to me. Twice." A smile twitched the corner of his lips, but his sapphire eyes were serious.

I pulled my hands from his grip. "I'm fine. Just...distracted."

A waitress in a short striped skirt and blue cyberfalls appeared at my side and slid a plate full of cheesy fries in front of me. "Loaded fries. And a steak sandwich." She placed another plate in front of Tristan. "Can I get you guys anything else?"

"No, we're fine," Tristan answered with a smile, his eyes on me as the waitress nodded and went on her way.

"Did...did I order these?" I pulled a fry from the plate and then dropped it as it scorched my fingers. "Ow. Hot." I put the tips of my fingers in my mouth to soothe them.

"No. I ordered them for you."

"Oh," I muttered from around my fingers. "Thanks."

"That's it, Lys. Eat your fries, then I'm taking you home."

"What? Why?" I felt a bit like a broken record. How many times had I said that in the past few minutes?

"You need sleep. Or...something."

I blinked down at my coffee. Now that he mentioned it, I felt... drunk. How much wine had I had? I tried to remember, but got lost in a memory of pale-gold eyes. I absently picked up a fry and hissed as I burned my fingers again. "Maybe you're right," I said quietly, and leaned my forehead on the table. "How much wine did I have?"

"Not enough for this. Eat."

"I'm trying. They're too hot," I whined.

He sighed and pulled my plate across the table with a scrape. He blew gently on my fries for a few minutes while my head spun. "Here," he said. I raised my head to find him holding out a bundle of fries to me. "They're cool enough now, I promise."

I opened my mouth and he fed them to me. They were good... salty, with lots of bacon and chives. "Mmm." I chewed happily and smiled up at him. He fed me a few more bites before I felt with-it enough to feed myself. We ate in companionable silence for a while, both focused on our food. I finished the fries and picked up the last bits of bacon and cheese that had collected on the plate before laying my head on the table again.

"We should get you home," Tristan said.

"No. Need to wait for Logan." I closed my eyes and tried to stop the spinning in my head. I heard him sigh and then his tux jacket settled over my bare shoulders.

There was a clatter to my left and someone jarred the table. I grumbled my disapproval and opened one eye. Logan had pulled a chair up to the side of the booth and was sitting in it backwards, his forearms leaning on the table.

"What are you doing here?" I opened my other eye and looked at him for an answer.

"I'm supposed to meet you guys here. Right? That was the plan..." He glanced from me to Tristan and back again.

"Yeah, but you were supposed to finish out your shift. Why'd you cut out early?"

He looked from me to Tristan again, and Tristan shook his head.

"What now?" I groaned, burying my face in my hands.

"I didn't cut out early. It's 12:45."

I sighed heavily and sat up, letting my head fall back. "Maybe you *should* take me home," I said, looking down my nose at Tristan. He shrugged in a manner that said *I told you so*. Or maybe I was reading too far into things.

"Is she drunk?" Logan asked.

"She's something." Tristan said, sipping his coffee.

"How much wine did she have?"

"I don't think it was the wine."

"Did someone drug her or something?"

My heart thumped in my chest, and my breath caught. I hadn't thought of that. Did someone drug me? Who would have done that? And why? We didn't know anyone there, so no one would have had reason to. What if someone was watching us and we didn't know it...

Logan read the panic on my face and held a hand out to calm me. "Whoa, whoa, hold on." He leaned down and pulled a small backpack from under his chair. He dug through the front pouch and pulled out what looked like a small silver pen with a flat, angled tip. "Here, give me your hand."

"Why?" I eyed him suspiciously through my haze, but laid my hand on the table in front of him anyway.

He took my fingers in his, turned my hand palm-up, and ran the tip of the device over the inside of my wrist, where the veins were closest to the surface. I yelped in surprise, earning a glance from the diners at the nearby tables and a scathing look from Logan. The device beeped once, and he watched the thin LCD readout on the side, frowning.

"What? What is it?" I asked breathlessly, pulling my hand back to my lap and absently rubbing my wrist.

He shook his head. "Nothing."

"Logan! Tell me!"

"No, I mean, it's literally nothing," he said, and Tristan leaned over to look. "No drugs in your bloodstream and barely any alcohol." He tucked the device back into his bag and both of them regarded me, Logan with his forehead scrunched up in confusion and Tristan with his eyes narrowed in suspicion.

"Maybe I'm getting sick?" I suggested, but it sounded weak even to me.

"Come on," Tristan sighed, pushing up from the booth and slipping his jacket back on. "Let's get you home. You can talk to Spikes here later."

Logan tensed, and then stared at me with wide eyes when I let out a loud laugh.

"Spikes," I giggled. "You know, 'cause your hair is spiky." I patted the top of his slicked-back hair. "Well, usually."

He took my hand from where it lay on top of his head and looked at me with worry in his eyes. "Go home. We'll talk tomorrow, okay?"

"Oh, fine," I huffed. I slid out of the booth and tripped over my high heels, but Tristan caught me by the elbow before I could fall.

"Easy there," he said, making sure I was steady before guiding me toward the exit. I waved my fingers at Logan over my shoulder.

Tristan led me to his fancy silver car, and I sighed as I sank into the leather chair and thumbed the seat warmer on, letting my head fall back against the headrest. The slam of the driver's side door started me and I let out a little shriek as it jolted me out of my haze.

Tristan raised an eyebrow at me, then buckled his seatbelt ever so slowly, as if he thought I would bolt at any sudden movements.

"I'm sorry," I said, putting a hand over my face. "I don't know what's wrong with me."

"It's okay. I'll take you home." He started the car and pulled out of the parking spot. "Which way?"

I opened my mouth to answer and then shut it again.

"Lys? Which way to your place?"

I pressed my lips together in a thin line, staring resolutely out the front window.

"Alyssa?"

"I don't want to tell you. You'll just stalk me or something and make my life hell again."

He threw the car into park and shifted in his seat until he was turned toward me. "Alyssa, look at me."

I didn't want to, but I turned toward him anyway. His blue eyes were black in the shadows of the car, and small curls escaped the hold of his hair product and fell forward into his eyes. He caught my gaze and held it, letting the silence stretch out for the span of a few heartbeats.

"I'm sorry." His voice was so quiet it was almost a whisper. "I don't know what else I can do or say, other than I'm sorry. I can understand why you don't trust me anymore, and I kick myself every day for being so dumb. You were the best thing that I had, and I screwed it up." He raised his hand to my cheek and trailed his fingers along my jaw to my hair at the back of my neck, making me shiver. "I don't expect you to ever forgive me. But please try to understand that I'm not that person anymore. Not really." He bowed his head and looked up into my eyes. "I'm so, so sorry."

His gaze traveled over my face, pausing at my lips. I wanted to say something, anything, but my head was still spinning and his fingers in my hair weren't helping me think. His eyes met mine again, and there was sorrow behind them.

With a sigh, he dropped his hand from my neck. I rocked forward, startled by the sudden absence of touch. He settled back into his chair, shifted the car into reverse, and twisted the car back into the parking lot.

"What are you doing?" I asked.

"Call Rose," he said, staring out the windshield with his hands tight on the steering wheel. "If you don't want me to know where you live, I understand. Call Rose and have her come get you. I'll wait with you here."

I watched him in the shifting shadows as he clenched his jaw and swallowed his pride. Maybe he really was sorry. This was the first time in years I'd seen a glimpse of the old Tristan, of the man I'd fallen in love with, rather than the arrogant mask he'd donned when we left Arcadia. My head was still spinning, but the memory of that Tristan pulled at my heart and warmed my cheeks.

"Left," I said.

"What?"

"Turn left out of the parking lot. Then I'll tell you where to go."

He turned his head and smiled softly down at me, then shifted the car into gear.

10

I rolled over and the sheets moved against my skin, soft and warm, as I slowly blinked my eyes open. My room was dark, but sunlight seeped in around the edges of my blackout curtains. My toes reached to the end of my bed in a long, languid stretch and I pushed my hair out of my face, trying to piece together the night before.

Most of the night was a blur, but I could vaguely remember Tristan driving me home and walking me to my apartment door. I'd tripped in my high heels, still unsteady from whatever had affected me. A memory surfaced of a hushed argument between him and Rose as I stumbled to my bedroom and fell into bed. Curious, I shifted again, peering under the covers. I was in my pajamas. Did Rose help me change or did I do it myself? My jewelry was gone, too, settled in a small pile on my bedside table. The sight of my silver WMA laying amid my necklace and earrings brought thoughts of Seraphina's hand on my waist as we spun across the dance floor.

My face warming, I slid out of bed and padded to the bathroom. She and I had done nothing more than chat and enjoy one dance together, but there'd been sparks there—literally. I'd never had that kind of reaction to anyone before. I showered, letting the hot water rush over me as I tried to decipher exactly what that meant. She'd given me her number. I could just call her and find out. We could get together and do…something. Just coffee or drinks. Low pressure, no expectations. I could do that, right?

Right.

I dried off, then dialed her and put the phone to my ear. It rang once. Twice.

"Hello?" Her voice was as I remembered it, low and smooth and sensual. It slid down my spine and chased all rational thought from my head.

"Uh," I stammered. "Seraphina? It's Alyssa D'Yaragen. We met last night at the gala?"

"Oh, Alyssa, I'm so glad you called." Even over the phone I could hear the genuine relief in her voice. "I was so upset with myself for not getting your number before you ran off last night. I was worried I'd never hear from you."

She was happy I called. That was good, right? I should have given her my number at the gala. Why didn't I think to give her my number?

"Would it be too forward of me to ask you to meet me tonight?" she asked. "I have some things I wanted to talk to you about."

"Things?" *Smooth, Alyssa.*

"Yes. It's about the new Arcadian Wing of the Botanical Gardens, and—well, I'll tell you more tonight. Does seven sound good to you?"

"Yeah, seven is good," I answered automatically, then winced as I realized I needed to go in to the shop until close. "Uh, actually, no. Would nine be too late for you?"

"Nine is fantastic. Do you have any place that you like to go?"

"Sure. Do you know Manny's? In District Five? It's a pub. Good food, good drinks."

"I don't know it, but I'll find it and meet you there. And Alyssa?" She paused. "I really am glad you called. Really."

My heartbeat pounded in my ears and I sat in dumb silence.

"See you tonight."

"Bye," I said softly, but she'd already hung up.

I arrived at Manny's shortly after nine, anxiety slipping through me as I strode down the damp sidewalk. It had rained earlier, and the scent of wet pavement filled the air, the passing cars kicking up a fine mist to make rainbows around the streetlights. The humidity was doing terrible things to my hair, so I pulled it up in a messy bun at the top of my head. My silhouette in the puddles told me it wasn't helping much—stray wisps of hair flew out at every angle, and I tried to tuck them behind my ears before giving up. Messy was in, wasn't it?

I stopped at the door with my fingers on the brass handle and took two deep breaths. I was being ridiculous; I wasn't some teenager out on my first date. There was no reason for me to be this nervous. Besides, it wasn't a date.

Maybe. Probably.

I took another deep breath and pulled the door open, stepping into Manny's and looking around the room. My eyes landed on Seraphina, her pale head shining, sitting in a booth on the far side of the room. She was wearing a lilac top over white pants, laughing and talking to...

Tristan.

Definitely not a date, then.

My heart sank a bit, but I forced a smile as she looked up and saw me. Tristan twisted around in his seat to follow her gaze, and smiled at me in return. There was a small flash of something akin to regret behind his smile before it quickly vanished. My heart twisted a bit at that. Pieces of his apology from the night before floated to the surface of my mind, though they were blurry. Had he almost kissed me? I couldn't quite remember.

Jeremiah was sitting in his normal booth in the back corner, and he raised a glass to me in greeting, a cigarette hanging from his lips. I nodded back.

"Hey," I said as I reached Seraphina's table, and tried to decide who to sit next to before Tristan slid over and patted the space next to him.

93

"I like your hair like that," he said with a grin as I sat in the open space. "Very JBF. Sexy."

I gave him a long, unamused look before turning to Seraphina. Her gaze took in my tousled hair, then traced its way down my jawline to my lips. Then she met my gaze and quirked an eyebrow in a way that made heat rush to my cheeks.

"Uh, so," I said, flustered. "What's up?"

"Well," she leaned forward, her hands laced in front of her on the table. "I wanted to talk to the two of you about the Arcadian Wing project." She looked from me to Tristan and went on. "I wasn't completely open with you last night, but it's because the Order and I agreed we needed an element of privacy in this whole affair."

Tristan tensed beside me, and I sat up a bit straighter in my chair. "I'm the liaison between Lucca and the Order of the White Hart," she pitched her voice for us alone. "I'm the one who's been handling negotiations and keeping the dialogue open. But," she paused. "I've been given approval to bring on others, if I needed to, or if I'd found those I thought worthy." She smiled, looking pleased.

I raised my eyebrows. "And…you mean us?" I glanced at Tristan, who quickly replaced a look of quiet suspicion with a grin.

"Sounds great," he leaned back in the booth with a self-satisfied smirk. "I can't think of two people who could be more worthy."

"What does this entail?" I asked, looking back at her. She dug through a small bag on the bench beside her, and produced a velvet pouch.

"Not a lot at the moment, honestly." She fingered the strings on the pouch, pulling it open slowly. "You'd basically just be helping me with any further negotiations. Also, you get these." She dumped the contents of the pouch into her palm and I gasped.

"Hart rings?" Tristan's voice held an edge of disbelief.

I felt the same way. Two silver rings nestled against her skin, shimmering in the dim light of the bar. They both had intricate knot-work engraved on the outside, the lines giving the impression of a leaping stag, and the inside of the band was decorated with the flowing hand of the Arcadian script. Doubt made me shift in my seat as I eyed the rings.

"These grant you certain…privileges, obviously," she said. "They signify that you work for me and, in conjunction, the Order. Other Arcadians would have to defer to you in any decisions regarding Americorp and the Botanical Gardens. And likely other decisions, as well." Her eyes glinted mischievously. "It's not a bad…what do you call it…'gig'?" She turned her hand over to show a similar ring on her index finger, only hers was made of gold.

"You barely know us," I said.

"I'd like to change that." Her gaze laid heavy on me, and my stomach flipped once before she went on. "I'm also excellent at reading people, and I think you two are exactly what I need. You were proactive last night, and I appreciate that in potential…colleagues."

My heart thudded, my mind going back to my dance with Lucca. Swiping his prints. If she had figured out what we were up to… "Last night?"

"Asking about the Sevenstar Orchid," she answered. "Part of the reason I was there last night was to evaluate the reaction from the other Arcadians. I knew it was going to raise some concerns, but you were the only ones actively asking around about it. The rest of them…" She waved a hand, her mouth pulled down in a mix of disappointment and…disgust? "They would do anything, as long as the name of the Order was invoked. You two, though, you look past appearances. That's good."

"Well, I'm convinced," Tristan said with a wink, and held out his hand. Seraphina smiled brilliantly at him and dropped one of the rings into his upturned palm. He slipped the ring on his own left index finger, and jumped when it shrunk down to fit snugly against his skin. "Well," he laughed shakily, "that was unnerving."

She turned to me, waiting for my answer.

A Hart ring was tempting. Really, really tempting. It would open doors for me in basically any Arcadian establishment. My voice would carry more weight in any decision. My opinion would matter, no matter what the situation. As a liaison with Americorp, it would give me access to Thomas Lucca.

Plus, any excuse to see Seraphina again looked really good right now.

But it was risky. I'd already drawn attention to myself by dancing with him. If I was going to go through with this run, I'd be stealing from him, and the more familiar he was with me the more chances there was for a slip-up. Lies would pile up, and the more I lied the more it meant keeping my story straight.

"It's all right." Seraphina reached over and took my fingers in hers. "You think about it. Hold onto this until you decide." She placed the ring in my palm.

A tingle of energy spread from the ring to skitter up my arm, raising goosebumps on my skin, and at the same moment there was a clatter and a cry from the far corner of the bar.

I looked up sharply. Jeremiah had dropped his tumbler of whiskey and was clutching his head. His curly hair stuck up between his fingers, and, as I watched, he pitched over sideways onto the floor of the bar.

I was up and running, reaching him before anyone else even had a chance to react.

"Jeremiah," I said, holding his head in my lap as his body starting seizing. "It's okay, Jer, I've got you. It will pass. It's okay."

His vacant eyes stared up at me, not really seeing me, and his pupils had gone milky white.

I'd only ever seen this happen to him a few times before. He was typically in control of his gift, but every once in a while a vision would assert itself without warning, and his body and mind would react violently, at the mercy of the premonition.

I wouldn't wish it on anyone.

The seizing slowed and his lips moved. I leaned my head toward him to hear.

"Smoke," His breath was hot on my cheek, strong with the scent of whiskey and cigarettes as his whispered. "Fire and smoke and blood. Don't open the door—no, it's too late, the enemy is inside. A bastard of light and darkness, born out of love and into hate. Twisted and warped by bitterness and jealousy." He moaned, and his body renewed its violent shaking. "Don't—"

Finally the seizing stopped altogether, and I sat on the floor with his head in my lap, smoothing his hair. Footsteps near me made me look up. Tristan and Seraphina stood above me, Seraphina watching with wide eyes. Tristan's expression was closed, unreadable.

"He'll be okay," I said to them, glancing around at the other patrons peering over their booth seats or from their places at the bar. "He's okay," I said louder, and one by one people went back to their meals.

Manny approached with a glass of water and a soft rag in his hand, placing them both down on Jeremiah's table before nodding grimly down at me. "Want some help?"

I nodded, tucked Seraphina's Hart ring in my pocket, and together we got him up off of the floor and into the booth seat. The bench was long enough that I could sit in the corner and keep his head in my lap. Let's hear it for antique workmanship.

Manny wiped up the spilled whiskey and took the glass back to the bar. Seraphina and Tristan hovered around me, watching helplessly from the edge of the booth.

"Can we do anything?" she asked, wringing her fingers absently.

I shook my head. "It'll be awhile before he recovers, but he'll be okay. You guys should go, I'm going to wait with him until he wakes up." I dipped the cloth in the water and wiped his forehead.

Tristan shrugged before walking back to their booth. I frowned after him.

She nodded. "You keep the ring. Let me know when you make a decision. There's no rush."

"Sure," I said with a soft smile. "Sorry things got crazy."

"No, it's not your fault. You take care of your friend, it's more important." She turned, then stopped and looked back at me. "Let me know if you want a rain check on tonight. I'd like to see you again, not just for business."

My heart pounded a few times and I smiled at her. "Sure. You pick the place next time, though."

She nodded, cast one last concerned look at Jeremiah, and walked back to her table.

I pushed Jeremiah's hair out of his face, wiping the cloth across his brow again. I slipped off his glasses, folded them, laid them on the table next to the cup of water, and thought over what he'd said while in the throes of his vision.

A bastard of light and darkness, born out of love and into hate. A door opening that shouldn't be. Was it the same as my door—the door that should not be opened? It would surprise me if it *wasn't* the same; there didn't tend to be a lot of coincidence when it came to prophesies. I mulled over the rest, chewing on my lower lip in thought. Smoke, fire, and blood. That seemed pretty self-explanatory, and it couldn't be good.

I didn't know much, but I did know one thing.

I would pay a fortune if just once I could get a vision that wasn't cryptic as hell.

11

The rain came down hard, pounding on the big window of Manny's Pub and cascading down in sheets. The bar patrons all spoke in hushed voices, hunched over their cups and casting worried glances out the window. Every once in a while, a peal of thunder would shake the building, setting the light fixtures and rows of glasses above the bar to rattling dully.

"Leave it to Georgia to have a thunderstorm in November," I muttered.

Seraphina and Tristan had left long ago, finishing their drinks and hurrying into the night just as the rain started. I was fleetingly jealous: they both had cars to run to. My motorcycle and I were going to have to wait this out.

Jeremiah stirred, groaning. I helped him sit up, keeping a hand on one shoulder until I was sure he wasn't going to tip over again.

"You alright there, Jer?"

He leaned his head into his hands and moaned unintelligibly. When I didn't reply, he spoke louder.

"Booze." His voice came out gravelly, his throat raw.

I nodded to Manny behind the bar, who'd been casting glances our way and waiting for Jeremiah to wake up. He nodded back and pulled a new tumbler from the shelf, filling it with a generous pour of amber liquid. He walked out from behind the bar and set it on the table next to Jeremiah, who scooped it up and drank down half of it in one swallow.

"Rough one?" Manny asked.

Jeremiah nodded and downed the rest of the drink, then pushed the tumbler back to Manny. "More."

Manny raised his eyebrows at me, but took the glass back to the bar to refill it.

I waited until he was sipping on his second drink before speaking again.

"Get anything useful?" I asked softly.

He shook his head, his eyes distant. "No. Damn it. What the hell good is this *gift* if I can't even tell what the hell I'm seeing?" His voice was bitter and he took another sip from his glass.

"Maybe it's in there and you just can't pick it out?"

"Same difference," he snorted.

I sat quietly, watching him swirl the whiskey around the sides of the tumbler. "You mentioned a door...is it *my* door?"

He stopped swirling the glass, paused for a few heartbeats, then took another drink. "I think so."

I cursed quietly.

"Yeah," he agreed.

"Did you...see *me*?"

His eyebrows pulled down in concentration. "I don't know. I couldn't really see anyone, it was just impressions. Which are *so bloody helpful!*" He yelled at the ceiling, his voice heavy with sarcasm.

As if in answer, a roll of thunder shook the building. That earned us several worried glances, and a few patrons quickly paid their tab and left, pulling coat collars up tight around their ears before rushing out into the storm.

"Keep this up and you'll run off all of Manny's customers," I said wryly, and he cast me a dark look. "Okay, not ready for humor. Noted."

"I don't know what's coming, Lys, but it's bad."

There was nothing I could say to that, so I stayed quiet, looking past him as the rain slowed and the window began to clear. When it seemed the worst was over, I sighed and put my hand on his shoulder.

"We'll figure it out."

He snorted.

"Or we won't. Either way, what's going to happen will happen, right?"

"Yeah," he downed the last of his drink.

"Then we can only brace for impact."

He slipped his glasses back on, ran a hand through his hair, and nodded grimly. "Better grab your ankles..."

I laughed softly, then bumped his shoulder with mine. "Scoot out. I need to get home before this storm starts back up."

He slid out of the booth and I followed, bouncing on my toes once before reaching out to hug him. He tensed a moment before hugging me back.

"Be safe out there," he mumbled into my hair.

"Always."

Outside, the night was cold and humid, and I could still hear rumbles of thunder. The clouds roiled around the tops of the skyscrapers, threatening to open up and soak me if I didn't hurry. I jogged to my bike, yanked my helmet on, and pulled out into the main street.

Being a Friday night, there were still a good number of cars and people on the street despite the rain. I made my way through traffic, mindful of the slick roads and careless pedestrians. I was about halfway home when my phone rang, the wireless headset in my helmet announcing the incoming call as Logan.

"Hey, techie, what's up?" I answered.

"Where are you?" He said, his voice breathless.

"I'm doing great, thanks for asking. How're you?" I rolled my eyes and turned onto a side street. He was silent for a moment.

"I have something to show you. I'm at your shop. Where are you?"

"Logan, it's after ten o'clock on a Friday night. I'm most decidedly *not* at work."

"Oh." He sounded crestfallen. "Do you think you could come here, though? I really want to show you this."

I sighed heavily. "Sure! Why not? Not like I'm doing anything else," I muttered.

"Okay, good. See you in a few." He hung up.

I sighed again, turning at the next cross street to angle back toward my shop. My mind was tired from everything that had happened tonight—and, hell, last night, too. Maybe it was good that I was going to see Logan. He and I could talk and work out plans for the Americorp run. We still hadn't decided on details—though I wasn't sure if I could focus on details tonight.

As I sat at a red light, something moved in my peripheral vision. I turned my head and searched the shadows in front of the dark store fronts, but nothing was there. The traffic light changed, and I chalked it up to reflections from the rain as I pulled forward. As I picked up speed, though, I noticed it again. Something moving along the side-walk, low and sinuous, but it was gone when I turned my head to look for it. *A cat?*

It had seemed too big to be a cat. But it hadn't moved like a dog, either. Too low to the ground, too fluid and twisty.

Unease shivered up my spine, and I pushed my bike to go faster.

As I did, the rain started again.

"Great," I muttered, as it plinked against my face shield and soaked into my pants. I slowed, but as I did, the slinking shadow to my right wove between a trashcan and the street light. I saw a flash of jagged teeth in the haze, then it reared up and hissed at me. A spray of slime emitted from its long mouth and I yelped as it barely missed my helmet. Then a drop landed on my bike and sizzled, sending up a small stream of acrid smoke that smelled like a welding shop.

"You've *got* to be kidding me," I yelled, and gunned the motor. My bike lurched forward, the tires squealing and sending up a spray of oily rainwater. By now the rain had renewed its force and was coming down in sheets. The creature kept pace and I cursed, wiping water from my visor. I couldn't use the Eldergloom here, there were still too many people on the streets who could see me. And I didn't have my gun. Dammit, why didn't I have my gun?

I made a silent resolution to always carry a weapon if I could just get through this. But what could I do? I couldn't fight an acid-spitting...whatever that was. I caught a glimpse of shining scales and a lizard-like head, and my heart dropped as I realized what I was up against.

Crap.

I hit a button on my handlebar and, inside my helmet, my phone rang.

And rang.

And rang.

"Dammit, Logan, pick up! Your phone's in your brain, it's not like you can miss the freaking call!"

"Hey, Lys," he answered.

"I'm heading your way," I yelled to be heard over the rain thundering against my helmet. "Something's after me. It's spraying some sort of acid and I don't have my gun."

There was a long pause. "What?"

"Dammit, techie, keep up!" I wove between two cars and blasted through a yellow light. "I'm incoming, hostile on my tail, likely non-humanoid and really damn fast. You got anything to handle this?"

"Non-humanoid?"

"Yes or no, Logan!"

"Yes! Yes. I've got you covered."

"Good. Heads up, I'll be there in less than two." I thumbed the button again and ended the call.

Then I focused on not dying.

Hey, sometimes it's harder than it sounds.

The next two minutes were a blur of rain, slick tires, close calls, and scales and fangs illuminated by the occasional flash of lightning. I hunched over my handlebars, relief flooding through me as I rounded a corner and my shop came into view, dark and vacant. My stomach dropped.

No sign of Logan.

Before I could look for him, a large, serpentine form reared up in front of me. My tires skidded on the wet pavement as I braked hard. There was no way I was going to stop in time. With a small prayer, I yanked my bike into a hard turn, and in a heart-stopping moment, my tires slipped.

I had two choices. My legs could get crushed between my motorcycle and the street, or I could try to jump free. And I had a split second to make the decision.

I chose to jump.

I leapt free from my bike and hit the ground hard, trying to tuck and roll to minimize the damage. My ankle wrenched underneath me and my shoulder slammed hard into the pavement. Then my head hit the road, sending ringing waves of white exploding across my vision.

Thank God for helmets.

With an awful sound of metal and fiberglass grinding, my bike careened toward the creature. Instead of getting cut down, the monster simply went up and over the hurtling motorcycle and headed for me.

I tried to sit up, shaking my head to clear my vision. There was a loud hiss and the creature hovered over me, front legs in the air and fangs bared, its head pulled back as if to strike.

Then there was a humming *zzzhhee-OOM* that I felt more than heard. A glowing blue mass shot over my head and took the creature square in the face. It flew backward ten feet, hit the pavement, and was still.

Gasping, I pushed my visor back and looked over my shoulder. Logan stood behind me with a plasma rifle braced against his shoulders, his hair dripping with rainwater. The seams of his motorcycle jacket glowed with blue EL-wire. The gun was matte black, but had a line of luminescent blue running down the side to the stock that matched his jacket. His face split in a huge grin and he let out a whoop.

"Got it! Did you see that? That was *awesome*. This thing was completely worth it." He hefted the rifle in satisfaction.

I simply stared up at him and waited for the stars to clear from my vision.

"Oh, hey, are you okay?" He let the gun fall to hang from a strap over his shoulder and rushed to me, reaching down to help pull me to my feet.

"Well," I said, gasping as pain shot through my ankle. "I'm alive, so that's good. I *am* alive, right?"

"Hell yes you are," he grinned. "And the way you jumped off your bike like that? That was bad-ass!"

I pulled off my helmet and gave him a grim smile of acknowledgment. "Thanks." The rain hit my hair and wove its way under the collar of my jacket. My head began to throb, my ankle ached. I rolled my shoulder and hissed at the jabbing pain that shot through my arm with the motion.

"What the hell *was* that, anyway?" he asked.

We both looked at the creature lying in a puddle on the other side of the street. I limped toward it, one arm braced on Logan's shoulder. "A storm drake, I think."

The creature was laid out on its back in the gutter. It was about five feet long from tail to…well, where its nose *should* have been. The blast from Logan's gun had taken its head completely off. The ragged edges of the stump glistened and smoked, sending up a rancid smell that burned my nostrils and made my eyes water. Its gray-green scales shone dully in the streetlight, lighter on its stomach and fading to almost black on its back. It looked like a giant, mutated lizard, its six legs sprawled out to its sides, and I jumped as one of the legs twitched.

"Should I shoot it again?" he asked, hiking his gun up to his shoulder.

"No. It's dead." As we watched, it began to collapse in on itself and the smoke increased. I coughed and put a hand over my mouth. "We'd better back up."

Logan coughed and nodded, helping me limp back across the street and sit down on the curb. He sat next to me, and together we watched the storm drake disintegrate.

"No one's going to believe me," he said with a quiet laugh.

"It's probably for the best," I said, testing my shoulder again with a slow roll. "Ow."

"How're you doing?"

"Me? Oh, I'm just peachy," I sighed. Just past the still-simmering puddle, my bike had slid to a stop against the store front. I let out a small whimper and put my head in my hands. My poor bike.

"So," he said, drawing out the word. "Do you get attacked by storm drakes often?"

"No, this is a first for me."

"Ah." He was quiet as we watched smoke swirl into nothingness. "Uh, so, um…what *is* a storm drake, anyway?"

"Sort of a miniature dragon. They thrive in storms, sort of an elemental creature, but not very powerful."

"That wasn't very powerful?"

"No, that was actually pretty weak as elementals go. You were able to kill it with a plasma rifle, after all."

"Yeah, but I can kill most things with a plasma rifle."

"Most of the things you're shooting at are from this plane of existence. They're easier to kill. Even elves," I added in response to his raised eyebrow.

"All right, then."

I let my eyes drift shut. Now that the adrenaline was ebbing, I was exhausted. My entire body ached; even the light pressure of my boot on my ankle hurt. I hoped desperately that it wasn't broken. I couldn't go on this run with a broken ankle.

"Uh, do you need a ride home?" Logan asked, and I nodded.

"Just let me put my bike in the alley. I'll look at it tomorrow." I started to push up off of the curb, but he stopped me.

"No, hey, I got it." He jumped up, gave the remnants of the drake a wide berth, and picked my bike up from the ground, wheeling it around the side of my shop and reappearing a few moments later with his own bike.

"How did it look?" I asked, bracing myself.

"Uh, I couldn't tell," he said, avoiding my eyes. "Too dark."

I groaned. It must be bad.

He pulled on his helmet, got on his bike, and held out a hand to me.

"Wait," I said. "What is it that you wanted to show me?"

"Oh." He pushed his visor up and grinned again. "This." He pulled the gun across his chest. "I was gonna tell you all about it, but I think getting to see it in action was more than enough."

"Techies and their toys," I sighed, then smiled. "Thanks. I'm not sure what I would have done if you hadn't been here."

"No problem. Thanks for giving me a chance to try it out on something other than the shooting range."

I smiled again, then pulled my helmet on and got carefully onto the back of his bike. "Let's avoid crashing this one, yeah?"

"Sure thing."

We both pushed our visors down and he drove us toward home.

T he storms had cleared out overnight, but the parking lot of The Grove was still dotted with puddles as Rose and I pulled up on her bike. It was early, just a hair after eight in the morning, and a cold fog hung in the air and wove its way between the buildings, clinging to our clothes and making everything damp. I was wearing working leathers today, just in case—leather pants, soft leather boots, leather jacket—and kept my eyes open for any stray storm drakes. Thankfully, nothing attacked us, and we made it to The Grove without incident.

Rose helped me down from her bike and gave me an arm to lean on as we made our way into the coffeehouse. She walked up to the bar to order a drink and I limped to the archway, whispering the password and stepping into Arcadia.

It had rained here, too, and the same mist hung in the trees, but where it had been cold and miserable in Atlanta, here it was warm, the air heavy like in a rain forest. A young Acolyte I didn't know scurried across the grass, the hem of his emerald robe damp from the dew. He bowed his lilac head to me.

"*Am'fialte,*" I greeted him with a smile. "I'm here for mending. Is there a Healer available?"

He nodded his head again. "I will check. What ails you?"

"Oh, lots of things," I laughed ruefully, then sighed when he simply frowned at my lame attempt at humor. "Head, shoulder, ankle." I took a few limping steps in demonstration.

"If you wish, you may sit and I will send some Acolytes out with a *luaven*."

"Thank you, yes," I sighed, lowering myself onto a stone bench beside the arch. "Also, if you see Keeper Lorelei, please inform her that Alyssa would like a word."

He nodded and scurried off again. I inhaled, breathing deeply the scent of flowers and new grass. The stone beneath me was damp, but I stretched my legs out and propped my injured ankle on top of the other. A few minutes passed and two Acolytes trotted out to me, led by the original Acolyte and carrying a small litter between them. They set the cushioned chair down. Once I settled into it, they lifted the litter and carried me off.

The healing ward was a large stone building toward the back of the grove, nestled between two ancient trees. We entered through double doors under a sweeping archway, into a long room with beds lining either side. Each bed was tucked back in an alcove with a round mirror in a delicately carved frame hanging on the wall above it. The ceiling was vaulted, with delicate pointed arches. Round windows let in natural light, and three chandeliers hung with candles were suspended high above our heads, lending a golden glow to the misty morning.

They put the *luaven* down next to one of the beds and one of the Acolytes helped me up. Once I was seated on the bed, the two carrying the *luaven* took it away and a Healer in white robes approached me. The original Acolyte nodded and turned to leave.

"Thank you..." I said, trailing off.

"Quin," he said.

"Thank you, Quin."

He smiled at me and followed the others. I watched them go, then turned my attention to the Healer. His dark hair was pulled back from his face in an intricate set of plaits that met at the nape of his neck to form one long, thick braid. His gray-green eyes were kind, and he smiled at me.

"*Am'fialte,* my name is Ciane. What brings you here today?"

"I may have broken my ankle. My shoulder is injured, too, and I hit my head. I may or may not be concussed."

He raised his eyebrows but kept any commentary to himself. "If you would, please remove your boots and your jacket and I'll look you over."

"And the price of this healing, for someone living outside Arcadia?" Arcadia ran on a very socialist-style system…normally, healing would be free for those living in and contributing to our society. Since I hadn't been in Arcadia for many years, they would no longer heal me out of the goodness of their hearts. And I didn't expect them to.

He paused, his hands in a basin of water on the bedside table. "A donation of time or coin to the Arcanum should suffice. Do not worry yourself over the cost. Our wayward brethren all find their way back eventually." He smiled softly and rinsed his hands. The motion always struck me as more ceremonial than sanitary, and the water that dripped from his fingers sparkled more than it should have in the soft light. I frowned at the implication that I was wayward, but did as he asked, pulling off my boots and dropping them on the floor. He stared as I pulled off my jacket and exposed my gun. I shrugged at him and folded my jacket at the foot of the bed, pulled my gun from its holster, and laid it on the small bedside table. After last night, I wasn't going anywhere unarmed.

I laid back, and looked up at the sound of the front door opening. Lorelei strode through the door and headed straight to me.

"Alyssa, what happened?"

I hissed as Ciane laid gentle fingers on my injured ankle. He cast me an apologetic look, then his eyes silvered as he pulled on the Eldergloom, sending tendrils of it through his fingertips and deep into the joint. I watched with a small pang of envy. Those who were Healers could access the Eldergloom to work wonders on the injured. They couldn't do much else with it, but it was an art I'd never perfected. Healing had always eluded me.

I tried not to dwell too long on what that might say about me as a person.

Lorelei stood quietly at my bedside, watching as the Healer worked.

"I was hoping you could help me figure that out, actually," I said with a grimace. "I was jumped by a storm drake last night."

Her eyebrows shot up, and Ciane faltered briefly in his work. "In Atlanta?" She asked.

I nodded. "I've never seen a storm drake in the city before."

"No. Too much iron for their liking." She chewed on her lower lip.

"I know. I could almost chock it up to the crazy storms we were having, but it specifically went after me. It chased me through blocks and blocks of the city, past plenty of other people."

She looked at me, hard and long. "You think someone summoned it."

I shrugged and then winced as pain lanced through my injured shoulder. "It's the only explanation I can come up with."

Her eyebrows pulled down in thought. "Have you angered any Elves lately?"

"No, I—" I stopped, and my eyes widened. "Eyja." I snarled.

"Who?"

"A Talmorin I met a few days ago."

"And you think she wishes you harm?

"I don't know. She was openly hostile to me and tried to screw me out of a job, but I didn't expect this. Though maybe I should have." Her words echoed through my memory: *You didn't tell me she was Alfheimer.* My lip curled. "One thing's for sure, she and I will be having a little chat when I get back."

Ciane moved from my ankle to my shoulder, his hands on my skin tingling like a thousand tiny shocks. I rotated my ankle and sighed happily at the lack of pain. Lorelei settled herself in the chair on my right side, folding her hands neatly in her lap and observing.

"Oh," I said. "I almost forgot. Has the Order said anything about endorsing an Arcadian Wing of the Atlanta Botanical Gardens?"

She looked at me sharply. "An Arcadian Wing of—no. Though the

Order doesn't share their every move with me." She frowned. "You have this on good authority?"

I nodded and flicked a meaningful glance from her to Ciane and back. Healers were generally tight-lipped about what they heard while their patients were in their care, but I didn't want to bring up the Hart rings to anyone but Lorelei. Though Seraphina hadn't said not to talk about it, until I knew the Order's actual intentions, I didn't want to be spreading potential secrets.

We sat quietly as Ciane worked, my bruise fading as his fingers moved over my skin. He finished with my shoulder and laid his hands on either side of my face, his fingertips on my temples. With one last, long exhale, he sent the humming energy through my skull. It spiraled behind my eyes several times, then dispersed through me with like a soft sigh.

"Your injuries are mended," he said, the Eldergloom fading from his eyes. "Do you require anything further from me?"

"No," I said. "Thank you. I feel ten times better."

He smiled gently at me. "Of course. It's what I do. Now, I will leave you two to your conversation. Stay as long as you need. Keeper," He nodded respectfully to Lorelei, tucked his hands into the sleeves of his robe, and turned on his heel to head back to the rear of the building.

I watched him go, then looked back at Lorelei. "I didn't spill any secret beans, did I?"

"Even if you did, Ciane is not one for idle gossip."

"Good," I sat up and swung my feet over the edge of the bed. "Because Thomas Lucca, the CEO of Americorp, announced the new wing publicly at a charity gala earlier this week. There were other Arcadians there, so I imagine it will start sifting back here soon if it hasn't already. Also, the intermediary between the Order and Americorp has Hart rings."

"Then there's no doubt that it's supported by the Order," she said. "I do not know why it's been a secret up until now, but it's within their purview to keep it as such."

"Lorelei, this new wing will have both human and Arcadian flora. Why would they agree to something like that? That makes no sense."

"I don't know," she said, her back stiffening. "But it's their decision to make."

I sighed heavily. "Okay, okay, I get it." She was giving me her official Keeper of the Relics voice, a title she held only by grace of the Order.

She gave me an apologetic look, her emerald eyes imploring. "I'm sorry, Alyssa. If the Emissary has Hart rings, it's official. I cannot question it...but that doesn't mean that you can't." A devious smiled flashed across her face and was gone again.

"I'll remember that." I grinned back. She handed me my boots and I slipped them back on, grabbing my jacket from the foot of the bed before hopping down to the floor. I spared a moment to enjoy the freedom that comes with two good ankles, and draped my jacket across my shoulders. "I should be getting back. I need to have a discussion with a certain Talmorin," I growled.

"I'll walk with you," she said, and we made our way out of the Healer's ward and toward the arches.

"Do me a favor," I said as we approached the standing stones. "Keep an ear out for anything suspicious? Jeremiah has been having some bad visions lately."

She nodded. "What has he seen?"

"Oh, you know, the usual. Blood. Fire. Death and destruction."

She made a low sound of acknowledgment. "That doesn't sound good. I haven't heard of anything from the Oracles, but I will check. Maybe his visions are localized?"

"Maybe. Between his visions and the elemental, though, I'm worried."

"As you should be. I'll see what I can find. Until then, be safe."

I gave her a quick hug, whispered *a'chara*, and ducked back through the archway.

13

I stepped out into The Grove, pushed my hair back from my face, and looked around for Rose. She was tucked in a comfy chair in the back alcove with her eReader in one hand and a large white mug in the other.

"How'd it go?" she asked without looking up.

"Well, I'm back in one piece, at least. My information-gathering was less than productive." I threw myself into the chair next to her, sitting in it sideways with one leg over the arm.

"Mmm," was her only reply as she sipped her coffee and pushed a second mug across the small table between the two chairs. "Extra whipped cream."

I grinned at her and lost myself for a few minutes in steamed milk and espresso. When I returned to the land of the living, I pulled my phone out of my pocket and turned it on.

Several notifications chimed in: three text messages, two from Logan and one from Tristan, and one missed call from Seraphina.

My heart did a little somersault in my chest, and I tried for casual as I queued up my voice mail message and put the phone to my ear.

"Hello Alyssa, this is Seraphina. I know it's early in the day, but I was curious if you'd thought over my offer—and was wondering if you would like to come to my place this evening for a meal and a few drinks. One is not contingent on the other. I'll be awaiting your answer." The message ended, and I realized I was holding my breath.

Rose cleared her throat pointedly, and I jumped, a blush rising to my cheeks as I fumbled to hang up the phone. She raised her eyebrows, but ignored my reaction.

"So," she said. "What's the plan?"

I stuffed my phone in my pocket and took a long drink from my mug. Logan had already made his stance on the tension between me and Eyja clear. He probably wouldn't help me call out his friend. He likely wouldn't even believe me. I was going to have to do that on my own. Plus, if Eyja was sending extra-planar creatures after me, I had no idea what she would do if I confronted her straight on. It would make more sense for her to deny it rather than go after me in public, but I knew next to nothing about the woman. I was going to have to be careful about this.

"I might need to go down to Café 1337 tonight," I said, my eyes serious. "You feel like coming?" Hopefully Eyja made it a habit of frequenting there.

"You need me to back you up on something?"

"Maybe. I'm not sure yet," I replied. "It won't be until late tonight, anyway. I'll let you know." Before I went to fight with the Talmorin, though, I needed to decide what I was going to wear to Seraphina's. I was going to have to taxi it, since my bike was busted, so I could wear a dress. I winced, remembering my bike, still in the alley behind my shop. "I hate to keep asking you to drive me around, but will you take me over to my store? I need to see what shape my bike is in."

"I'll take you wherever you need to go if you let me finish my coffee and my chapter first."

"Deal."

I sipped my coffee and watched the morning crowd, some relaxing on a Saturday morning, others rushing in and out on their way to work. Thankfully, I could relax—Cinda ran the shop on Saturdays. With the amount of time she'd spent picking up my slack lately, I might as well just sell the shop to her. She'd probably laugh at me if I offered, though. She loved her job, but she saw the stress I went through every month around the time I had to pay bills.

I scrolled through my phone, checking the texts from Tristan and Logan.

Logan's read: *Let me know when you want to talk shop.*

I sighed and chewed the inside of my lip. We really needed to get this Americorp ball rolling, but now there was dinner with Seraphina...

I flicked to Tristan's message.

Just checking in. Let me know you're okay.

I scrunched my eyebrows at that. It could be real worry, or it could be his attempt at re-establishing contact with me. I glared at my phone as if it were the reason for all of my ills, then quickly tapped out a message.

I'm fine.

Hopefully he'd leave it alone, but I knew Tristan, and I knew he liked to push. I should never have gone with him to the gala, but I never expected Seraphina to give him an excuse to stick around town.

Why couldn't things ever go as planned?

I sighed again, and Rose shot me a look before going back to her eReader.

A thought occurred to me.

"Rose," I said.

"Hmm?"

"You never asked me about the gala."

"Nope." Her eyes never left her screen.

"Why not?"

"I figured you'd talk to me about it when you were ready." She raised a finger to the eReader screen, turned the page on her book, and continued reading.

I watched her for a long moment, my eyes narrowing. "I come home drunk with my ex-boyfriend and you have nothing to say about that?"

She shrugged one shoulder. "Should I have something to say?"

"Considering you never pass up a chance to lecture me, I'd assumed you'd have a presentation prepared. A monologue at least."

"Things must have gone at least moderately well, since you haven't been cursing or throwing things. Tristan drove you home and seemed genuinely concerned." She finally met my gaze, one eyebrow raised.

"I—yes." I picked at the cardboard sleeve on my coffee mug, avoiding her gaze. "He drove me home, and was a gentleman about it."

"Yes, he was," she said, and I glanced up at her sharply. She met my eyes with a serene gaze. "I was surprised."

I looked back at my coffee cup, mulling that over.

"And the rest of the night?"

"It went well. We got what we needed. And I...met someone." Heat crept up my neck again.

"Oh?" She sat up a little straighter. "Do I know them?"

"I don't think so. Her name is Seraphina. She's an elf, working with Lucca and the Order of the White Hart on a big project at the Botanical Gardens. She actually invited me over for dinner tonight."

Rose set her eReader down. "And Tristan?"

I sighed. "He might be sticking around for longer than I'd hoped. Seraphina invited us both to help with the project."

She grimaced. "Oof. Awkward."

"To say the least," I replied wryly.

"What are you going to do? Can he keep it professional?"

"Hell, I'm not exactly 'keeping it professional.' Makes it hard for me to throw stones."

"Good point." We both sipped our drinks. "You're not getting too close to Lucca, are you?"

"I hope not, but that's the only reason I haven't accepted her offer yet."

She nodded, stretched, and stood. "Let's go see the damage on your bike, shall we?"

We left the shop and made our way to my store.

My bike was a mess. I took one look at it and called my mechanic.

Back in my apartment, I sprawled across my bed, my head hanging off the mattress backwards as I tried to figure out what to do. My bike sat in the shop, and I had no idea how long it would be until I got it back. On top of my lack of transportation, there was the issue with Eyja. If the Talmorin *had* sent the storm drake after me, I needed to know why. If I walked into a confrontation with her without having more details, it was possible she'd escalate things in public. A fight amongst a gaggle of innocent bystanders was not my cup of tea. So I had to be careful, and I needed information.

My obvious choice was Logan, but I really didn't want to fight with him about his friend. Though, if I told him my suspicions, he might be eager to clear her name and so be that much more willing to talk about her. I chewed the corner of my lip and turned the thought over in my head a few times. It might work.

And then I had Seraphina.

There was no denying she'd captured my attention. My eyes drifted shut to the memory of her hand on my waist as we danced, gentle but insistent as she guided me across the floor. I barely knew this woman, but there were sparks there for sure. Dinner tonight would help me figure out if this was just some silly schoolgirl crush or if there was more to it than that. I'd never put much stock in love at first sight, but attraction at first sight?

Oh, yeah.

Besides, I still owed her an answer about the Order.

With a start, I realized I'd left the ring in my pants pocket in the chaos of the night before. I rolled onto my stomach and grabbed my torn jeans from the pile of clothes next to my bed, shoving my hand into the pocket. My fingers touched the cool metal of the ring and a tingle of power ran across my skin. I pulled it out and turned it over in my hands, watching the sunlight gleam off the intricate knotwork.

The problem was, I still didn't know what I was going to tell her.

I pushed up off of my bed and walked to my dresser, digging

through my jewelry box and coming out with a simple, naked chain. I slid the ring onto the chain and secured it around my neck.

My phone rang.

Logan.

"Hey, techie. What's up?"

"Hey. What're you doing?"

I sighed. "Just considering the existential crisis that is my world right now."

"…what?"

"Nevermind. What did you need?"

"I wanted to see how you were doing. How's the head?"

"It's good, actually. I'm good to go for the run, so don't stress yourself about that."

"Are you sure? We can push it back a few days if we have to, in case—"

"Logan," I interrupted. "I'm fine. Trust me."

There was a long pause before he went on. "Okay, if you're sure. I thought we could get together to discuss the run tonight. I don't want to put this off too long in case something goes wrong and we need to bail until another night."

"Yeah, that's probably a good idea." I twisted a curl around my finger absent-mindedly. "I sort of already have plans for tonight. I can do it this afternoon or tomorrow."

"Sure, I can meet you this afternoon. Where would you like to work?"

"We can work in my back office. Manny's may be a little public for this sort of work."

"All right, awesome. I'll meet you at your shop around two. Sound good?"

"Yeah, that's fine. Sorry about tonight."

"No problem."

"Actually, I have something I need to talk to you about, anyway," I tucked the stray curl behind my ear and opened my closet, eyeing possible outfits for the evening.

"Uh oh. That sounds like you're breaking up with me or some-thing. You're not ditching the job on me, are you?"

"No, no, nothing like that." I pulled a long, flowing blue dress from my closet and held it up to myself, turning to look at my reflection. "It's about Eyja, actually."

"Alyssa—"

"Just let me talk to you about it before you start yelling at me, okay? It may not be what you think." *Or it's totally what you think.*

There was a long pause before he spoke. "Fine."

"Thank you."

"See you this afternoon."

I hung up the phone and stared at myself in the mirror. Then I queued up Seraphina's number and put the phone to my ear.

"Hello, Alyssa," her voice purred from the other end of the line. "Did you get my invitation?"

I swallowed and tried to calm my heart, which had started hammering the moment she spoke. "Yes. I'd love to come over."

"Oh, good. What time works for you?"

"I have something going on this afternoon and I'm not sure how long it'll take. Can we maybe schedule it for later in the evening?" *Or I could come over right now if it's all the same to you.* Ugh, why did I have obligations?

"Of course. Does seven sound good? I can have dinner ready when you walk in the door and have you out in an hour if you need to."

"I don't need to rush," I said quickly. "I can stay for a few hours if you want to, ah…do…things."

"Very well, then," there was a smile in her voice. "Then be here at seven and we'll eat eventually."

"Okay. Seven. I can do that."

"Excellent. I'll send you my address and see you tonight."

"Okay."

"Goodbye, Alyssa."

"Bye."

I turned back to the mirror, phone in one hand and dress in the other. Seven. Sure.

Now I just needed to figure out how to hide a gun in this dress.

W hen I walked in to the shop a little after two, Cinda and Logan were leaning across the counter, laughing at a projection on the glass top. They glanced up at me then looked back down, their heads inches apart, and laughed again. I peered over Logan's shoulder to see a video of a puppy growling at a tennis ball.

"All right, techie, playtime's over," I said, smacking him lightly on the shoulder. "Let's get to work. Heya, Cinda."

"Hi, Alyssa." She stood and shook out her short blond curls. "How's the bike?"

I winced. "Not good. It's going to be a few days in the shop. I'm stuck with taxis until then."

She pulled a bottle of glass cleaner from under the counter and began to wipe the surface. "You can always call me if you need a ride, you know."

"I wouldn't do that." I smiled at her. "You deserve to spend your free time doing something other than shuttling me around. But thank you for the offer." I moved around the counter toward the back of the shop. "We're doing some work in the office today. No visitors, okay?"

"Sure thing. Oh, before you head back, a package came this morning. We weren't expecting a shipment and it was addressed to you personally, so I didn't open it. It's in your office."

"Thanks."

I led Logan to the back, thinking. We *weren't* expecting a shipment, and I hadn't ordered anything for myself recently, being on a tight budget and all. Maybe that supplier had finally sent me those MP3 players I'd—

A large wooden crate roughly five feet long and four feet high sat in the middle of the floor.

"Huh." That was...not what I was expecting. I approached the crate cautiously, looking it over.

The return address read "Atlanta Botanical Gardens."

My eyes narrowed. "Hey techie, grab my pry bar from the bottom desk drawer, will you?"

Logan tossed me the pry bar and, with a few deft movements, I popped the front off the crate. Foam pieces tumbled onto the floor, and I was left staring at a painting wrapped in thick, protective plastic. The image was barely visible through the cloudy sheeting—a circle of stone arches beneath a full moon.

With a quiet sense of awe, I crouched down, carefully slit the plastic and pulled it away from the painting, exposing the artwork. It was even more beautiful up close—it was easier to see how each delicate brush stroke enhanced the image and lent the whole thing an air of ethereal beauty. I settled back on my heels.

I hadn't placed a bid on the painting—it had been way outside of my expendable budget. Someone else must have purchased it and then gifted it to me.

I looked up at Logan with an arched eyebrow, but he seemed only vaguely interested.

"Did you buy this?" I asked him.

"Buy what?"

"This," I gestured at the painting. "It was up for auction at the gala."

"Oh." He looked it over once, only slightly more interested than before, and flopped into a chair. "No, wasn't me."

I chewed on a fingernail, thinking. It could have been Tristan. He seemed to have no problem bankrolling his trip to Atlanta—between the fancy car and the tickets to the gala, he'd dropped a lot on this little excursion.

Or...maybe it had been Seraphina.

I shook my head and stood. That was silly. Seraphina had no reason to buy gifts for a random woman she just met, even if she *was* interested in me, which I didn't even know for sure that she was. I balled up the heavy plastic and threw it toward my tiny wastebasket by my desk, but the plastic unfurled and fell in a heap to the floor a foot from its target. I took three long strides, snatched it up, and stuffed it in the trash can.

Logan watched me intently as I walked across the room, his eyes pulling down in confusion as I sat down across from him.

"You really *are* fine, aren't you?"

I stared. "Why Logan, you sure know how to sweet talk the ladies."

"No, I mean," He waved a hand, indicating all of me, and I quirked an eyebrow at him. He looked even more flustered and a light blush filled his face. "You're not hurt."

I laughed once and settled back in my chair.

"How are you not hurt?"

I shrugged one shoulder and grinned at him. "Magic."

"Fine, don't tell me." He sighed and cued up his projector on my desk top. I leaned forward and studied the floor plans for the Ameri corp plant, and we got to work planning various strategies.

An hour later I straightened up, stretching my back and letting out a long sigh. "I think that's it," I said. "Anything we missed?"

He tucked his holoprojector in his pocket and shook his head, his gaze lost in thought. "No, I think that's it for planning. You said you wanted to talk to me about Eyja."

I nodded, avoiding his eyes, and sat in my chair. The old leather creaked as I pulled myself up to the desk. I set my hands on the desktop and laced my fingers together.

"I think Eyja sent the storm drake."

He looked at me with blank eyes and blinked once. "I...that doesn't make any sense."

"Storm drakes are elemental creatures. They thrive in storms, but even with that they wouldn't voluntarily come into the city—too much smoke and iron. And it was obviously after *me*. The only reason it would have behaved the way it did was if someone summoned it to attack me."

"Okay," he drew the word out long. "So, ignoring the *why* for now, *how* exactly does one summon a storm drake?"

"There's several ways," I said noncommittally, not wanting to tell too many elfy secrets. "I don't know which one she used, specifically, but it usually takes an elf to do that sort of summoning."

"You said 'usually'." He sat up straighter, seeing a chink in my argument. "So it *could* have been a human."

"Yes," I admitted, trying not to lose my patience. "There's an incredibly infinitesimal chance it could have been a human. Maybe if they had some elf blood, or had trained for a long time or managed to find one of our artifacts—" I stopped myself, realizing I was revealing more than I should about Arcadians. "But the chance it was a human is miniscule, and Eyja's the only elf I've pissed off lately. The strife between the Arcadians and the Talmorin goes back generations, Logan. She could just have targeted me because I'm of the light and she's of the dark."

"Don't describe her like that. *Of the dark*. She's not *of the dark*."

"Fine. But the point is, she's the only one it could be." I laid my hands palm up, imploring him to see my side. "I'm not accusing her of this lightly, Logan. This is serious. I need to talk to her and get this worked out before someone gets hurt."

He shook his head. "Eyja wouldn't do something like that. I'm not saying she doesn't have some sort of grudge," he said as he held up a hand against my protest. "I'm just saying if she wanted to kick your ass, she'd do it herself. She wouldn't summon some sort of creature to do her dirty work for her. It's not her style."

I sat back in my chair. "Will you at least set up a meeting so we can get the air cleared?"

He looked at me for a long moment, then nodded. "But it waits until after the run."

I considered arguing for a moment, then conceded with a nod. "Thank you."

"I'll let you know after I talk to her. And I want to do the run on Monday night. It gives us a good cushion of time afterward."

"Okay. I'll be ready then."

We both pushed up from my desk. "Do you want to go get a drink at Manny's or something?" He asked. "I could use something to eat."

I glanced at the clock ticking loudly on my wall and considered. It was only three, and I was meeting Seraphina at seven. "Sure. But you have to drive me."

Manny's was crowded, as I'd expected, but the booth Logan and I had used at our first meeting was open, so we made ourselves at home. It was too early for Jeremiah to have taken up his spot in the back booth, and it was occupied by a group of Arcadians sporting a rainbow of hair colors. We ordered drinks, Logan ordered food, and we settled in to chat.

"So what made you decide to be a runner?" He asked around a mouthful of burger.

I sipped my beer and shrugged. "Let's just call it my rebellious phase. I'd just moved to Atlanta and was looking to do something a little more risky. Something my parents wouldn't approve of, something that was totally out of character for me. Then I met Rose, who'd been doing it for about a year. She pulled me on a few jobs, and I was hooked."

"Running is out of character for you? But you're so good at it!"

I laughed. "It was out of character for me *then*. And I have a few secret weapons at my disposal. Some might consider it cheating."

"What weapons?" He took a swig of his beer and another bite of his burger.

"I can't tell you. Then they wouldn't be secret anymore." I grinned. "Anyway, you beat me, so I can't be *that* good."

"No, you're good. I'm just better."

I scowled at him and threw my balled-up napkin at his head. He batted it aside without even looking up.

"See? Better."

I scowled again. "What about you, techie? Why'd *you* become a runner?"

"The money." He grinned. "Plus, it's fun as hell."

I laughed.

He swallowed his mouthful of food and his expression turned serious, the grin melting away. "Can I ask you something?"

I eyed him suspiciously, thrown off by his change in demeanor. Then I nodded.

"What's up with you and Tristan?"

I took a deep breath, then let it out in a long sigh, turning my beer around in my hands and watching the condensation drip down the sides of the glass to pool on the table. "That is a really long, complicated story."

"Can you give me the condensed version?"

"Sure. We were engaged. He cheated on me a lot. We broke up, I moved to Atlanta. The end."

He set his burger down and sat up straighter. "Ah. I assume that explains the 'rebellious phase' you were talking about."

I nodded again, a little slower this time, still not meeting his gaze. "The day he walked into my shop was the first time I'd seen him in five years."

"Wow," he said. "You should have let me kick him out."

"I'd have done that myself, thanks. No, it's okay. It's in the past. Maybe...maybe he's changed. Maybe it's for the best that he came back into my life. It's my chance to reconcile all of this."

"Guys like that don't change, Alyssa," he said, his voice very low and soft.

Old anger surged in my chest, the almost-Pavlovian response to defend Tristan, but I stopped myself cold. I knew what Logan was saying was right. It was something I'd told myself a hundred times. But the regret in Tristan's voice the other night, the kindness he'd shown me...he was there, somewhere, behind that arrogance and short-sightedness. Not the playboy and the serial cheater, but the *real* Tristan, the one I'd fallen in love with in Arcadia. He *had* changed, when we'd left Arcadia and come to the human world. Maybe he could change again, back to who he'd been before. Maybe he was already changing, realizing who he really was.

Or maybe he'd just gotten better at faking it.

"I know," I said heavily. "It's not as if I'm inviting him back into my life as a romantic partner. I just want to reconcile and finally move on. Get past this lingering...whatever this is." I gestured at myself, and he quirked an eyebrow at me. "Look, you worry about Eyja, I'll worry about Tristan, okay?"

He looked at met, his gaze intent on mine. "Fine."

"Good. Thank you." I took a long pull from my beer and glanced at the display on my phone. "I need to go soon. You heading out, or should I call a cab?"

"I can drop you at home, no problem. Let me finish my burger."

I nodded and sat back to finish my beer and contemplate my life choices, glad Logan was here even if he was quiet company.

Sometimes staring into the abyss requires moral support.

I stepped out of the cab and stared up at Seraphina's building, tugging my duster closed over my dress. The huge skyscraper loomed above me, sheer panes of deep blue-black glass reflecting the lights from the other buildings like stars. It was in the heart of the downtown district, surrounded by trendy and NeoFuturist architecture, with a lot of colorful LEDs in the neighboring buildings' windows. The lights blinked and faded from one color to another, causing the shadows to shift and jerk erratically. Electric cars hummed by; the pedestrians sported the latest and best in fashion, from classy and understated to loud and proud.

A thick red carpet extended across the sidewalk from a set of glass double doors to the curb. The doors were covered by a deep blue awning with "Azure Gateways" stitched across it in gold thread. A doorman in a black uniform opened the large glass door for me as I approached, giving me a polite smile and a little bow of her head. I smiled back, flustered. Was I supposed to tip her? I'd never been good at remembering those rules. I fiddled with my small black purse, but when she turned away I dropped my hands and walked into the building.

The lobby was as equally impressive. Its vaulted ceiling towered three stories above me, ornamented with elaborate scroll work along the crown molding and silver decorative tiles, with a large crystal chandelier filling the space. Plush oriental rugs covered the tiled floor, and dark blue couches and chairs sat arranged in small clusters around deep mahogany coffee tables.

Someone politely cleared their throat, and I jumped. I flushed as I realized I'd stopped just inside the door and was staring around with wide eyes. At the desk along the left wall, a receptionist stood smiling at me.

"Can I help you, miss?" He said it in a way that managed to question my presence without being overtly offensive.

My back tensed at his tone. "Yes," I said, turning and walking to the desk. "Hi..."

I glanced at his name tag. "Hi, James. I'm here to see Seraphina Dubhan. Do I need a permission slip to get in?" I quipped. "Or is there a secret handshake?"

His lips twitched, though I couldn't tell if it was in amusement or annoyance. "No, miss, I just need your ID and I'll dial up to her."

I produced my license with a little flourish, but he simply took it from my fingers and looked it over. Then he lifted a slim phone from the desk, punched a few buttons a put it to his ear. He spoke quietly into it, then hung up and smiled at me. "Go right ahead. The elevators are to your left and right. The last one on either side will take you straight to the penthouse."

I raised my eyebrows in surprise. "Thanks, James." I waved my fingers at him, my high heels loud on the tile floor as I crossed the lobby. Then I stepped into the elevator and did something I'd never done before.

I pushed the button labeled "PH."

I stood, watching the numbers tick by, and smoothed my skirt, feeling the reassuring weight of my tiny gun tucked in an inner thigh holster. It wasn't much, but it was better than nothing. It wasn't the most comfortable thing, either, but unless I wanted to waltz into Seraphina's flashing a shoulder holster, it was the best I was going to get in this outfit.

I ran my fingers through my hair for the billionth time, checked my make-up in the metal door, caught myself fidgeting, and forced myself to be still. This was so ridiculous. I was too old to get nervous over a date. And besides, this wasn't even a date.

Was it?

Of course it wasn't. Seraphina invited me simply to share some time with another elf. This was just a...a friend thing. Nothing more. I wasn't even sure which way her tastes ran; I shouldn't jump to silly conclusions.

Before I could work myself up into a fresh ball of panic, the elevator dinged to a stop. My heart skipped a few beats, and then the doors slid open.

I stepped into a small lobby-like area with another elevator across from me. One end of the lobby held a door marked "stairs" and the other could have been the front door of any house, complete with knocker and a small arrangement of potted ferns next to it. I stepped up to it and rang the doorbell.

A few moments passed. I stood debating whether or not I should ring again, when the door finally opened, and Seraphina stood smiling in front of me. She wore a long black dress with high halter neckline, and her hair hung loose and stick-straight around her shoulders.

"Alyssa, come in." She stepped back and gestured for me to enter.

"Thanks," I said, stepping into her apartment—her *penthouse* apartment. The scent of rosemary and warm olive oil filled the air, presumably from the airy kitchen area to my left. A large bank of windows dominated a far wall, with a set of charcoal gray couches arrayed for conversation but also for enjoying the view. Gauzy black drapes hung in swaths from the ceiling in a semi-circle around the couches, lending them some privacy. The drapes were lit with blue lights from...somewhere. I couldn't tell if it was from above or below, but it gave them an ethereal glow.

"I can take your coat," she said, and I slid out of my duster and handed it to her. I stood, trying not to fidget, as she hung it in a coat closet by the front door. She turned and smiled at me. "It's okay, I'm not going to bite," she teased, and walked past me and down two small steps to the sitting area. "I hope you like wine and fancy cheese."

"Who *doesn't* love wine and fancy cheese?" I scoffed, and followed her down the stairs.

She laughed, low and throaty, and heat colored my cheeks at the sound. "I admit, I hesitated in setting them out. It seemed so clichéd. But then, it's a cliché for a reason, right?"

She led me around one of the curtains. In the center of the circle of couches stood a black glass-and-wrought-iron coffee table. A silver tray of cheese sat in the center, with several small bowls of cut fruit around it, and two slender glasses of white wine beside a bottle. I perched on the end of one of the couches. She handed me a glass and then settled on a chaise, leaning back and regarding me over her own glass.

There was a long, drawn-out silence as we sat, simply looking at each other. Her lips slowly curled into a smile, and I tried not to squirm under her gaze. I glanced away, and she laughed.

"Oh, Alyssa. You are darling."

Darling. Was that good? "I, uh…" I stammered. Gods, I was *so smooth*. I cleared my throat and started again. "I brought the Hart Ring with me." I tugged at the chain around my neck, pulling the ring from where it was nestled inside my dress. "I still haven't decided if I'm going to accept it fully or not yet, but if you'd like it back until I do, I—"

She sat up straighter and waved a hand in dismissal. "Oh, I didn't invite you here to discuss business. We can leave that for another day. I'm in no rush. This invitation was purely for pleasure." She smiled.

I blinked.

"I hope you don't mind me being so forward. I find that the ambiguity that generally accompanies such things usually leads to misunderstandings and misconceptions, and in turn, hurt feelings. Let me be perfectly clear," she leaned forward, her elbows on her knees. "I invited you here this evening because I'm interested in you. You've captured my attention entirely, Alyssa D'Yaragen, yet I find I barely know anything about you. I wish to change that."

My breath caught in my throat and my heart pounded in my ears.

"If you've come here with the misunderstanding that it was purely for business, and have no wish to pursue this any further, you can leave and I will not hold it against you. If, somehow, I've misread you, and you're previously committed or otherwise uninterested, the fault lies with me." Her golden eyes searched mine, her white-blond hair falling forward to frame her delicate face. "But," she said softly. "I hope

I have not misread you, Alyssa, and that you desire to know me as I desire to know you."

Several pounding heartbeats passed while I watched her in silence, my mind reeling. Then I set my wine on the coffee table and stood. A flash of disappointment flickered across her face.

"I understand," she said, and for the first time I heard uncertainty in her voice. She set her wine on the table and stood as well, smoothing her skirts and avoiding my eyes. "I'm sorry for the misunderstanding. I—"

I took three long steps around the table and stopped inches in front of her. I took her face in my hands, hesitated long enough to see the spark of desire in her eyes, and lowered my lips to hers.

14

Her lips were soft but earnest, and I spent a moment simply savoring them. A tingle of energy ran between us wherever our skin touched—my lips on hers, my fingertips against the curve of her jaw—and as her lips parted and her tongue darted against mine, it increased to a shock that hovered right at the pleasant edge of painful. I pulled back and gazed at her, my blood rushing in my ears.

"Do you feel that?" My voice came out breathy, and I trailed my fingers into her hair.

Her eyelashes fluttered and she nodded, trailing her hands up my arms and leaving lines of fiery sensation in their wake.

"What is it?"

"I'm not sure," she breathed. "Magic, I think."

"The Eldergloom?"

She nodded again, looking at me with half-lidded eyes.

"It's never felt like this before. Why would it—"

"Shh..." she said, running her fingertips over my shoulders. "Stop talking." She raised her lips to mine again.

I happily obeyed.

Sometime later I became aware of a soft beeping. It wasn't quite an alarm bell, but I pulled back, trying to get my swirling mind to make sense of the noise. Seraphina smiled up at me apologetically.

"Dinner's ready," she said. "I should go take that out of the oven."

I nodded absently as she gently extracted herself from my arms. I followed in a haze. Her kitchen was surprising large, with plenty of counter space and a double oven against the interior wall. She pulled a casserole dish from the upper oven and a loaf of bread from the warming drawer next to it.

"Go ahead to the table, I'll bring this right in." She gestured past the kitchen to a small dining area, where a table was set for two.

"Candles and everything," I smiled. "So this *is* a date!"

She laughed deeply and the sound warmed me all the way to my toes. Trying not to grin like an idiot, I took the far seat and watched her bring in two plates of food. She set one in front of me and one at the other seat, then placed a bowl of steaming bread in the middle of the table.

"Oh," she said. "I also have something special for dessert—if you want to stick around that long." A mischievous sparkle flashed in her eyes.

I considered and discarded one lascivious remark after another, and just settled for raising my eyebrows at her.

"You'll have to wait and see." She grinned.

We focused on our food, a tender chicken breast over a bed of rice and a side of asparagus. The sauce on the chicken was light and the asparagus was cooked to perfection, with just a hint of crunch. I ate, absently appreciating the meal while my mind spun out of control. That kiss earlier. It had been…it was…not what I'd expected when I'd planned this evening out in my head. It's what I'd wanted, sure, but I never thought it would happen. If I was being honest with myself, Tristan really screwed up any sort of expectations I had in regards to relationships and my self-esteem. I couldn't tell when people were into me anymore, always doubting or second-guessing. Part of me would never forgive him for that, though hopefully I could start to rebuild. I'd hoped that five years was enough time, but apparently not.

Seraphina cleared her throat. I looked up from pushing a grain of rice around on my plate to find her watching me with a soft smile on her face.

"What were you thinking about?" She took a bite of chicken, her delicate lips sliding across the fork in a wonderfully distracting way.

"Just tonight," I answered a bit too quickly, mentally kicking myself for letting Tristan distract me even here. "This is…nice." I gave her something resembling a smile, then looked back down at my plate. "It's been a while for me. I didn't realize how much I missed it."

There was silence from the other side of the table, then she pushed her chair back and walked to my side. "Come with me," she said, and held out a hand to me.

I took her fingers in mine. She pulled me up from my chair and led me down a long, wide hallway off the back of the dining room. It curved slightly to the left as we walked, until we came to a set of glass double doors.

She opened one of the doors and led me into what could only be described as a conservatory.

Plants of all types filled the room. The air was warmer here, humid and heavy with the scent of lavender, jasmine, and other flowers I couldn't identify. Statues sat among the greenery, and trees towered above me, their top-most leaves brushing against a high glass roof. Small, thin tendrils hung from the ceiling, and I stretched a hand up to touch the tip of one dangling just above my head. My fingers just barely brushed it, but the tendril jerked and rolled up as if escaping from my touch.

I gasped, pulling my hand back. "You have a *mira finuana?*"

"I do." She glanced back at me with a gleam in her eye. "Some-times—rarely, mind you—someone will bring one of our plants out of Arcadia and into the human world. Obviously, these plants sell for a considerable amount, but I make it a point to scoop up as many of them as I can before they fall into human hands." She led me a few steps further into the room. "You remember this one, I'm sure." The Sevenstar Orchid from the charity gala sat nestled in amongst the other plants in a raised bed, its petals glowing faintly in the shadow of the trees.

"I was wondering who'd gotten that."

Her eyes sparkled and she continued down the stone walkway, reaching out a hand here and there to adjust a leaf or brush a petal from a statue. Up ahead, the path widened and the foliage opened up into an atrium. As she dropped my hand and moved out of my line of sight, my attention was pulled to the middle of the room.

A large, circular plot of grass sat within the stone ring of the path. The grass was lush and inviting, and I longed to take off my high heels and walk in that cool, green carpeting, or to lie down and feel each delicate blade against my arms and the backs of my legs.

In the center of the grass, a tall archway made of rough, natural stone stood about eight feet tall. It was made in the stacked-stone style of the old cairns, with a large, smooth keystone carved with swirling Elvish script.

Speak Friend and Enter.

"This..." I trailed off in awe, slowly scanning the arch. "Is this..."

"Yes," she said, and I could hear the smile in her voice. "It is."

"But...how?" I took a few steps forward and held out a hand, my fingertips hovering less than an inch above the stone surface.

"I made it. It's been my pet project for years."

I let my hand drop and turned to her. She stood looking longingly at the arch, one corner of her lip curling up wistfully.

"Why?"

She blinked and turned her attention to me with effort, like someone waking from a dream. "What?"

"Why? Why has this been your project?"

Her eyebrows pulled down in confusion. "Why not? Haven't you always wanted a door home?"

"I guess I never thought about it." I turned back to the arch, letting my gaze travel across the carved script. "So...it's done?"

"As done as I can get it. I've finished everything I can. I just need to find a Weaver to activate it for me."

Tension snapped through my body, and I fought to keep my stance and expression free from any tell-tale signs as I glanced to her. Is this why she'd asked me here? Did she know?

But she was looking the arch longingly, her eyes flicking to mine only briefly, with no hint of expectation.

"Why would you show this to me?"

She shrugged one shoulder. "Why not?" she repeated. "It seemed appropriate. I think, maybe, it symbolizes my own loneliness." She turned her golden eyes to me, and I could see a deep sadness in them that tightened my chest. "It's been a while for me, too."

Our eyes locked for a long moment, and then I looked away. She sighed, a sound heavy with emotion: longing and sorrow and regret and a thousand subtle variations. "Come," she said softly. "I have something else to show you." She circled around the far side of the arch. I followed.

Tucked away in an alcove, surrounded on three sides by a raised garden, stood a tiny circular table with a soft white tablecloth and two cushioned, wrought-iron chairs. On the table sat a wine bottle nestled in an ice bucket and two fluted glasses next to two delicate bowls. The bowls practically overflowed with black cherries, each fruit glistening like a garnet in the light from the single candle in the center of the table.

"Dessert, as promised." She gestured for me to sit, and pulled the bottle from the ice bucket, uncorking it and filling my glass with a generous pour of white wine. "The cherries are simply to enhance. The wine is the 'something special' I mentioned earlier."

I lifted my glass and took a small sip. It was light and sweet, just a little dry, and with a wonderful bouquet that told me it could only be one thing.

"Elderflower?" I asked, and she gave me a knowing smile.

"I bought it from an Arcadian who had smuggled it out several years ago. You can't get good Elderflower wine from anywhere else. The humans are too heavy-handed with the plants."

I nodded and took another sip, savoring the flavor as it rolled across my tongue. "This must have cost you a fortune."

She poured herself a glass and smiled. "I find that the finer things in life are worth it. Money is fleeting and ephemeral. Experience is everything. Don't you think?" She leaned back in her chair, took a sip of her wine, and regarded me with an expression that brought heat to my cheeks. The corners of her lips curled up in a small smile, and she went on. "I hope you don't think I'm showing off. I struggled with whether to pull out all the stops and end up making myself appear arrogant, but the other choice was to *not* offer you the best I had, and that was simply unacceptable."

I laughed, both flattered and slightly embarrassed. "I certainly will never complain about being spoiled."

"I'll keep that in mind," she said. Her voice was low and husky, and the look in her eyes made my head spin and the earth shift under me.

Seraphina's eyes widened and the bowls on the table rattled, and I realized the earth really *was* shifting underneath me. I wondered briefly if this was what an earthquake felt like, and then the soil in the garden next to our table shifted, the earth pushing up from underneath to form a huge mound. Dirt fell away to reveal an enormous head, a set of broad shoulders and a hunched, expansive back followed by arms as thick as tree trunks and hands that were too large for their body. The hulking figure continued to emerge from the earth, and I simply watched in awe until it stood towering over us.

The creature turned, squinting down at Seraphina over a large, bulbous nose. Its heavy eyebrows pulled down in confusion and it shook its squat head. It pursed its lips in thought, which only emphasized its yellowing, oversized lower canine teeth protruding like tusks to almost touch his cheeks. Then it turned, fixed its beady eyes on me, and grinned with satisfaction.

"Crap," I said, and dove backwards as the troll swung a huge, meaty fist at me.

I came up from my backwards roll with my gun in my hand, proud that I only got tangled in my skirts a little bit. That little bit was all the troll needed to step from the garden and take another swing at me before I had a chance to aim, and I dove to the side as his fist smashed into the stone walkway with a boom that sent shockwaves through the entire building.

I followed my roll into a crouch and fired three bullets square into its back, the pop of the gun reverberating through the trees and bouncing back to me from the glass ceiling.

The troll fell forward onto one knee, scooped up a large stone paver, and hurled it at me in a backhanded throw. I got out of the way and heard Seraphina shriek as the stone crashed into the table, sending shards of glass flying.

"Hey! I wasn't done with that!" I yelled, and hit the troll with three more shots to the knee.

It stumbled for a second, then turned toward me and howled in anger.

Okay, so bullets weren't going to work. Noted.

Where was a plasma rifle when you needed one?

I glanced back at the table to see Seraphina pushing up from the floor, blood trailing down her arm and one cheek, one hand on her overturned chair.

Her chair. Her *wrought-iron* chair.

A troll was a fae creature, a creature of faerie blood, kindled with magic and sprung from the earth. If there was one thing the fae couldn't handle, it was iron. I wasn't sure if the chair had a high enough iron content in it to hurt him the way cold iron would, but it was my only option unless I wanted to lead a troll on a wild goose chase through a high rise full of innocent people.

I rushed to Seraphina's side, pulled her to her feet, and whispered, "*Run.*" She shook her head fiercely and I made a noise of frustration. "Fine. But I need to borrow this." I grabbed the chair with both hands and turned in time to see the troll barreling toward me, his fists raised high above his head.

I held the chair in front of me as if taming a lion, let out a cry of challenge that left my throat raw, and charged the troll.

He blinked his beady eyes, obviously confused by my change of tactic. I ducked low and braced myself as the legs of the chair slammed into his midsection, letting out a huff of air as the back of the chair hit me in the ribs and knocked the wind out of me.

The troll fell back with a piercing howl. The legs of the chair embedded themselves into his gray stomach, and anywhere metal touched his flesh there was a thin stream of hissing, acrid smoke. I followed him to the floor, leaning my weight on the chair and forcing the legs even further into his abdomen. He swung his fists blindly, and I ducked and twisted each time one came close to hitting me.

"Enough!" he wailed, his voice sounding like rocks in a blender. "I yield! I yield!"

I blinked and stayed where I was, struggling to catch my breath past the ache in my diaphragm.

"Mercy!" His eyes glittered like chips of glass as his gaze found mine. "Mercy, mighty warrior! The iron! It burns! Mercy!"

It took my brain a minute to catch up to his words, then I scrambled off of the chair until my feet touched the ground, keeping my hands on the metal as my thoughts whirled. I looked at Seraphina, but she simply watched the exchange with wide eyes. "I will grant you mercy—*if* you tell me why you're here."

"I will tell you! Mercy! Please!"

"You swear?"

"I swear on the mountain that birthed me! Mercy!"

I adjusted my grip on the chair, and with a heave, I pulled it from his stomach. The legs made sucking, slurping sounds as they came free of his flesh, and they dripped dark blood onto the shattered stone floor.

He let out a cry as the metal slid through him, and then sagged with relief. "Thank you, mighty warrior. You are as benevolent as you are skilled in battle."

I glared down at him, trying to look intimidating even though he was a four-hundred-pound monster that could probably rip off my arms if he felt so inclined. "I've shown you mercy, now talk."

"What do you wish to know?"

"Who summoned you?"

"I do not know their name or their face. I only know the taste of their hate and their magic."

"Their magic? What magic?"

His gaze flicked between me and Seraphina where she leaned against the broken garden wall. "A deep magic, wielded by the dark elves, much like that of your kind, only the inverse. The Eldergloom was used to pull me forth from my sleep and bind me to this task. It reeks of decay and cold, dead earth stripped bare of its riches."

Hate and death magic could only point to one thing. A Talmorin.

I looked at his flat, wide face with a surge of pity. If he'd been summoned and bound, he would have had no choice but to do what he'd been told. I couldn't imagine what it would be like to have that free will stripped from me, to be forced to do someone else's dirty work whether I wanted to or not.

Suspicion roiled in my chest. "If you were bound to kill me, why did you yield? *How* did you yield?"

"I was bound to attack, not to kill. You've bested me, so I need not fight any longer."

I set the chair down beside him and he flinched at the clang it made as it hit the stone. My mind spun, my thoughts chasing themselves in circles behind my eyes until I was dizzy. "What is your name, troll?"

"Egger Steinson, lady warrior."

"Egger," I inclined my head in greeting. "I'm Alyssa D'Yaragen." He nodded his head in return and I chewed my lip. Perhaps I could bind him, have him track down the source of his original summoning. But that would require the use of more magic than I was comfortable with in front of Seraphina. And I already knew who it was.

Eyja.

"Egger, you may leave, but remember that I granted you mercy."

"You have my thanks." As the last word left his lips, his skin split down the center of his face and he dissolved into a thousand tiny pebbles that melted like wax and disappeared into the cracks in the stone pathway.

15

I stood staring at the spot where Egger had been mere seconds before.

"Um," I said.

"What... just happened?" Seraphina's voice was breathless.

"Um." I leaned on the back of the chair and sat down hard in the seat, my eyes still on the ground.

"Was that a troll? Did you just fight a troll? And survive? How did that happen?"

"I guess wrought iron *does* have enough iron in it." A giggle escaped my lips. I wasn't even sure what was funny, but the laughter bubbled up through my chest anyway.

"What?"

I shook my head and let the giggles subside before looking up at her. She had a neat cut on her left cheekbone, and blood trickled down her face and neck to the collar of her dress. Her right arm dripped blood, though it was smeared from where I'd pulled her to her feet. I looked down at my own hands to see rusty red streaks, and anger replaced the laughter in my chest.

"I'm going to kill her," I snarled, jumping to my feet.

"What? Kill who? Alyssa, *what is going on?*"

"It's kind of a long, complicated story. Actually, no, it's not that complicated. There's a Talmorin. She doesn't like me. I think she sent the troll, and the storm drake last night."

"Storm drake?"

"I was trying to be polite for a friend's sake, but this..." I cupped her face in my hand, tilting her chin so I could see the cut. "This is too far. I'm not concerned with polite anymore."

She clasped my hand in hers. "He said the Eldergloom was used. Are you going to fight a Talmorin Weaver? This may not be wise. What if—"

"Don't worry about me. I'll manage. You go get yourself cleaned up. I'll handle this, and then I'll see if I can find you a new bottle of Elderflower wine, and we'll do this again. *Without* the uninvited guest next time."

She nodded and leaned in to place a light kiss on my lips. "I'll walk you to the door," she said.

The lobby of Seraphina's building was in a state of near chaos. Residents gathered around in clusters, speculating on what had happened. Had there been an earthquake? Was there an explosion? Several people gathered around James at the front desk, demanding answers from the poor frazzled clerk. I shoved my blood-smeared hands deeper into my duster pockets and walked quickly out the front door.

I hailed a taxi and slid into the back seat, telling the driver to take me to Café 1337, then pulled a packet of wet wipes from my purse and cleaned my hands as well as I could. I might be getting more blood on them later, but there was no reason to walk around making people suspicious.

The taxi pulled up to Café 1337, and I studied the people on the sidewalk for a moment before the cabbie cleared his throat and I stepped out. It was still fairly early, and even if the Talmorin was going to come out tonight, she might not be here yet.

That's okay. I could wait.

I pushed into the café and spotted Logan almost immediately. He was sitting in a booth, bookended by two girls with neon-pink nylon cyberfalls and lots of EL-wire woven into their clothes. His hair was extra-spikey tonight, and he wore black vinyl pants and boots with a blue shirt that glowed softly.

"Hey, techie," I said as I reached the booth, raising my voice to be heard over the throbbing music. "Where's Eyja?"

He and the two girls looked at me, and he raised his eyebrows. "Look at you, all dressed up. Did you have a date or something?"

"Yes." His face fell ever so slightly, but I ignored it. "Where's Eyja?"

"She's not here. Who'd you have a date with?"

"I need you to take me to her. Come on." I turned on my heel and walked back out of the café to the cold street. A few moments later, Logan pushed out of the door and walked straight to me.

"What's going on?" He asked.

"I told you. I need you to take me to Eyja. Where does she live?"

He crossed his arms and pressed his lips together.

"Oh, for the love of—Logan, I'm sick of these games! Look at this." I shoved my hands into his face. "Do you see that under my finger-nails? That's Seraphina's blood. Eyja sent another elemental after me this evening and she got hurt. I'm not going to tiptoe around your sensibilities while others get hurt because of me, so *take me to Eyja*," I snarled.

Doubt flashed in his eyes. I could see him struggle with his loyalties, weighing the possibilities against one another, and then he dropped his arms and sighed. "Fine. I'll get her down here. Then you two can *talk*." He placed heavy emphasis on that last word, his gaze intent on mine.

I nodded once and he spun on his heel, taking a few steps away from me as he slipped his Neurospecs from his pocket. Half of me was offended that he felt our meeting needed to be in a public space, and the other half of me didn't blame him. I wouldn't start blowing things up if it meant other people would get hurt, but I wasn't sure that I could say the same for Eyja. If the past few nights had been any indication, she had no care for who else got hurt as long as she could get to me. I'd heard that the Talmorin were coldblooded, but even I was a little surprised at how ruthless she'd been over nothing.

143

Logan pulled his Neurospecs from his eyes and walked back over to me, his big boots clunking against the concrete. "She's on her way. Why don't we head back inside and have something to drink before she gets here?"

I nodded again and followed him back into the café. The two girls were still in the booth, and they frowned at me when we walked up.

"I've got some business to handle," he said to them. "Can I catch up with you guys later?"

"Sure," the girl on the right said. "We're going out dancing anyway. Join us later if you're done with business?"

He nodded. They slid out of the booth and I took their place, positioning myself so I could see the entrance. He chewed his lip, his eyes distant.

"You want a drink?" he asked.

"Sure. Surprise me."

He walked to the bar at the far end of the room, returning a few minutes later with two thick, teal-colored drinks in martini glasses. I took a tentative sip and made a surprised sound. It was good, espresso blended with a white chocolate liquor of some sort. I smiled briefly at Logan, then we both sat in silence, watching the people around us.

A few minutes passed before he finally broke the tension.

"So," he said. "You had a date with Seraphina?"

"Yep." I took a sip from my drink, ignoring his gaze.

"And? What happened?"

Heat crept up my cheeks. "That's not really your business."

He stared at me, then laughed once. "No. I meant the attack."

Whatever blush I'd managed to fight off surged to my face in full force. "Oh. Uh, we were attacked by a troll."

He stared at me again. "A troll?"

"Yeah."

"Okay," he drew the word out. "And those can be summoned, too? Like the storm drake?"

"Yeah. They're earth-based elemental creatures. More intelligent than storm drakes. And bigger. It came after me. Seraphina got caught in the crossfire."

"She okay?"

"I think so. Just some cuts from broken glass. But the thing was hurling stone pavers like Frisbees. It could have been a lot worse."

He nodded, eyes still on me.

"I can't promise this talk will stay peaceful, Logan." My voice was low, my eyes on the drink in front of me. "If she's really sending these things after me, there's no guessing what she'll do when I confront her about it. And if it is her, and she does turn violent, she can probably do some damage. Especially here." My gaze skittered over the patrons, many with Neurocomms and various levels of built-in tech. If a Weaver started throwing power around in here, the fall-out could be catastrophic. I tapped the base of my glass with one fingernail, doubting the choice of venue.

"Why? What's special about this place?"

I paused in my tapping, then shook my head. "The why isn't important. Not now, anyway. We'll see what happens."

He let out a heavy sigh and sat back in the booth, and we proceeded to ignore each other, each of us lost in our own thoughts. I stared down at my fingernails, the blood under them drying to a rust-red. Seraphina had been hurt because of me. She'd invited me over for pleasure, not business...a wistful smile played across my lips, but melted into a frown.

Business.

I reached up and undid the clasp of the chain around my neck.

The Hart ring slid off the silver strand and settled in the palm of my hand. If Seraphina and I were going to be involved, there was no real reason to say no to the ring and the position at this point.

Plus, if I was being honest with myself, there was a certain swell of pleasure at the idea of wearing her gift.

I slipped the ring onto my finger and was prepared when it shrank down to the perfect size. Even though I'd been expecting it, it was a strange feeling, a little zing of magic followed by the tightening of the metal on my skin. My imagination ran away with the thought and I almost panicked as I wondered what would happen if the resizing enchantment was tampered with. If it just kept shrinking and shrinking, until it pinched my finger off at the knuckle.

I shuddered at the thought and rubbed my hands together to ward off the goosebumps that followed. I forcibly turned my thoughts back to the issue at hand.

Eyja was the prime suspect, but I still felt like I was missing something. Nothing jumped out at me, but a small, nagging feeling at the back of my head told me I was overlooking something vital.

Then Eyja walked into the café, and the nagging voice was silenced as she narrowed her eyes at me.

I tensed and Logan sat up straight in his chair. "Easy, Alyssa," he muttered. "You said you wanted to talk."

"As long as she keeps it to talk, I'm fine with that," I hissed through bared teeth.

Eyja stopped in front of our table and cocked a hip, looking down at the two of us. She wore a pair of leather-and-mesh leggings and a maroon, asymmetrical zippered vest under a long black jacket. "Logan," she said, still tinged with an accent I couldn't place, "you didn't tell me you had company."

"Actually, I called you down here because she asked," he smiled apologetically and gestured for her to join us. Her gaze flicked to me for a brief second before she slid in to the booth, with him between us.

"You said it was important, so I am here."

"It is." He looked at me. "Alyssa?"

I stared across the table at the Talmorin. Her crimson eyes met mine, and my heart skipped a beat.

I suddenly realized the thing I'd been missing this whole time.

Ever so faintly, over the iris of her left eye, was the golden web of a Neurolense.

"It's not you," I whispered, and sat back in my seat.

"I do not understand." She looked from me to Logan and back again.

"Do you have a Neurocomm?" I asked, even though I already knew the answer.

She blinked at me, then nodded, turning her head so I could see the small silver pushbutton behind her ear.

I cursed, putting my head in my hands. "It's not you."

"Logan?" She looked at him for an explanation.

"Alyssa," Logan said. "What do you mean? How do you know?"

I ran my hands through my hair, trying to figure out where to start, or what I could explain without giving up my secret. "I…can't really explain it. Not to you, Logan. Sorry." I turned my full attention to Eyja. "Someone has been summoning elemental creatures to attack me. I falsely assumed it was you. I'm sorry."

Her eyes widened, and she absently touched the button to her Neurocomm in understanding. "They have been summoning them to the city?"

"Yes."

"And you thought it was me. Why?"

"I was told it was a Talmorin who called them. I…don't really know any other than you, so you were the only one I could think of that would want to see harm come to me. It may have been hasty of me." I winced as Logan raised his eyebrows at me.

"I understand," she said, bowing her head slightly. "Old prejudices are hard to overcome. But now that you know it's not me, what will you do?"

"I don't know." My voice held a note of helplessness. "This just… makes no sense. I don't know who else would be doing this."

"If you need assistance in tracking them down, I would be happy to help you. *Alfheimer* or not, you're a friend of Logan's." She smiled slightly. "It speaks highly of you."

I fought my knee-jerk reaction at the Talmorin term and forced myself to smile. "Thank you. I'll…" I'd what? Eyja had been my only lead. I had no other suspects.

My frustration must have shown on my face, because Logan laid a hand on mine. "Hey. We're here. We'll help you figure it out."

I smiled at him in thanks, unable to tell him there was nothing he could do.

I was pacing a rut in the kitchen floor when Rose got home. It was getting late—nearing two in the morning—but I was too wound up to sleep. She gave me a once-over as she closed the door behind her, and quietly hung up her wrap.

She slipped off her boots. "You don't look happy. Did the date not go well?"

I shook my damp hair out of my face and looked down at my hands. They were clean now, but I could still feel Seraphina's blood on them. Guilt and frustration slid tendrils through my stomach and wrapped around my heart, pulling tight and making it hard to breathe.

"Out, damn spot," I muttered to myself, curling my nails against my palms.

"What?"

I shook my head. "I just can't put the pieces together." I shoved my hands in the pockets of my over-sized flannel pants.

"Okay. Not the date, then?" She hung her jacket in the closet and moved across the kitchen, pulling two tea pods from a drawer and popping them into the brewer on the counter.

"I was attacked again tonight by an elemental. While I was with Seraphina. So, no, you could say the date didn't go well at all."

"Oh no, Lys," she slid two mugs into the brewer and turned toward me, leaning against the counter.

"I confronted Eyja, but it's not her." I slammed my left hand down on the counter, my Hart ring hitting the wood with a hard *clack*. "Dammit! I just don't understand. I'm missing something."

She set the steaming mugs on the table, dropping herself into a chair and gesturing for me to do the same before she pushed one of the teas across to me. I wrapped my hands around the warm ceramic and raised the mug, breathing in the calming scent of chamomile.

"Sleep on it," she said, settling back with her own mug. "Give your brain time to process and sort everything. You might wake up in the morning with the answer."

I stared at her and blinked. "That's not a bad idea," I mused. "I… have something I can do that might help with that, actually. Ugh." I laid my forehead on the table. "Sometimes I'm so dense. Shut up," I said playfully when she let out a small snort of laughter. I raised my head and looked at her. "Thanks, Rose."

"You're welcome," she said, with a smile on her lips.

"You don't mind if I burn some incense in my room tonight if I keep the door shut, do you?"

"Nope. Do your elfy thing, girl. Just don't burn down the apartment."

"Don't even joke about that," I ran my hands through my hair with a sigh. "The way things have been going lately, I'll accidentally summon a fire elemental in my censer."

She laughed.

"Are you off tomorrow? Would you want to help me pound the pavement if I come up empty on my own? I have to be at the shop at eleven, but I'd wake up early for this."

She winced. "I'm visiting with Jonah tomorrow. I can cancel if you need me to."

"No," I said quickly. "No, go. How is he, anyway?"

"He's great," she grinned. "He's halfway through his first semester. Grad school's kept him busy, but managed to squeeze some time in for his big sister."

"Neuroscience, right?"

"Yep. He's going to have every mega-corp beating down his door in a year or two. The kid's a genius."

My heart warmed and a bit of my stress melted away. Rose and her brother had grown up with an absentee dad and a deadbeat mom who spent her time ignoring the fact that she had two kids. Rose had basically raised herself and her brother, and despite their broken home and limited means, both of them had excelled in school and gotten the hell out of their town. If Rose and Jonah could claw their way out of their terrible childhood and make it to where they were, I could manage this.

"Tell him I said hi." I stared down into my mug and swallowed back tears.

"Of course. You're welcome to join me, you know."

"No. Thank you, but you deserve your bonding time. Besides, I need to figure this out *and* prep for the run on Monday."

"Monday, huh?"

"Yeah. Gives us a few days just in case."

She nodded. "You let me know if you need me. I can sit sentinel or work communications."

"I think we're set, but I'll let Logan know. I doubt he'd want to bring in another runner this late in the game unless it's an emergency."

"I got ya. Just wanted to make sure you knew the offer was out there. I'd hate for you guys to get in a tight spot and not have me."

I grinned. "The pay's not bad, either."

She grinned back, her ice-blue eyes sparkling over her mug. "That is a nice perk. You tell Logan to come visit sometime."

"You know you can just talk to him yourself, right? You're both grown adults last time I checked."

"Oh, I know. But it's more fun this way."

I laughed and shook my head, finishing off my tea in a long swallow. "You're a mess, Rose. You know that, right?"

"Naturally."

I stood and set my mug in the sink. "I'm going to bed," I yawned, exhaustion and the warmth of the tea seeping into my bones. I padded softly to my bedroom door, weaving my still-damp hair into a loose braid down my back. "Night."

"Night, Lys. Sweet dreams."

Once in my room, I pulled a carved-wood box out of the top shelf in my closet. I dug through the contents, emerging with a mortar and pestle and several small sachets.

I sat cross-legged on the floor, arranging the items in front of me with the mortar and pestle in the center and the small bags in a semi-circle behind them. I laid my hands on the floor, took a few deep breaths, and focused on centering myself.

Casting small magic like this wasn't hard, but it took a singular attention to come out right. If you let your mind wander while you were working, you could spoil the spell. Right now I needed to focus on getting answers, but to do that I needed to let all of my frustration seep out of me. I needed a clean mind for working. If it was a more detailed spell, I'd take a long bath first with the appropriate oils and work nude or in a light cotton shift. This wasn't nearly that complicated, so I figured my flannels and t-shirt should be fine.

Always observing the formalities. That's me.

After a few minutes of deep breathing and meditation, I opened my eyes and focused on the task at hand, pouring a palm full of dried mugwort into the mortar and grinding it together slowly and rhythmically. After it had been worked down to a fine powder, I added a few pinches of resin and kept grinding until they were evenly mixed. I reached for the small stone censer on my dresser, glad I had cleaned and filled it with fresh coals after I'd used it last. It wouldn't do to have bits of the old incense contaminating the spelling mix.

I tossed the new incense into the censer, then tugged on the Eldergloom and breathed fire into the charcoal bed. A soft red glow spread through it, and a light scent like leather and wood sifted up from the resin and leaves.

I set the censer on my bedside table, slid under my blankets, and flicked off the light.

I was asleep within minutes.

I was standing in Arcadia, in the circle of stone arches. Dark gray clouds billowed and roiled above me, and I knew with bone-deep certainty that something was very, very wrong. I turned, taking a step toward the Atlanta gate, when it burst into flame and collapsed into a pile of stone at my feet.

I let out a small cry, jumping back in surprise, then the next gate fell in on itself in a charred heap. This continued all the way around the circle, until all of the exits were cut off and I was left staring at the trees as rain began to fall.

The Hall of Relics rose up around me. Aisles of books and artifacts stretched out into the gloom, the high ceilings and heavy walls out of the reach of the light from my single candle. Shadows shifted and leapt as I walked slowly down the center aisle. I was looking for something. I couldn't remember what it was, but I knew it was in here. I just had to *find* it.

A low, pale humanoid figure skittered across the aisle in front of me on all fours. I gasped, startled, and then a small face peered around the shelf at me. Wild, white hair twisted with leaves and twigs framed a face dominated by large, dark eyes and a slash of black lips. The creature tilted its head at me quizzically, then quirked a beckoning finger in my direction and scuttled down an aisle.

"Aisling," I whispered, and took a tentative step forward.

Aislings were wild fae, unaligned similar to the way elementals were their own breed of fae. They visited in dreams, offering visions to those who needed it.

Sometimes the visions lead you down the right path.

Sometimes they lead you astray.

You could never quite tell what you were going to get with wild fae.

I followed the Aisling, but when I turned the corner, it was gone. The aisle stood empty in front of me, the shelves packed with old, musty tomes, locked boxes, and soft silk pillows holding ancient artifacts. On one shelf, a long wand of yew wood sat on a stand amid a cluster of carved knuckle bones. On another, a sphere of crystal was nestled in a small box and pulsed with a faint emerald light. A golden sickle rested beside sprigs of holly and mistletoe that looked freshly cut, though somehow I knew it had been centuries since they'd been shorn from their bushes.

A rustle from above made me glance up. The Aisling perched on the top-most shelf, clutching a white drawstring bag to its chest with long fingers. Runic sigils I didn't recognize glowed, stitched into the fabric of the bag. With a jerk of one hand, the Aisling threw the parcel down to me. I lunged forward to catch it, but just before it touched my outstretched fingers, the bag vanished.

A sound rumbled through the darkness, so deep it shook the

ground under my feet. I shifted my stance, expecting another troll, and then I realized what the sound was.

Laughter.

Long and low, it seemed as if it were coming from nowhere and everywhere all at once. The Aisling seemed as surprised as me, and then its mouth stretched into a grin too big for its face—a crescent of impossibly long, pointed teeth shining in the candlelight like a feral Cheshire Cat.

The blood drained from my face in pure, primal terror, and the shadows began to press in.

My candle sputtered once, then went out.

16

The laughter followed me out of my sleep before fading into the darkness. I pushed up onto my elbows and stared wide-eyed at the shadows of my room, seeing writhing shapes there until I blinked a few times and finally pulled free of the dream.

I fell back against my pillow, trying to slow my pounding heart. Next to me, the incense was letting off the last bit of its smoke, and I set a small lid on top of the censer to extinguish the coals.

At least the spell had worked. There was only one problem.

I had no idea what any of it meant.

That was the issue with visions. You didn't always get a straight answer. And the Aisling complicated things. I didn't know if it was being helpful or harmful. That smile certainly hadn't seemed friendly.

A shiver ran down my spine at the memory. I threw my blankets off and forced myself out of bed. My clock said it was nearing ten, and I needed to get ready for work.

I pulled on a pair of tight jeans with tall black boots, a dusty cerulean v-neck with three-quarter-length sleeves, and lots of silver bangles on both wrists. Rose offered to drive me to work and I happily accepted. This taxi thing was getting tiring. And expensive.

As we climbed onto her bike, I said, "Just keep an eye out for anything weird. I don't know when the next elemental attack is coming."

"If it's even coming."

"Oh, it's coming," I answered, my voice low.

The day at the shop was pretty slow, though I made a few decent sales. Sundays were always our slow days, a hold-over from the time when Georgia was ruled by the Bible. As it was, the store was only open from noon until eight, and I was getting ready to flip my old-timey "Open" sign to "Closed" when Logan walked in.

"Hey, techie," I said, locking the front door behind him after he walked in. "I'm closing, but I assume you didn't come here to shop."

"You feel like getting a few drinks and waiting to get attacked by an elemental?"

I blinked at him. "Excuse me?"

"Well, I figure, if it's going to happen again, it's best to be prepared, right? And these things seem to follow you around. So, why don't we go get a six-pack from Manny, camp out somewhere away from innocent bystanders, and wait for this thing to come? I brought my plasma rifle with me," he said in a lilting, sing-song tone.

A small smile pulled at my lips. "Any excuse to use that thing, huh?"

"Well, what's the point in buying it if I don't get to shoot bad guys with it?"

I cocked my hip, my eyebrows in my hair as I gave him a pointed once-over. "Don't know if you noticed, Logan, but we're runners. Technically, *we're* the bad guys."

"Well sure, if you're going to look at it that way. But I'm the hero of my own story, thank you."

I shook my head, chuckling softly and heading back toward the register. "Okay. Give me about a half-hour to close and then we can go."

"Excellent!" He clapped his hands once and bounced on his toes.

"I'll go ahead and get the supplies from Manny, and then come back here to get you. You have an idea of where we can go?"

I peered out the front windows. The night was clear, but I could tell there was a chill in the air. We needed to be away from people and somewhere that would minimize property damage if I could help it. "There's several fire pits down at Piedmont Park. If we can snag one of the more isolated ones, it should be well away from any other people."

"Aww. No abandoned warehouse or something?"

I looked at him for a long minute, glanced down at myself pointedly, and then back at him. "Do I look like the kind of girl who hangs out in abandoned warehouses?"

"Not when you act like that, no," he said, his voice holding a hint of petulance. "Fine. Park it is. You sure you're not a greeny?"

"At this point, I'm thinking about converting so people will stop asking me that."

"Be back in half an hour." He grinned and dashed out into the cooling evening.

I locked the door behind him again and then set to counting out the register. I had just finished cleaning all of the counters and windows when there was a rap on the front door. I looked up, expecting to see Logan, but found Tristan smirking at me from the other side of the glass.

I considered leaving him standing out in the cold. Instead, I decided to be gracious and opened the door.

"Are you here to tell me you're leaving Atlanta?"

"Why would I do that?" He breezed past me into the shop and I stifled a surge of irritation.

"The store is closed, Tristan. That's what the 'Closed' sign on the door means."

"I'm not here to shop, I'm here to talk to you." He wore jeans that were just tight enough to be flattering and a double-breasted wool coat the color of storm clouds, with the collar popped up against the chill.

"Of course," I threw my hands in the air in frustration. As if I didn't have enough on my plate. "What are we talking about now?"

"Well, for starters, I was curious if they ever delivered the painting."

I stared at him, dumbfounded. He sent the painting. Of course he did.

"Don't tell me they didn't deliver it," he said.

"You sent the painting? Why?"

He shrugged one shoulder and gave me a crooked smile as he leaned back against the counter. "Do you like it?"

"Excuse me?"

"The painting. Do you like it?"

"Yes, but—."

"Good."

"No, not good. You can have it back. I don't want it."

"No, you keep it. It's a gift. No strings attached."

I let out a snort of laughter. "Why do I *not* believe that?"

"I'm serious." His expression sobered and he crossed the space between us. "I'm trying to make amends here, Alyssa. For real this time. I know I can't buy you back or anything like that, but I want to try and at least give you a few more good memories of me. Just in case you decide to throw me out again." He gave me a shadow of his crooked smile and took my hands in his.

At this distance his eyes were very, very blue. Part of me wanted to pull away from him, to reclaim my hands and tell him goodnight and goodbye. But the warmth of his hands in mine was familiar. I hadn't realized how much I'd missed it. The lights cast strange shadows over his face, emphasizing the angles of his cheekbones and square jaw. In fact, in this light, it looked almost as if…

"Are you hurt?" I pulled a hand from his and laid my fingers on his face, tilting his head so I could see the purple bruise that spread from his jaw back to the hairline at the nape of his neck. "What happened?"

"Nothing." He pulled away from me, then grabbed my hand in his again and looked down at it with a small intake of breath. "You accepted the Hart ring?"

"So?" I pulled my hand out of his. "So did you."

"I know, but Alyssa—"

A sharp rap on my front door startled us both and I peered through the glass to see Logan waiting with a six-pack of beer, a gun, and a grin. The grin faltered a bit as he saw Tristan, and I waved at him to wait.

"If you'll excuse me," I said to Tristan. "I have some business to deal with."

"But—"

"Thanks for the painting. I really do love it." I said it to distract him, but I was surprised to find I meant it.

He smiled softly, and the look in his eyes set my heart stuttering. "You're welcome."

My jaw clenched in frustration as I silently scolded my circulatory system for its inappropriate reaction, and I turned from him before he could see the reaction on my face. "You can see yourself out, I'm sure. I need to get my things. Have a good night." I hurried to my office without waiting for an answer and grabbed my jacket, slipping on a shoulder holster and checking my gun before I put the warm, heavy leather on over it. Tristan was gone by the time I reentered the store, so I locked the front door and turned to Logan.

"Ready?" He bounced on his toes again.

I nodded, eyeing the few pedestrians still on the street as I climbed onto the back of his bike. Tristan was nowhere in sight. Two retropunks laughed as they walked arm and arm down the street, their bright clothes almost glowing in the dimming light. Another punk in black leather stood on the opposite corner, the bottom half of his face hidden behind a black bandanna printed like the jaw of a skull. I stayed alert as we pulled away from the shop, hoping we got somewhere isolated before we were jumped.

I didn't realize how much tension I was holding in my shoulders until we pulled up to the park and Logan rolled to a stop in a parking spot. I was stiff from the stress of anticipation, and I rolled my neck and shoulders as I slid off the bike, trying to loosen up. Logan opened the side panel of his motorcycle and I watched, impressed, as the plasma rifle unfolded from inside a hidden compartment. With a crooked grin, he looped the strap over his shoulder, then followed me across the street and down a sidewalk that cut through the trees of the park.

"This way," I said, stepping off the path and walking across the open grass. After a few minutes we reached a circle of benches carved from stumps. A fire pit sat in the center of the ring of benches. I grabbed a few logs from a small pile nearby and threw them into the pit. "You want to set up a quick perimeter while I get this started?"

He nodded and took off into the trees.

I glanced around to be sure I was alone, then blew gently on the base of the wood, tugging on the Eldergloom the way I had the night before with the charcoal. By the time Logan returned, a decent flame was going and I was sitting back in a chair, my feet on the edge of the pit and a beer in my hand.

He noted the fire with an impressed look and flung himself into a chair across from me. "So," he said, mirroring my posture with his feet on the stone as he popped the top off a beer bottle. "What sort of baddie should we be expecting this evening?"

I shrugged, staring into the flames. "It could be anything, really. It will be strong, if last night's attack was any indication. And smart."

He looked at the fire for a long moment. "There's a lot going on here that I don't understand," he said softly. "I get that there's stuff you can't tell me, and I respect that. I'm not going to force you to give up information or anything. But if there's anything you *can* tell me that would help, now would probably be the time."

I watched the light flicker and reflect in his eyes, struggling with the urge to protect him and the need to keep myself—and my people's secrets—safe. He looked up from the flames and must have seen the frustration in my face, because he raised a hand.

"Don't make yourself nuts over it, Lys. I can't imagine the stress you're under. Just...think about it, okay? The more I know, the more help I can be."

I nodded. "It's...complicated," I started. "Not everything is my secret to tell. My people are very private by nature, even now. The elder Arcadians pride themselves on being enigmatic and indecipherable. It's kind of their thing." I gave him a crooked grin. "And it's worked for them. But that means I can't really go around revealing all of our secrets."

"But, why not? Why do they insist on being so mysterious? Don't they understand that the more humans know about them, the less afraid they'll be?"

"Don't be so sure about that," I whispered.

He looked at me long and hard, his face slowly sobering.

I took a drink from my beer.

"So you guys are scary? I'm sorry, but I don't buy it."

I raised my eyebrows and he put a hand up as if to forestall any argument.

"You can summon elementals and do some woojy stuff. I get that. That's *really cool,* by the way. But I have a *plasma rifle.* The leaps and bounds tech is making these days…I wouldn't be surprised if we can mirror your magic soon, or at least keep up in terms of weaponry."

I shook my head, but he went on.

"And even then, that's nothing to be scared of. You live in our society, you abide by our rules. Attacking me with a troll is no worse than attacking me with a hired thug."

"Can the hired thug shrug off bullets as if they were pebbles? Because the troll can. You saw the storm drake—it took a plasma shot to the face to take it down."

"But I *did* take it down. And you managed the troll. This is the same stuff the humans pull, only a different flavor. Magic instead of mods."

"You still don't get it," I said. "These things—these elementals? It's way more than the normal human sees on a day-to-day basis, and it's still just a fraction of what my people are capable of."

"Your people came out of hiding when humans got too close to your borders. If they're so capable, why were they afraid of a drilling company?"

"My people were afraid, yes. But not for themselves. They were afraid for *you,* Logan. For the humans. We could have turned your teams away, one after another, but it would have taken more and more aggressive means. Eventually someone would have gotten hurt. We are a peaceful people. We did not wish to incite a war." That was mostly the truth. In reality, many of the Arcadians *did* want to use violent means to repel the humans, to keep ourselves hidden and our secrets safe. They were in the minority, thankfully. Another portion wanted to chase off the humans and go back to pretending they didn't exist, but humanity's curiosity is relentless. If they knew we were there, they would keep looking until they found us, whether we wanted them to or not.

So, some of us emerged and joined them. But the issue was far from settled. Some humans wanted access to Arcadia, claiming it was only fair—we got to join them, why couldn't they join us? The Order had managed to make excuses for nearly fifteen years, but I wasn't sure how long they would be able to hold out. Anti-elf movements had popped up almost immediately when we'd come out, and the more secrets the Order kept, the more people those movements recruited.

Maybe Logan was right.

"You're a peaceful people," he said, interrupting my thoughts, "Yet someone is summoning elementals to kill you."

"No," I said through my teeth. "A *Talmorin* is summoning elementals to kill me. I do not speak for them, and they are far from peaceful."

"Hmph." He took a drink of his beer and stared into the fire.

We sat in silence for a while, each of us nursing our beers and our thoughts. I tried not to let my frustration simmer, but it ignored all of my deep breathing techniques and insisted on hovering right under my skin. I rubbed my hands up and down my arms, trying to warm the sleeves of my jacket and ward off the goosebumps prickling the surface of my skin. I shivered and stood, pacing in a tight path between the chairs and the fire, holding my hands to the heat of the flames.

"Are you okay?" Logan asked. "Are you cold?"

I looked at him. He was leaning back, relaxed, with his jacket open and his hand wrapped around the cold beer, and I stopped in my tracks. He seemed comfortable next to the fire.

I turned, realization hitting me as I stared out into the darkness of the park. The goosebumps weren't from the cold. "Something's happening."

He stood and looked out at his side of the circle, the runner's instincts kicking in. "What?"

"I don't know. Magic."

We both stood, his hand on his rifle and mine under my jacket, on the butt of my gun, and waited.

And waited.

And waited.

Nothing came howling out of the darkness at us. Nothing dropped from the trees and attempted to eat me. Just...nothing. The wind sighed through the leaves. The stars winked above us, oblivious to our conundrum.

I let my hand fall from my gun and just barely resisted the urge to stomp my foot. "I don't understand," I huffed.

"Maybe the magic was unrelated? It's not always about you, you know."

I searched the darkness once more. Other than leaves blowing under the occasional street lamp, all was still. The magic had been too familiar, though. "No. It was about me. I just don't know how."

He let his rifle slide to the ground and opened another beer. "It's after ten. How long do you want to stay out here?"

"Midnight." I said. "If it doesn't attack by midnight, it's probably not attacking. Feel free to leave if you want to, techie. I can grab a cab."

He shrugged. "Hey, this was my idea, remember? I'm in it for the long haul. At least we're well-stocked. Cheers." He raised the bottle to his lips, draining half of it before setting it down and wiping his mouth.

I quietly wished for something warmer than beer, but made do with raising my body temperature with alcohol as we sat beside the fire. I kept my back to the flames, not wanting to ruin my night vision any more than it already was. The fire was a beacon at our backs—if the point was to draw an attack, we couldn't be more obvious or vulnerable out here in the middle of the deserted park.

Midnight arrived and still nothing came.

As Logan and I walked back to his bike, I couldn't decide whether I was relieved or frustrated. Not getting attacked was a good thing, for sure, but it would have been nice for it to happen when I was ready, for once. It could have been that the attacker didn't want to get too predictable, and decided to skip a night to throw me off. Or it could be they'd given up after I'd defeated the troll.

"Alyssa? You with me?"

I looked up to see Logan storing his rifle in the compartment on the side of his bike. He smiled at me with his crooked grin.

"You must be tired," he said.

I really was. A bone-deep weariness had seeped into me. I was sick of this, of having no answers. "Just thinking."

"About?"

"Trying to figure out what the game is. It doesn't seem over to me, but why did nothing show?" I glanced around, noting each dark corner. It was late, so there were few pedestrians, and I slid out of the way as a punk in black leather and a skull bandanna walked too close to me and cut across the street. His arm brushed mine, and a tingle of warmth and magic ran over my skin. I must have been more tired than I thought, because it took my brain a minute to catch up, and I gasped.

The punk had reached the far side of the road by the time I realized what was happening. He turned toward us and raised a hand in front of him, almost as if in greeting. I had a glimpse of a glowing red glyph carved into his palm just as the slight hint of sulfur tickled my nose. With a small cry, I tackled Logan. He let out a grunt as we hit the pavement.

A ball of fire flew through the air inches above us, the heat scorching even through the leather of my jacket. I cursed as I tried to disentangle myself from Logan, only to be knocked back down to my hands and knees as the fireball hit the wall at the end of the alley and exploded in a blast that left my eardrums ringing.

I blinked away the after-images and lifted my head. The punk set his feet in a wide stance, threw his head back, and *roared*. A gout of flame spewed from his mouth into the dark sky.

"What the hell is *that?*" Logan gasped from the pavement.

"A fire elemental," I whispered.

The punk lowered his eyes to us. Smoke tricked from his nostrils and his mouth twisted into a grin as he held his hands out to his sides. Fire blossomed in his upturned palms.

"Um," I said. "Run."

We pounded down the alley away from the walking barbecue, and cut left at the end of the building just as another fireball *whooshed* passed us. It hit the already-smoldering brick and threw us into the back wall of the building, nearly knocking us off our feet.

"Go!" I hauled Logan out of his half-sprawl and shoved him into a run.

For a few minutes there was nothing but the sound of our feet on the pavement, punctuated by our gasping breaths and the occasional explosion. We wove our way through the back streets and alleyways, but every time it seemed like we were gaining ground, we'd take a turn only to have our heels scorched as he caught up with us.

"Dammit!" I gasped. "How the hell is he keeping up?"

"Why don't you go back and ask him?" Logan snarled.

My reply died on my lips as we took a turn and hit a dead end.

"You have *got* to be kidding me," I muttered. "Clever boy."

"What?"

"He drove us. Like cattle. Straight into our pen." The brick wall towered in front of us. It stood only four stories tall, but it may as well have been twenty. "Uh, I don't suppose they've invented some sort of super-powered leg mod that lets you leap tall buildings in a single bound?"

Logan eyed the building. "It's actually a leg replacement, but the science is still in the prototype phase. Besides, it's way out of my price range."

"So, you don't have it, then. Great." A growl from the alley behind us pulled me around. It rolled across us, deep and low, not quite animal, but not human either. I felt it in my feet as much as heard it. "Oh, this is so not good."

"You think?"

Okay, Lys, think. What are your options? I furiously took in our surroundings. Two large, industrial-sized trash cans heaped with garbage. Three brick walls. One long fire escape that was too high to reach. Maybe Logan could lift me? No, by the time we got the ladder down, we'd be completely exposed as we made our way up the side of the building.

I could use the Eldergloom to hide both of us, but there was no promise that the elemental couldn't see through my veil. Plus, Logan was loaded with tech. I could hide us, but if I fried his brain in the process, the end result would be the same as if I'd just let the elemental have its way with him.

I had to fight.

Turning to Logan, I took him by the shoulders. "Ok, look, I can get us out of this. I think."

"You *think?*"

"Shut up, you left your rifle at your bike, so this is the best option we have right now. Unless you have a fire hose hidden in one of those pockets of yours?" He raised an eyebrow at me but I talked over his response. "I can get us out of this. But you have to promise you won't say anything to anyone about what I'm about to do."

Another roar shook the buildings around us. His eyes widened at the sound and he pulled a pistol from his holster at the small of his back.

"Logan, it's a freaking fire elemental! Bullets won't hurt it! I don't have time to explain, just, please. Promise me."

A red glow shimmered from the far end of the alley, causing strange shadows to leap up from around the corner of the building. His eyes flicked from me to the glow and back again. "Yeah, sure. I promise."

"Okay, good. Now, get behind me." I took three steps forward and planted my feet, squared my shoulders, and closed my eyes.

I took a deep breath and pulled on the Eldergloom.

I can't quite explain what it is that I do. It's like trying to explain walking to a fish. The simplest way to put it is I reach across the veil and pull the life energy into myself, spool it through my mind, and then weave it into the form I want it to take. This time, I wanted it to take the form of a wall of energy between us and the elemental. I exhaled, and a soft, silvery haze shivered from my fingers and eyes and lips. It spun across the floor of the alley, up the walls, and, with the faint sound of a temple bell, sealed shut in a shimmering, translucent barrier.

Then the elemental stepped around the corner.

It had all but given up whatever glamour it had been using to disguise itself. Instead of a punk in leather, it was now seven feet tall, vaguely humanoid...and on fire. Its skin was volcanic rock, darker on the surface where it cooled against the air, with veins of molten lava woven through it. Its eyes were pure flame, and when it opened its mouth to roar, the air around it shimmered with the heat. It threw out one arm-like appendage, and fire sprayed toward us.

The fire hit my wall of Eldergloom and the impact nearly threw me off balance. He was packing a lot more power than I'd expected. My wall held, but I could already see cracks starting to form. With a deep breath, I channeled more energy into it with my left hand, willing it to hold.

In my right hand, I gathered a separate set of energy and wove it into a ball, slowly but surely wrapping the Eldergloom over and over itself until a glowing sphere of frigid energy hovered just above my palm. The cold radiated against my fingertips, and still I willed it colder.

I staggered as my wall started to give way under my divided attention, and I pushed just enough into it to make it last just a few more seconds. The timing needed to be just right. If I dropped the wall too early, the sphere wouldn't be powerful enough. If I dropped it too late, my own attack would hit it and shatter, and my efforts would be wasted. Not to mention it would probably shatter the shield wall as well, and Logan and I would be toast. Literally.

So I held the wall and spun my sphere even colder. "Logan, when I say 'down,' you hit the pavement, got it?" There was silence behind me. Dammit, I couldn't spare the glance over my shoulder to make sure he was okay. "Logan!"

"I—Right!"

"Ready..." I slowly released my hold on the wall, diverting all my will into the sphere. It shone a silver-blue, making my hand ache from the cold. The wall began to crack in the center, the energy wavering as it was undone by the elemental's heat. Just a bit longer... and..."Down!"

I shoved my right hand forward and let fly. My ball of super-chilled Eldergloom barreled toward the wall, and for a split second I thought I'd mistimed and let go too early. I held my breath, but just before the sphere reached the barrier, the wall fell, dissipating with a clang. The frozen projectile flew through the now empty space, impacted with the elemental's flame, and kept going.

I hit the pavement just before the sphere collided with the elemental, and I threw my arms over the back of my head as the flames, now unimpeded by my wall, blasted above us.

Have you ever dropped an ice cube into a cup of hot tea, or tried to wash a cold glass under a stream of hot water? The violence with which they crack is nothing compared to the reaction created by the meeting of a fire elemental and a ball of frozen Eldergloom.

The *crraaa-BOOM* of the exploding elemental echoed off of the walls of the alley and shattered the windows in the nearby buildings. Smoldering bits of pumice and obsidian rained down on us, scorching my skin where they hit. A small piece landed in my hair, and I shook my head with a shriek to dislodge the ember before it could set my whole head on fire. As it was, I could smell burning hair. Hopefully it wasn't too bad.

I turned as Logan picked himself up off the pavement, also shaking his head free of any stray bits of elemental. The whites of his eyes showed large around his irises as he looked from the smoking remains at the end of the alleyway to me. His pistol hung limp in his hand, forgotten.

"What…what just happened?" His voice was high and thready.

"I took care of the elemental." I turned my head toward the street as the far-off wail of sirens cut the air. "That's our cue. Let's go."

Logan simply stared at me.

"C'mon, techie, you're not going wobbly on me now, are you? We've got to get the hell out of here before the cops show, Logan."

He blinked, then shook his head. "Right. Yes." He tucked the pistol back in his holster, and took off in a jog back the way we'd come.

I followed, and flashing red and blue lights came into view just as we slipped out of sight.

We ended up at my shop. Our run through town had put us closer to there than to his bike, and we needed to get cleaned up before we went out anywhere. I pulled a small first aid kit out from underneath the counter and made my way to the back office, where Logan was sitting in one of the battered leather wingchairs in front of the cold fireplace. I sat in the one across from him, popped open the lid on the kit, and tossed him some disinfecting swabs. We quietly cleaned our wounds and patched the burns with second skin, neither of us meeting the other's eyes.

Finally, as I was applying a bandage to a burn the size of a quarter on the back on my hand, Logan cleared his throat and spoke quietly.

"So," he said, his voice taut. "Do you want to tell me about it?

I shrugged one shoulder, meeting his eyes and looking away quickly. "Not much to tell. I can do magic." I raised my hands, wiggling my fingers, and plastered a wide, fake smile on my face. "Surprise!"

"Not much to tell? Lys, there's *tons* to tell. Like, how can you do that? Can all elves do that? Why can't I tell anyone? Why didn't I know?" He stood and paced the small space in front of the fireplace. "Why didn't you blast *me* like that on our first run?" I looked up at him and he held up a hand before continuing. "Don't get me wrong, I'm glad you didn't, but you *could* have. You could have taken the prize from me, easy. So, why didn't you?"

"Because I'm not in the habit of killing people."

He stopped, looking down at me. "Yeah, but wasn't there something else you could have done? You didn't have to kill me, right? I'm not a fire elemental, I wouldn't have exploded like that."

"No, but…" I sighed. "Hang on a minute." I stood and walked into my dark store. After looking around, I grabbed a small, lime green mp3 player from the shelf and went back to the office. I thumbed it on and placed it on the side table between the chairs.

I took a deep breath and found Logan's eyes with mine, holding his gaze as I pulled the Eldergloom through me. His eyes widened as my irises silvered.

"This is the Eldergloom. It's life energy. I can weave it and twist it however I like. I can make a tree grow from a seed in a day. I can call lightning from my fingertips. I can freeze water or thaw ice. I can even do this." With a slow exhale, I wrapped the Eldergloom around myself.

He gasped as I disappeared from his sight.

Slowly, I circled the chairs. "I can do all sorts of things," I said softly, and he jumped, searching the room with his eyes. My voice sounded strange in my ears, with a humming echo as it filtered through the eldritch power, and I wondered what it sounded like to him. "But things like this are never as simple as they seem. You asked why it was a secret?"

He nodded, turning as he followed the sound of my voice.

"Because people would be afraid. Because they wouldn't understand. And humanity always seeks to destroy that which it doesn't understand—or seeks to control it. I do not wish a war between the humans and the elves. Nor do I wish to be used as a weapon. So it's secret." I dropped the veil as I returned to the table. He took an involuntary step back as I reappeared. "Even *you* are afraid."

He shook his head, his blue eyes earnest. "No."

"You should be." I smiled coldly, the Eldergloom still in my eyes. "You asked me why I didn't use it on you, and I said I didn't like to kill. Yes, I could have tried to restrain you instead of kill, but it could have turned out that way anyway. Watch," I said, pointing to the player.

I placed my index finger on the table top and breathed out slowly. A shimmering line of Eldergloom skittered across the surface and wrapped around the player. The small green square sparked once, twice, then emitted a thin stream of acrid-smelling smoke. I released the Eldergloom, gingerly picked up the player between my thumb and forefinger, and turned it over. A melted black hole simmered in the back. I held it up for him to see.

"Pretend that's your Neurocomm," I said, my voice grim.

His face paled.

I tossed the player back on the table and lowered myself into the wingchair with a sigh.

"That's why you're low-tech," he said in realization.

I nodded. "My...*talents*...don't get along well with tech. It seems the more advanced it is, the more violent the reaction. So, I can use a handgun and keep myself hidden, but if I tried to veil myself while wearing Neurospecs, I might lose my eyes."

"The Eldergloom," he spent a second on the new word. "You use it to summon elementals?"

I nodded again.

"And Eyja has tech. That's why it couldn't be her."

"She could probably work around it, but it's unlikely. It's a tricky thing. And risky. Very risky."

He stared at the melted MP3 player. "So, what now?"

"Now? Now my job tomorrow will be a little bit easier if I'm not worried about showing off the Eldergloom in front of you. It's *so handy* on a run," I sighed.

"Your secret weapon," he said, and I smiled slightly.

"That is, if you still want me on the run with you. I shouldn't go. I'm a liability."

"What do you mean?"

"What happens if one of these elementals manifests in the middle of the Americorp building? How exactly are we supposed to deal with that without getting caught or killed? I don't fancy dodging security guards *and* fireballs."

He shrugged. "After seeing what you can do tonight, I'll take that chance. And who knows, maybe it'll serve as a distraction."

"It's a dumb risk, Logan."

"And it's my run," he said, his voice firm. "If I want you there, that's my dumb choice to make."

I looked at him for a long moment, then nodded. "Okay," I said. "In that case, it's time to go home and get some rest. I'll meet you here at eleven tomorrow night."

He nodded, pushing to his feet. "Do you have a way to get home?"

"I'll call Rose or a cab. It's no big deal. You need me to call you a cab?"

He shook his head. "I'll manage. See you tomorrow night. And Alyssa?"

"Yeah?"

"Thanks. For saving us and trusting me. It means a lot."

I shrugged one shoulder, avoiding his gaze.

"See you tomorrow night."

I let him out the front door, then locked it behind him. Once back in my office, I went to the large bureau in the back corner, slid a large silver basin from the bottom drawer, and set it on my desk. I pulled a bottle of water from my mini-fridge beside my chair and emptied the contents into the basin, then lit two candles, one on either side. I waved my hand over the basin three times, clockwise, then touched my ring finger to the surface and said *"Etta es,* Lorelei."

A soft, clear chiming filled the air and a moment later the ripples in the water settled. Lorelei looked back at me from the surface of the water.

"*Am'fialte*, Alyssa," she said. "This is unusual—and very late. To what do I owe the rare pleasure of a scrying from you?"

"*Am'fialte*. Have you had any luck with the Oracles?"

"No. They have seen nothing as of late. Why? Has something changed?"

"The elemental attacks are still coming," I said, laying a hand on either side of the basin and letting my head hang forward. I was exhausted. "A troll last night, and a fire elemental about an hour ago."

"They're increasing in power," she mused. "This is not good."

"You're telling me." I sighed, rolling my head to stretch my neck and shoulders. "The Talmorin I suspected is innocent. And the troll...I managed to question him. He didn't know much, but he was able to tell me that a Talmorin Weaver was behind this."

"A Talmorin Weaver?" Her voice was incredulous, and she peered up at me intently. "Alyssa, what *have* you been doing lately?"

I laughed once, harshly. "Oh, you know me. Making friends everywhere I go."

She shook her head. "I will increase my investigations with the Oracles. In the meantime, be very careful."

I nodded, stray pieces of my hair trailing in the water, causing her image to waver. "I will. It was close tonight though, Lorelei. Others are getting hurt because of me. I need answers."

"Do you think it is because of the Order of the White Hart? What sort of questions have you been asking?"

I started, staring down at my left hand where it lay splayed across the desk top. The silver Hart ring gleamed in the candlelight. "I hadn't considered that angle. The attacks *did* start the night I got my ring."

"You were given a Hart ring? You didn't tell me that when you were here."

I nodded. "The Emissary asked me to take a ring and aid her. I saw no reason to say no at the time."

"I think this certainly bears looking into then, don't you? Perhaps there's more to this Botanical Garden issue than we first thought. I will speak with the Order. If their emissaries are being attacked by the Talmorin, they'll wish to know."

"Tristan," I whispered as a sudden thought struck me. I wasn't the only one helping Seraphina. If I was being attacked, maybe he was, too.

"What about Tristan?"

"He's also helping with the project." I held up a hand at her disapproving gaze. "It wasn't my choice to include him, but I need to make sure he's okay. I saw him earlier today and he had a bruise on his face...damn it, I didn't even make the connection."

"You're worried he may have been a target, as well." She pressed her lips together in thought. "Very well. You go. Make sure he is unharmed. I will see what I can discern from the Order."

"Thank you, Lorelei," I said.

"No thanks are needed, Alyssa, just be safe."

Our gazes held for a long moment, then I nodded once. She waved a hand, and the image rippled and was gone.

I dialed Tristan's number. It rang several times before going to voicemail. I cursed quietly and dialed again, but he didn't answer. I sat heavily in my chair, rubbing my temples with my fingers. Maybe he was at a club and couldn't hear it over the pounding music. He could be asleep, the phone silenced for the night.

Or he could be laying in a gutter somewhere, bleeding.

I stood and paced, worry and helplessness making my legs itch. I had no idea where he was staying while he was in town, nowhere to start my search. The only potential place I could think of was The Grove, but they'd closed hours ago. The city was too big for me to just drive around with no destination. I'd never find him that way. So, I could run around looking for him, or I could go get some sleep and start in the morning when I was freshly rested and thinking straight.

I called a cab and climbed into the back, exhausted beyond words, and told the cabbie to head toward my apartment. As the tires hummed across the blacktop, a longing filled me. I was tired, and burned, and bruised.

I just wanted to fall asleep in someone else's arms instead of my own empty bed.

"Actually," I said to the cabbie. "Take me to Azure Gateways."

We pulled up to Seraphina's building and I paid the cabbie and got out, wrapping my arms around myself. Maybe this was a mistake. It was the middle of the night. She was probably asleep and wouldn't appreciate me dropping by unannounced.

But...maybe she knew where Tristan was staying. I had a legitimate reason to be here other than my own loneliness. I walked into the foyer, nodding my thanks to the doorman, and stepped up to the counter. Tonight it was manned by a pretty Arcadian with a powder-blue pixie cut.

"Alyssa D'Yaragen to see Seraphina Dubhan, please." I laid my license on the counter between us. She looked it over and tapped at a small touchscreen behind the counter.

"You're on the approved list. You can go up," she said, gesturing to the elevators.

I blinked once, startled. "Thanks."

I ran my hands through my hair as I rode up to the penthouse, trying to make sense of the singed tangles the fire elemental had made. The desk clerk must have some excellent customer services training—she hadn't reacted at all to my appearance. I was kind of a mess.

The elevator dinged and I stepped into the hall.

I hesitated at Seraphina's door, my hand raised halfway, before I sucked in a deep breath and made myself ring the doorbell.

There was the sound of movement from deeper inside the penthouse, then the clatter of something falling over and a muffled curse. Seraphina opened the door. Her hair was disheveled as if she'd been sleeping, though she was in a deep purple dress that clearly wasn't a nightgown. She stumbled as she opened the door wide, and leaned against the frame to steady herself.

And she was...giggling.

My brain, slow as it had been all night, had trouble processing that.

Then she raised her eyes to mine and the smile slid off of her face.

"Alyssa?" She glanced behind her briefly, then back to me as an expression somewhere between confusion and panic took the place of the smile.

"It's okay, nothing broke," came a voice from inside the apartment. "Who is it?"

My heart sank. Oh no. Not again. No, no, no.

Tristan stepped into view, shirtless, his hair tousled.

I spun on my heel and ran.

18

There was no way I was waiting for the elevator, so I fled to the escape offered by the stairwell. I almost tripped once or twice before I even got five stories down. The door at the top of the stairwell creaked open, and Seraphina called my name. Tristan's voice followed hers, and their tentative footsteps echoed off the cement stairs. I dove for the nearest door, pushing out into a hallway lined with apartments, and ran across the expensive tile floor. My feet skidded on the carpet as I rounded a corner. Out of sight of the stairwell door, I slid to the floor, my breath heaving and a sob catching in my throat.

No. I would not cry over this. Not this time.

I swallowed my tears, pushed to my feet and looked around. A building this size should have more than one stairwell. Sure enough, at the far end of the hall was a sign with a picture of a little stick figure man running out an open door.

Exit.

The long expanse of hallway held the hushed quiet of the wee hours, the tenants in the surrounding apartments sleeping and unaware. I walked toward the stairs calmly, like I had every right to be there, then made my way slowly down to the first floor.

It was a long walk down.

At the bottom, I didn't even bother going out the lobby door. Part of me was afraid that Tristan and Seraphina would be down there already, waiting to head me off before I could leave.

Another part was afraid they wouldn't be.

Instead, I pushed out the door labeled "Emergency Exit Only—Alarm Will Sound."

They did not lie. A siren sounded, wailing loud and rebounding off the walls of the stairway.

I ignored it all, walked two blocks down, and hailed a cab. My phone rang, and I looked at it only long enough to turn it off.

Back at my apartment, I crept quietly through the door and slipped off my boots, not wanting to wake Rose if she was home. Only once I was safely curled up under my blankets did I let myself really think about what I'd seen.

Seraphina. With Tristan.

Of course it had been Tristan.

I had been so, so stupid.

I shouldn't have allowed myself to get wrapped up in her so quickly. I didn't even *know* her. She and Tristan were the same. To think I'd been sitting in her apartment the night before, confessing feelings I didn't even understand. Hell, she'd confessed to me first. And we'd kissed. And...

It shouldn't hurt this much. I'd known her all of a handful of days. We hadn't committed to each other or made any promises of exclusivity. She was free to see who she wanted. I was free to do the same.

My brain recognized all of these as being perfectly valid and reasonable. My heart, on the other hand, was not so easily swayed.

I was just really tired of not being good enough.

That's what it really came down to, I realized. Being lied to hurt, yes, but worse than that was the implication that I wasn't enough. That they needed to supplement me with others in order to be satisfied.

As the concept finally solidified, I felt both lighter and heavier. It felt good to finally be able to put these feelings into words after so long. It was a relief to be able to point to the exact thing that was bothering me, and to be able to verbalize it rationally.

But that didn't make it hurt any less.

I would not cry over this, dammit.

I pulled my blankets up to my chin, and rolled over, staring at my window and the pale square of yellow around the edges, where the street lights managed to filter through. A siren wailed in the distance, and every once a while a car would drive by on the otherwise deserted street. A door slammed somewhere deeper in my building, and muffled footsteps sounded from above.

I closed my eyes and let the noises of the city carry me off to sleep.

I was proud of myself. I didn't cry.

M y shop was closed on Mondays, so I took the opportunity to mope, staying in bed until the afternoon. Rose finally coaxed me out of my room with the savory scent of pancakes and sausages.

I gave in to the rumblings of my stomach and forced myself out of bed, took a quick shower, and was at the table just as she finished cooking.

"I figured this might get you up," she said, spearing a stack of pancakes with a fork and dumping them on my plate, followed by a pile of sausage links.

I grunted noncommittally and poured a generous amount of syrup over everything. I cut a large wedge from the stack of pancakes, snagged a sausage with the end of my fork, and shoveled it into my mouth.

"You feel like talking about it now?"

I nodded, holding up a finger while I finished chewing, and then washed everything down with a large swallow of coffee. "I went to see Seraphina last night and found her with Tristan at her apartment." I took another bite and gave her a significant look, making sure she understood the implications of that "with."

Her eyes widened, and she shook her head. "Oh, Alyssa, I'm sorry."

I shrugged and chewed, determined not to be upset about it.

"What did they say?"

"I didn't exactly give them a chance to explain. They didn't need to. It was obvious. And Seraphina and I aren't a *thing*, not really. Neither of them owe me an explanation."

"Like hell," she snarled. "That's a crap way to treat you, and you know that. Seraphina obviously knew how you felt. Did Tristan?"

I shrugged again. "I wasn't exactly having girl time and pouring my heart out to him. I just figured, after what he said the other night…" I shook my head and sighed. "The point is, I was stupid and should have expected it. I'm going to move past it and worry about other, more important things. Like my run tonight."

"That's right, that's tonight. I'm glad I waited until two to make breakfast then. Did you get enough sleep?"

I nodded. "I think I'm going to go over to the shop and get some new inventory on the shelves. I got a shipment in a few days ago and it's been sitting in boxes in the back. It'll be nice, mindless work. Help me get focused on tonight."

She nodded, her mouth full of sausage.

We finished our breakfast in companionable silence.

She hugged me tightly as I was heading out the door. "Be careful tonight," she said softly into my shoulder. "Don't get caught. And don't die."

"I'll do my best," I said, hugging her back. The warm, clean scent of shampoo and vanilla body wash filled me, and I closed my eyes and let the hug linger before breaking away and giving her a smile. "Thanks for breakfast."

She smiled back. "Anytime. You know that."

I turned my phone back on when I was settled in the back of the cab, bracing myself for the barrage of text and voice messages—or lack thereof. My heart fluttered before my phone caught up with itself, and a notification popped up.

Seven missed calls. Six new voicemails. Ten new text messages.

I opened the call log and scrolled through the list. Tristan, Seraphina, Seraphina, Tristan, Tristan Seraphina…and the repair shop. I queued up voicemail, skipping over Tristan and Seraphina's messages, and stopped when I heard my mechanic's voice.

"Hey, Alyssa, good news. Some of the bikes in line before you took less time than we thought, so yours is ready for pickup today."

I let out a little *whoop* of happiness, startling the cabbie. I grimaced in apology and hung up my phone.

"Sorry," I said. "Can you take me to Borelli Brothers Garage over on Ponce instead?"

She nodded, making a quick U-turn at the next light, and took me to pick up my bike.

I was practically bouncing on my toes as I paid for the repairs—just as pricey as I expected, but not unreasonable—and a short, dark-haired man brought me my keys.

"Tony, I could just hug you," I said, relief heavy in my voice.

"I won't complain," he said, and laughed as I wrapped my arms around his neck.

"I seriously needed this today, you have no idea."

"I'm glad I could be the bearer of such good news. You scuffed her up real good, though, so just be gentle with her for a while, deal?"

I beamed at him. "Deal."

I grinned from ear to ear and wove my way down the streets toward my shop. It felt so good to be back on my own bike again. I took the turns a little faster than I needed, laughing out loud at the pure delight in the ride.

My good mood vanished as I pulled into the alleyway beside my store and saw Tristan leaning against the back door. Heat surged to my face, my heartbeat thundering in my ears, causing the edges of my vision to close in as I turned off my bike and kicked down the stand. He watched me in silence as I pulled off my helmet, shook out my hair, and walked straight toward him.

"You're in my way," I growled.

"You didn't answer any of my messages." His tone was nonchalant, but there was an edge of tension in his shoulders that betrayed him.

"That's probably because I didn't check any of them. Now if you'll please excuse me, I have work to do."

"I can explain, Alyssa."

"Don't bother." I fought to keep my voice low and neutral. "Please. I really don't care to hear it. I'm tired of these games, Tristan, and I have more important things than you to worry about."

"You don't understand," he said, pushing off of the door and taking a step toward me. "It wasn't—"

I took a step back from him. "I said *don't*. Seriously, Tristan, don't push me on this."

"No, you need to know—"

"Stop!" The suppressed anger finally broke free, surging in my chest, and I violently pulled on the Eldergloom and threw a gust of wind at him, slamming him back against the door. I stood with my feet apart, my eyes glowing and my hair flying around me as if in a gale. "No more, Tristan! I'm tired of the excuses, and the explanations, and all of the ways you pass off the blame to everyone but yourself! I. Don't. *Care.*" I flung power at him again, pushing him to the side and making him stumble away from the wall and toward the entrance of the alley. "Now go, before I do something I might regret."

He steadied himself and looked at me, something akin to desperation in his eyes, then ran his hands through his hair in frustration. "You're always so damn stubborn!" He raised a hand to stop me as my fists clenched and my hair swirled with renewed anger. "At least listen to my messages. Please. I'll go. Just...listen to them."

With that he turned on his heels and walked toward the street. He glanced back at me once, then turned the corner out of sight.

***

I spent the next few hours unpacking boxes and reorganizing shelves. I'd never been much of a neat freak, but cleaning helped me clear my head. It gave me something to do when there was nothing I *could* do, or kept me from doing things that I shouldn't.

I didn't listen to Tristan's messages. I didn't read his texts, either, or Seraphina's. I almost deleted all of them in one fell swoop, but hesitated at the last minute and just shoved my phone into my back pocket, focusing on pricing and organizing a full set of hardcover novels by an early twentieth-century author. They were all signed, too, and would bring a great price from the right buyer.

My stomach growled loudly at me around seven, so I finished up my last box and headed out to Manny's for dinner and a drink before the run. I parked my bike in the side alley and walked in, immediately relaxing in the warm, comfortable atmosphere. I waved to Jeremiah, ordered a club sandwich with fries and a beer at the bar, and then joined him in the back booth.

He had dark circles under his eyes, barely hidden by his glasses. His skin was pale and his fingers shook as he raised his cigarette to his lips.

"No offense, Alyssa, but if you brought any more visions with you, I'm going to need to you to just walk right back out that door." He exhaled and met my gaze briefly before looking away.

"They haven't stopped?"

He ran a shaky hand through his soft curls. "If by 'stopped' you mean 'occasionally let up long enough for me to get wasted,' then yes." He raised a glass tumbler to his lips and downed the rest of the whiskey in the bottom. "Luckily for you, you caught me at a lucid, non-seizing moment, but I'm not up for doing any favors at the time being."

"I'm not here for a favor, Jer," my voice was soft. "I have a run tonight. Just wanted to check on you and have a good meal before getting ready to head out."

He grunted in response, taking another drag from his cigarette. "What else is going on with you? You don't look like you're doing much better than I am."

I shook my head, smiling when Manny set my beer on the table as he walked by. "Just relationship drama. Oh, and the occasional elemental attack. You know, the usual."

He raised his eyebrows at that, perking up a bit. "You'll have to tell me about that second part some time. Glad to see you still in one piece, though."

"Yeah, well, came close a few times." I took a long drink of my beer and sighed contentedly, leaning back in the booth bench. "My bike fared far worse than I did, though I got it back from the shop today. Tony does great work."

"He does, indeed."

Manny set my sandwich in front of me and I set to work devouring it. Jeremiah occasionally stole a fry off my plate, but I pretended not to notice. I finished my beer around the same time I finished my sandwich, and sat back in my seat, smiling. I pushed my plate to Jeremiah, wordlessly offering him the rest of my fries. He raised his whiskey glass in thanks and picked one up, dipping it in ketchup before popping it in his mouth.

"So," he said around the fry. "Risky job tonight?"

"You could say that." I glanced around the room, but no one cared to listen in to our conversation. "We're as ready as we're going to get, though."

"Good luck. Don't get caught. And don't die."

I smiled at him, amused by the runner's mantra coming from his lips. "I'll do my best. I'll swing by tomorrow and let you know how it went."

"Do that," he said, stubbing out the butt of his cigarette in the little glass ashtray. "You can buy me dinner."

"Deal," I grinned, then sobered. "Get some rest, Jer. Let me know if I can do anything."

He waved a hand dismissively, not meeting my eyes. "Don't worry about little ol' me. Sounds like you've got your own problems to worry about. Just take care of yourself. I'll be here when you're done."

I nodded, dropped some cash on the table for my bill, and slid out of the booth, giving Manny a little salute as I walked passed the bar and out the door.

Back at my shop, I changed into my leather running gear, leaving all my jewelry in a little pile on desk and tucking my equipment into its various pockets and holsters. Then I took a moment to savor the excitement that comes just before a run, letting it course through me before taking a few meditative breaths and settling my nerves.

As the clock on my mantel chimed midnight, there was a short, staccato rap on the back door of my shop.

I peered through the small security peep-hole in the door before undoing the deadbolt and stepping back to let Logan in.

"You got your bike back already?" He asked, tilting his head in the direction of the back door and the alley behind it. "That was fast. Who's your mechanic?"

"Tony, down at Borelli Brothers."

"Nice, I might have to try them."

"They do good work, and they don't try to gouge me on it, which is nice. I've used them for years."

He grunted, nodding, and followed me to my office. He was wearing much the same outfit that I saw him in the last time: all-black, ripstop nylon. He had his hair pulled back in a French braid, tight against his head, and his knit hat tucked into his belt. He wore Neurolenses, and I was sure he had his Neurospecs tucked into one of his many pockets.

"You get ambushed by any elementals yet tonight?"

I shook my head. "No. Look, Logan, it might be safer if I—"

"No," he said. "I already told you. It's worth the risk. Besides, it might be fun to watch an elemental tear through the Americorp building."

I scooped a small earpiece from the top of my desk and tossed it to him "We can use that to communicate if we get separated. It calibrates the microphone to your voice so it picks up your speech only. You can practically whisper and I will still hear you over any background noise."

He turned the piece over in his hand and then slipped it into his ear. I did the same with mine, pressed the small button on the side, and said, "Lysistrata in."

"Grendel in," he said, his voice pitched low. I nodded as I heard his voice through the earpiece.

"You're loud and clear, techie. You ready to do this?"

"Hang on," he said, and reached into the pocket of his jacket, producing a small metal cylinder. He unscrewed both sides and set the resulting shot glasses on the table, then screwed off the small top and poured a clear liquid into both glasses. "It's a pre-run ritual of mine. Helps take the edge off." He lifted one up in a "cheers" motion. "Don't get caught."

I picked up the other one, mirroring him. "And don't die."

We clinked the glasses together and then downed the shots. The alcohol burned my throat, the warmth spreading to my limbs as it hit my stomach.

I handed the shot glass back to him and he pocketed the set, zipping his jacket up after him.

"Let's go," I said.

We headed out into the night, to potentially the biggest payout of our lives.

19

We parked our bikes between some large dumpsters in an alley about a block from the Americorp complex. Grendel looped his plasma rifle across his back and slipped on his Neurospecs as I set my helmet on my bike and pulled on a ski cap. It was a straight shot from the alley to the tall chain link fence that surrounded the entire complex. We crouched beside the dumpsters, eyeing the layout. A small security camera was mounted on a tall pole about fifty feet inside the perimeter. Grendel looked at me and nodded once.

I could take out the camera with the Eldergloom, but there was no promise it wouldn't take out more than that. If every camera on the circuit went down at once, it would garner more attention than we wanted. Instead, I nudged a few stray rocks and bits of asphalt with the toe of my boot before settling on a stone the size of a quarter—oblong, with a good, solid weight.

I pulled a small sling out of a pocket and slipped the rock into the pouch. Rising from my crouch, I took a step into the mouth of the alley and spun the sling by my side. It made a soft *whoosh*ing noise as the cords cut the air, and after taking careful aim, I gave it one last spin and let fly.

The stone rocketed across the distance and hit the side of the camera with a clang, knocking it off kilter. I winced at the sound, hoping it didn't carry too far. At least now the camera wouldn't be pointing in our direction, and if we were quick we could get through the fence and to our destination before a guard ambled by to check out the noise.

A quick sprint took us across the street and to the unguarded service gate we'd seen while virtual scouting. Grendel laid his RFID lockpick against the small, plastic reader and hit a few buttons. The light on the reader blinked red a few times, then switched to green, and the gate jerked into motion. The chain link rattled as it rolled to the side, and we dashed through the opening.

Getting in was easy. Getting out would be the hard part.

We ran across the parking lot, empty except for several cars belonging to security guards or employees up against a deadline. We approached the side of the main office building, aiming for the blind spot between the cameras at a blank expanse of wall, where no doors or windows offered easy access. Our feet were nearly silent against the blacktop and we made it to the building without incident.

Grendel leaned casually against the wall, raising his grappling hook gun with a grin. I did the same, and with two soft *pops*, our hooks shot up six stories and over the edge of the building. I tugged experimentally on mine, then clipped it to my belt and pushed a small button, and the cable wound into itself, lifting me to the roof.

We pulled ourselves over the ledge and quickly re-holstered our hooks, looking around. Gravel and tar paper stretched between us and the stairwell door, the expanse dotted with industrial-sized HVAC units, and we ran from one to the next, using them as cover. A half-sphere of a security camera was mounted above the door, so we approached it from behind. Grendel pulled a small thumb drive and a set of tools from his pocket, winked at me, and took three deep breaths before dashing around the side of the building. If he did this right, he would have the camera running on a recorded loop before any security guards noticed something amiss. In fifteen seconds he was back, a grin on his face.

"Good to go," he whispered.

The door had no handle, meant to prevent anyone from getting in from the outside. He slid a long, thin piece of metal between the door and the jamb, and after a moment of work the door popped open with a *click*. He held it with a gloved hand and gestured for me to go first, then eased it shut behind us.

The interior of the stairwell was dark, and he flicked on a small pen light, angling it at the steps. We made our way down one flight and paused at the door to the sixth-floor hallway. He raised a hand for me to wait, slowly looking from right to left along the stairwell wall, scanning the hallway with his Neurospecs for heat signatures. He nodded and I pushed open the door, edging out of the stairwell.

A long stretch of hallway spread out before us, and another angled off to the left. With a tilt of his head, Grendel indicated that we needed to head straight, and together we dashed down the hall, low and silent.

The office was to our left, three doors down. An RFID lock awaited us, and I gestured for Grendel to have at it. He pulled an electronic pick from his pocket, laid it against the pad, and grinned. A few seconds later there was a soft *click* and he pushed open the door.

We slipped into the room and shut the door quietly behind us. The security lights in the hallway filtered through the small glass window in the door and gave us plenty of light to see by.

Logan and I stopped and stared.

The room was standard office fare: a desk facing two chairs, with frames holding diplomas and awards arranged on the wall behind it. A large swivel chair sat behind the desk.

But the perimeter of the room was lined with tall filing cabinets, each one with haphazard stacks of papers piled on top.

"Wow," he whispered. "Are they all full?"

I picked a cabinet at random and slid open a drawer. It was packed tight with manila folders stuffed with papers. "Looks like it."

He shook his head in disbelief and walked across the office, sliding into the desk chair. A small computer cube sat on the corner of the desk, and he flipped it on. A projected keyboard and display blinked into existence on the desk in front of him, requesting ID validation. He slid a small memory stick into the port, and his fingers flew across the keyboard. Then he placed his thumb, with the fabricated fingerprint, on a small reader on the side of the cube.

I held my breath as the display flickered. The moment of truth.

He watched the display, then looked past it to me and grinned.

I let my breath out in a *whoosh*, and turned to keep an eye on the hall.

For a few minutes, there was nothing but the sound of our breathing and the *pat-pat-pat* of his fingertips on the desk. We were actually going to pull this off. Data theft from *Americorp*. A long way from stealing statues in small office buildings, that was for sure. Pride swelled in my chest.

Then Logan cursed softly.

I turned my head and looked at him, questioning.

"It's not here," he whispered.

I blinked. "What?"

"The file's not here. I can't find it anywhere in the system." His fingers tapped a little harder.

"Did you double check?" I moved across the room and looked over his shoulder at the display. Rows of file names and numbers filled the screen.

"Yes, I *quadruple* checked. Either Reed gave us the wrong file number, or they've gotten rid of it."

"Look again."

His fingers pounded out the file number—*K12-PP1434.*

No matches.

"*Dammit,*" he spat. "I can't believe it. All that work and we have a bad file name."

I shifted my weight onto my heels in frustration. This didn't make any sense. Why would Reed send us out with bad information? Unless it was some sort of trap, or another one of his stupid *competitions*. I silently vowed to zap each and every piece of Reed's expensive tech myself if it turned out to be another test. My eyes skittered around the office, searching for the answer among the diplomas, stacks of papers, and filing cabinets.

"Grendel," I said, my eyes landing on a filing cabinet. "What was that file name again?"

"K12-PP1434. Why?"

I walked to the filing cabinet. A small white label on the front of the drawer read "C." I pulled open the drawer and thumbed through the files. Each manila folder was labeled with the cabinet letter and a number—C12, C13, C14—in ascending order. I glanced up at Logan.

"Find cabinet K."

He stared at me. "You're kidding."

"Nope. Finish the job, techie. Let's go."

He jumped to his feet, and we scanned the cabinet labels. Each had a letter of the alphabet on the front, though they seemed to be arranged in a random order. I finally found cabinet K wedged between X and M. I yanked the drawer open and pawed through the folders until I found the one labeled K12. It was overstuffed with papers, which slid to the floor in a pile when I pulled the file free.

"You have *got* to be kidding me," I grumbled.

Together, we picked the scattered papers up from the floor and sorted through them.

Two minutes later, Logan pulled his breath in through his teeth.

"I think I found it," he breathed.

I looked over his shoulder. In his hands was an interior schematic for a first-generation Neurocomm. The page was numbered "1434" in the top right corner.

"Why would Reed want first gen Neurocomm plans?" I asked.

"Don't know, don't care. As long as this is what he wants and we get paid for it."

I nodded, and he gently folded the paper in half and then in half again, and put it in the interior pocket of his jacket. Then he zipped up his coat and patted the spot on his chest where it rested.

"Let's jet before security gets wise," he said with a grin.

I couldn't help but smile back.

I put the papers back in the folder and refiled it as he powered down the computer. My heart pounded, but this time with the adrenaline of victory. I couldn't pull the smile from my face as I watched him slide his memory stick into a small pants pocket, and my steps were light as I walked across the office and opened the door.

"After you," I bowed, giddy.

"Gee, and I thought chivalry was dead," he replied with equal giddiness, and stepped into the hall.

There was a soft pop, and his left shoulder jerked oddly. He turned back toward me and frowned.

"I think we have a problem." His voice was oddly disconnected as he raised his hand to his shoulder.

His fingers came away bloody.

Then his eyes rolled back in his head and his legs gave out under him. He hit the floor as sirens began to wail.

2 0

I gasped and grabbed Grendel by the leg and dragged him back inside the office, crouching below the line of windows and slamming the door shut behind him. I twisted the lock, and stood slowly, peering carefully through the small window. A cluster of tactical security guards crouched at the end of the hall with muzzles trained in our direction.

The safety glass of the window shattered with a crunch as a bullet pierced it an inch above my head. I ducked back down with a curse.

Grendel lay unconscious on the floor, a pool of blood slowly spreading beneath him. I opened his jacket to see a seeping red hole near his collar bone, just above the line of his vest. It was either a very good shot or a very lucky one. I fumbled at my belt for a small, blunt syringe filled with packed gauze and a gel coagulant. I pulled the cap off, shoved the rounded tip into the bullet hole, and pushed down on the plunger. His body spasmed slightly, and went limp again. My mind spun in panic. That would stop the bleeding temporarily, but he needed to get to a hospital, and soon.

I looked back at the hole in the window. I doubted the guards would listen to reason. I also doubted they'd take a peaceful surrender, seeing as how they shot Grendel without so much as a warning.

Even if I could carry him out of here—which I wasn't sure I could do—if I tried to walk out of the office door, I'd end up shot and then we'd both be dead. I looked around the office, willing another entrance to appear. Of course, none did.

I didn't have a whole lot of options.

Staying in a low crouch, I scuttled across the office and pushed the rolling swivel chair back across the room to where Grendel lay. Then I lifted him into the chair as quickly as I could, painfully aware that the guards outside were giving me an inordinate amount of time before they burst in with guns blazing. *No time to question it now.* After I had him settled, I dropped his plasma rifle in his lap, pulled out the ear-pieces from both of our ears, disabled them, and shoved them in my pocket. Then I reached behind his ear and found the small button to his Neurocomm.

I switched it off.

"Sorry, techie. Hope this doesn't hurt too much," I whispered, and tucked a stray piece of blond hair back under his hat, sending up a small prayer that his Neurolenses would deactivate when the Neuro-comm went offline. Then I pulled in the Eldergloom, wrapping it in a bubble around the two of us, cloaking us in shadow and silence. I reached out with one hand and pulled the office door open.

To the left, five armed guards in full tactical gear were arranged at the far end of the hall, three crouching and two standing behind them, all with rifles aimed toward the door. They made no move toward the office, confident we had only one way out—through them. To the right, there was nothing but a long expanse of hallway ending at the stairwell door. If we'd tried to make a run for it without the Elder-gloom veiling us, it would have been pathetically easy for them to take us down before we made it anywhere near the end of the hall.

I laid both my hands on the ground, took a deep breath, and sent the Eldergloom skittering across the carpeting to the guards.

The floor underneath them simply collapsed. All five guards fell to the floor below with shouts of surprise and a clatter of guns and debris.

Well. That was that.

I grabbed the chair and Grendel and wheeled him down the hall at a jog. At the stairwell door I stopped, laid my hand against the carpeting, and sent a line of Eldergloom slithering back across the floor. When it reached the pool of Grendel's blood, it burst into flame.

You could never be too sure.

Besides, the alarms were already raised. Might as well throw a little smoke into the mix to confuse things. *Bring on the sexy firefighters.*

I opened the stairwell door as quietly as possible and shut it behind us. Then I stared dumbly at the stairs.

I'd gotten past the guards, but I had no idea how I was getting Grendel down six flights of stairs in a rolly chair.

Maybe I didn't need to get him down six floors. Maybe I just needed to get him up one.

"Here goes nothing." I looped the strap of his plasma rifle across my chest, then hoisted him onto my shoulders in a fireman's carry.

Holy *hell*, he was heavy.

I looked up the stairs, immediately regretting my decision.

By the time I pushed open the door at the top of the stairs, my thigh muscles were burning. The door closed behind me and I leaned my shoulder against it, trying to catch my breath. I wasn't exactly out of shape, but I wasn't used to carrying a hundred and eighty pounds of techie, either.

I half ran, half stumbled to the side of the building where we'd come up and peered over the edge to the parking lot. Security guards prowled the edges of the buildings, and clusters of them waiting at each door. Even with a shroud of invisibility up, getting past them was going to be tricky. I could hide us, but I couldn't muffle any sounds, and hitting the ground from here was going to make at least some noise.

I set Grendel down against the low half-wall at the edge of the building and jogged back across the roof to the other side. Then I picked some random sap's car and sent a tiny ball of flame toward it.

It hit with an explosion that sent the car twenty feet into the air, where it flipped before landing upside down with a crash.

"Sorry, dude," I muttered, then went to retrieve Grendel.

Things went my way for once, and the guards all ran toward the explosion, leaving our side of the building unguarded. I pulled Grendel's grappling hook from his belt, hooked it to the edge of the half-wall, and did the same with mine. I took him in my arms, took a deep breath, and rolled us off the side of the building.

For a brief moment I thought we were going to fall, but then the cables caught and lowered us gently to the pavement. I released both hooks and tucked them back into place before lifting Grendel back to my shoulders. He groaned in pain, his eyelids fluttering, and I held my breath as I waited for him to regain consciousness. Then his head fell forward again, and I sighed, moving as quickly as I could across the vast expanse of blacktop.

My legs were shaking when I reached the service gate, and I cursed again. I couldn't use the RFID pick and maintain my hold on the Eldergloom. I'd likely just short the whole thing out and end up locking us in.

I looked back over my shoulder. The guards were gone from this side of the complex, likely searching around the burning car on the other side of the building.

Still, I had to be fast.

I laid Grendel down by the fence and dug through his pockets until I found his RFID pick. Then I cautiously approached the reader, glanced back at the building one more time, and dropped the Eldergloom.

I slapped the lockpick against the reader, hit the appropriate buttons, and prayed.

"C'mon, c'mon..." The light on the pick blinked red once. Then twice.

Then it blinked green and the gate rattled into motion.

I threw the Eldergloom over us again just as a shout echoed across the parking lot. My muscles screamed as I struggled to lift Grendel onto my back again, and I stifled a cry of frustration, lurching forward into a stumbling run.

By some miracle, I made it to the bikes.

I settled him in an awkward sitting position in front of me and straddled my motorcycle. We'd have to leave his here and hope that the guards or cops didn't find it before we could come back for it. The Eldergloom dropped as I engaged the run-silent mode on my engine and drove us out of the back of the alley and away from Americorp.

I sat next to Logan, watching the line on the heart monitor move up and down rhythmically. His fingers were cool and limp in my hand, and I shifted my weight in the hard plastic chair, straightening the edge of the sheets around the bandage on his shoulder.

The small room was clean, sparsely furnished, and not exactly legal.

I couldn't take him to a hospital, as they were required to report all gunshot wounds they treated and Americorp would be monitoring any and all emergency rooms for exactly this kind of thing. Thankfully, Rose knew a fairly reputable street doctor. So, here we were, in the basement of a warehouse that otherwise served for holding dry supplies for a bulk-foods store.

The scent of antiseptic tickled my nose as Dr. Tara Gupta checked his vitals and injected a syringe full of medication into his IV drip. The good doctor stood just under five feet tall, with short-cropped brown hair and cream-and-coffee skin. Her eyes were an unsettling gray-green, standing out starkly against her complexion. I bit my lip and watched her work, bouncing my toe impatiently and trying not to bother her.

"Well," she said, "he's stable. The bullet nicked his subclavian artery, otherwise he wouldn't have dropped so fast. Surgery went well. And you should be proud of yourself."

"Me? Why? Because I got him shot?"

"If you hadn't stopped the bleeding as quickly as you did, he may not have made it. As it is, he's going to be out for a while. It's probably for the best. He's going to be in some pain and he'll have to take it easy so he doesn't tear anything back open. I'll get him some pills to take as needed for pain at home, but I suggest you let him spend the night here if you can risk it."

I nodded. "Did you…did you notice any damage to his tech?"

She looked at me, her face professionally neutral. "Like what?"

"His Neurocomm or his lenses. Was there any…malfunction? Anything that hurt him?"

She studied me a moment longer, then pulled out her ophthalmoscope and checked his eyes. "His lenses and eyes seem fine," she said. "I can't check his Neurocomm without a scan. Would you like me to do one?"

I thought about it, chewing on my lower lip. "No. I guess we'll find out when he wakes up, right?"

She didn't answer right away, then nodded once and left the room, closing the door behind her.

I squeezed his hand and laid my head on the crisp white sheet. My hair spread in a wide, curling fan across his lap, and I let my eyes close as my brain ran itself in circles.

That had been close. Really, really close. I replayed the events over and over in my head, trying to figure out where we went wrong, what we missed. Maybe there was a sensor on the rooftop door we hadn't noticed. Or maybe a motion detector in the hallway. It could have been any number of things we either hadn't seen or that hadn't been listed on the schematics Logan had lifted from Zeus Security's database.

Whatever it was, it didn't matter now. We got the prize, and more importantly, Logan would be okay…I hoped. The night hadn't exactly gone as planned, but now that we were out of harm's way, it was salvageable. We'd still get paid. As long as he woke up.

And we could say we'd successfully gotten into and out of Americorp. I didn't know any other runners who'd done that.

I frowned. It seemed too easy. Americorp was one of the biggest mega-corps on the planet. It didn't make sense that the two of us could get in and out like that.

I mean, Logan *had* been shot. There was that. And the guards probably still had no idea how I'd collapsed that floor out from under them. But I'd expected worse.

I'd expected an elemental attack.

My eyes sprang open and I sat up. I hadn't been attacked yet tonight.

I looked around the small room at all of the delicate medical equipment, then at Logan, lying unconscious on the small hospital bed, small red stains seeping through the stark white bandages on his shoulder. If an elemental showed up for me here, there was no telling the damage it could do.

I squeezed his hand once and slid my fingers from his, then crept quietly out the door. I found Dr. Gupta at a small desk, her fingers tapping over a projected keyboard.

"I...I have to go," I said quietly. "Will you tell him I'm sorry? Tell him there was too much technology and I couldn't risk it. He'll know what you mean."

I could see judgment in her gaze, though no surprise. She thought I was splitting on my partner.

"I'm not bailing on him, I swear. Please, just tell him? I'll come back if I can."

She simply nodded and went back to her work.

Guilt tugged at me. I could only imagine what it would look like to him when he woke up. Hopefully he would be lucid enough to understand my message.

Now I just needed to make it back to him in one piece.

I couldn't go home, or to my shop or Manny's, and risk bringing the elemental there. Instead, I went back to our spot at the park and rekindled the embers of a fire left in the pit, stretched out on a bench in my working leathers, and waited.

I didn't even realize I'd fallen asleep until the sounds of the city pulled me awake. Even though the sun was still below the horizon, there was the feel of the city coming to life around me. Lights turning on in apartment windows, commuters waiting at red lights, cafés and restaurants opening their doors for the morning rush. I sat up and stretched, my muscles protesting the combination of the run, heavy lifting, and a night spent on a hard bench in the cold November air.

I hadn't been attacked.

Okay, now I was really confused.

I threw my hands in the air in surrender, wincing at the aches in my back and arms. I ran my fingers through my hair. "I give up," I muttered to myself. Now I had even less an idea of what was going on, and that was saying something.

I pulled my phone from my pocket and switched it on, listening to the new voice messages as I walked to my bike.

"Hey Alyssa, it's Logan." His voice was rough, sounding like he'd swallowed ground glass. *"I got your message. I just wanted to tell you not to come back to Gupta's. Eyja is getting me and taking me home. I'll call you later."*

I sagged a little in relief. Then I hopped on my bike, swinging by The Grove to get a large, quad-shot vanilla latte with extra whip to go before heading toward my store. We were open today, and Cinda wouldn't be in until noon, so I needed the caffeine and sugar.

After all, I had a business to run.

"Alyssa?"

My head snapped up at Cinda's voice, startling me out of my almost-sleep. I grabbed the edge of the counter as I nearly tipped off my stool behind the register, and my heart pounded in my ears and reverberated through my chest.

She winced. "Sorry. I just...why don't you go home? We're super-slow right now anyway. I can close up, it's no problem."

My eyelids were heavy and gritty. I felt greasy and gross, having bathed myself in the bathroom sink before opening the shop. Every now and then the faint scent of smoke would waft from my hair. My shoulders were stiff, my back sore, and my thighs protested every time I even thought about walking anywhere. Going home sounded fantastic, but...

"You've been picking up so much of my slack lately, Cinda."

"It's okay, really! I need the hours. Anyway, I *may* have a week or two off planned in the near future to spring on you without notice." She grinned at me conspiratorially.

Even my laugh was tired. "Okay, okay, I'll go."

I collected my backpack full of dirty runner's gear, and left through the back door to the alley where my bike sat waiting. The engine turned over with a roar. I slid on my helmet, lifted my head, and froze.

Seraphina stood at the mouth of the alleyway, her fine, blond hair rippling in the afternoon breeze.

I cut the engine and dismounted, removing my helmet and setting back on my bike. Three deep breaths later, I lifted my head again to see her still standing there, waiting patiently for me to come to her.

My footfalls echoed down the alley, hard and staccato. I stopped a few feet from her, staring down at the toes of my boots. Another deep breath in and out, and I raised my eyes to hers.

She flinched when our gazes met, and wrapped her arms around her middle.

The cars rushed by at the end of the alley, and a few crows cawed in the fire escape overhead.

"Did Tristan talk to you?" she ventured.

"He tried."

"Oh."

"He's not exactly your best ambassador if you're looking to apologize for what happened. We kind of have a *history*." I hissed the last word, lashing out with it as my hurt bubbled to the surface and made me angry.

"I know that's...that's why I came, myself. I owe you an apology."

I crossed my arms over my stomach, mirroring her, and waited.

"I'm sorry. I let myself get carried away with Tristan. There was too much wine, and he was..." She stopped and bit her bottom lip.

"Well, those are all just excuses, aren't they? I'm sorry, I owe you better than that."

I waited. I wanted to hear the whole thing, straight from her. The breeze picked up, sending a chill up my arms and flinging her hair out behind her like a silken banner.

"I invited Tristan over so he and I could talk, so I could get to know him better. Not like that," she said hastily, raising a hand before I could misinterpret her meaning. "Not like you. His invitation *was* purely business. Things just...went too far." She dropped her hands to her sides and sighed. "I'm sorry. This is the worst apology ever."

"Not quite the worst," I said softly.

A small, hesitant smile played across her lips. "I know I'm messing this all up, but could you consider forgiving me? At all?"

"Maybe a little. I could possibly be convinced to forgive you more." I quirked a small, mischievous smirk, but it slid from my face a moment later. "Maybe I have no right to be so angry. We hadn't...I mean, we weren't..." My mouth was dry and I swallowed a lump in my throat. "This is the only time, Seraphina. I can't do this again. I've done it too many times in the past and I refuse to be played the fool over and over."

She nodded earnestly. "It is. The only time, I swear."

"Don't make promises," I said. "Just know that if it does happen again, I'm gone. No more forgiveness after that."

She nodded again.

The tension seeped from me and I sighed.

"Do you...want to come over?" she asked. "We can start over. Have a date that's not interrupted by things breaking." The hope in her eyes made my stomach do little summersaults. I wanted to accept her invitation, I really did, but...

"What I want to do is go home and go to bed. Well, I want to shower first, *then* go to bed. I had a really late night," I explained as she looked at me quizzically.

"You know," she said thoughtfully. "I do have a shower at my place. And a bed." She held my gaze for a long moment, then looked away.

"Just a thought." Spots of pink colored her cheeks and she tucked her flowing hair behind a pointed ear.

I pulled in a shaky breath. Did I really want to dive head-long into this again? We should take it slow, make sure we really wanted this...*us*...to happen before we did anything we'd regret.

The little, rational voice in the back of my head said all these things, but I could barely hear it past the thundering heartbeat in my ears. A smile slowly spread across my face, betraying me.

She smiled back, heat in her eyes.

"Sure," I said, my voice husky. "Why not?"

———

The sound of slow, measured breathing beside me pulled me out of my sleep. I rolled over, feeling the comfortable shared warmth as the sheets slid against my bare skin.

I'd forgotten what it was like to wake up next to someone else.

I opened my eyes and let them adjust to the dim light, a lazy smile spreading across my lips as I let my gaze wander over Seraphina's sleeping figure. Her hair was strewn across the pillow, her face tilted ever so slightly in my direction. The gentle swell of her chest rose and fell softly with her breathing, her arm draped across her stomach. Her dark lashes stood out against her pale cheeks, her delicate lips parted slightly.

How did she manage to look so amazing, even while asleep? There must be a rule against that or something. I was lucky if I didn't drool all over my pillow.

I ran a hand over my mouth self-consciously, relieved to find it drool-free, and ran a hand through my tangled, still-damp hair.

Somewhere on the floor next to the bed, my phone rang. I cursed, scrambling to find it in the pile of discarded clothes. I slipped to the floor and pulled it from the pocket of my jeans.

Logan.

I answered it to stop the ringing, then dashed to the bathroom, and only once the door was shut behind me did I put it to my ear.

"Techie. What's up?"

"Dinner tonight, Deacon's Downtown." He sounded tired. "Reed wants to take us out as a thank you. I think he just wants to meet in a public place, but whatever. As long as he pays us."

I whistled, long and low. Deacon's was one of the pricier restaurants in the city. "You don't think it's weird that he'd be willing to be seen in such an upscale place with a couple of lowlife runners like us?"

He snorted. "Everything Reed's done up until now has been weird. I'd be wary if he started doing things by the book all of a sudden."

I couldn't argue with that.

"Anyway, dress nicely. Dinner's at eight." He hung up.

The display on my phone blinked back to the clock. Six o'clock. I sighed, wrapped my arms around my bare middle, and snuck back out into the bedroom.

Seraphina was waiting for me, lying on her side and smiling, sleep making her eyelids heavy.

"Sorry," I said softly. "Work call. I had to take it."

"I was wondering where you'd run off to." She rolled onto her back and stretched distractingly. "I thought perhaps you'd snuck out, but your clothes are still here, so…"

A blush spread all the way to the tips of my ears.

"Come back to bed."

My eyes traveled down the long length of her body, tracing the curve of her hip under the thin sheet. "I can't. Work calls."

She pouted, then sat up, and gathered her hair in a knot at the base of her neck. "Very well," she sighed. "But come back when work is done. We still have things to…discuss."

"Uh," I stammered, my heartbeat thundering in my ears. "Sure."

A hungry smile spread across her lips and heat filled her eyes.

I turned away, flustered, and quickly dressed myself. By the time I pulled my shoes on the blush—and my hormones—had quieted, and I placed a soft kiss on her upturned lips.

"I'll be back as soon as I can," I promised.

The cab pulled up to the restaurant just at eight. I stepped onto the red carpet on the sidewalk, wrapping my light shrug around myself as

I hurried to the meager protection of the red awning. A doorman held one of the double doors open for me, and the frigid air whipped into the foyer and tangled the hem of my dress around my ankles. I kicked free of the emerald fabric and walked to the hostess stand where a petite, red-haired girl stood. She wore high-waisted black pants, a classic tux shirt, and a black bowtie. As she smiled up at me from her place behind the stand, I could see gold Neurolense webbing on her purple contacts.

"Good evening. Welcome to Deacon's Downtown. Do you have a reservation?"

"I'm meeting someone here. He's, um..." I peered over her shoulder further into the restaurant, searching for Logan's blue-and-blond head. The wind gusted in behind me as the doors opened again, blowing strands of my carefully styled hair into my face. I tucked them back behind my ear and turned; Logan stood, grinning at me. His hair was loose, the long ends trailing across his shoulders, and he wore a dark blue suit. As he turned, I could see subtle strands of glowing blue in a delicate pattern across his tie.

"Could you possibly *not* match just once?" I said.

"Now where would be the fun in that?" He grinned wider, though there were dark circles under his eyes, and offered me his right arm. His left was in a black sling, braced tightly against his chest. "I believe our reservation is under Reed," he said to the hostess.

"Oh! Reed, of course." I raised my eyebrows at Logan as she gathered up her menus. Then she led us across the restaurant, seating us at a four-top table in the far corner. Logan held my chair out for me and I made a face at him as I sat, smoothing my skirts. The hostess handed us our menus and went on. "Jenna will be your waitress this evening. The rest of your party should be joining you shortly."

We both smiled at her and looked over the menus, a comfortable silence settling over us. After a few moments, I glanced up at Logan.

"How's the shoulder?" I asked quietly.

He started to shrug, then stopped with a wince. "It's okay. Still stiff and sore, but the pain pills the doc gave to me are helping. Just poke me if I start to fall asleep in my soup, okay?"

I smiled slightly in sympathy, letting my gaze run over the line of his neck and shoulder. The shirt and jacket hid any bandage he could have been wearing, but I could tell he was holding himself a bit straighter than normal.

"Good thing we're getting paid tonight," he said. "The good doctor is not cheap."

I winced and nodded. Motion to my left caught my eye, and I looked up to see Reed walking up to the table, his smooth, businessman grin on his face. He wore an expensive suit much like the one he'd worn the day he'd appeared in my shop. Logan and I rose to shake his hand, but he took a small step to his left.

Behind him stood Thomas Lucca.

I froze, my smile stiff on my face, stifling the urge to jump up from the table and start shooting our way out, and frantically tried to figure out what to do. I slid my left hand—the hand with the Hart ring on it—discretely behind a fold in my skirt, then glanced sideways at Logan and found his expression similarly frozen.

"Reed," he said, his voice guarded but neutral. "What is this?"

"Why don't we have a seat and we'll discuss it," Reed said, his expression never wavering from its bland, professional smile. "Logan, Alyssa, this is Thomas Lucca, CEO of Americorp."

Lucca held out his hand to Logan, who hesitated for a fraction of a second before taking it. When Lucca turned to me, he let out a small laugh. "Ms. D'Yaragen. Of course." He shook my hand firmly, smiling pleasantly. "I enjoyed our dance at the gala. Ms. Dubhan has had nothing but wonderful things to say about you."

"Th-thanks," I stammered, letting my hand slide back out into view. No point in hiding it now.

"I'd like to say I'm surprised to see you here, but it all makes sense now." He smiled again and settled in his chair.

"I'm glad things make sense to *you*," Logan said, a hint of venom in his words. "Mr. Reed has kept us in the dark on your joining us tonight."

"It's because I told him to."

I looked around the table at their faces, trying desperately to piece things together. Obviously Lucca wasn't going to have us arrested, or he would have shown up with cops, not with a boardroom smile. But why was he here with Reed? The answer spun just out of reach of my whirling mind.

"I'm sorry," I said, spreading my hands in front of me. "Mr. Reed, do you mind explaining? All of my interactions with you have been incredibly...irregular. I can't tell if you're brilliant or clueless."

Reed and Lucca laughed, then looked at each other. Lucca gestured for Reed to speak.

"My name is Charles Wu," he said, tilting his head apologetically, acknowledging what I'd suspected that first day in my office—that he'd given me a fake name. "I'm the head of security for Americorp."

Logan and I sat in stunned silence.

"The run you performed last night—successfully, I'm told—was a test. An interview, you could say. May I see the document?"

My heart pounded in my chest as Logan reached into the inside pocket of his jacket and produced a thin envelope. He handed it across the table to Reed—er, Wu, his face pale. Wu tore the top open with his butter knife, glanced at the document, and then handed it to Lucca.

I waited for cops to jump out of the potted plants and arrest us, but none did.

Hooray for small victories.

"Exactly what I thought," Wu said with a smile, looking from me to Logan and back again. "When we'd heard of your success, Mr. Lucca insisted on coming to this meeting. We were both incredibly impressed. And it's my pleasure to offer you both positions as professional security consultants for Americorp."

"Professional security consultants," I repeated.

Logan laughed once. "You want to hire us on as corporate runners," he said.

Wu and Lucca smiled at each other. "We prefer the term 'security consultant,' Mr. Turner. It looks better on the books."

"Of course it does," I muttered.

"What about our pay for this run?" Logan asked.

"Oh, that's not contingent on you accepting the job," Wu said, digging through a small briefcase. "That would be incredibly unprofessional of me." He pulled a small micro-thumb drive from the briefcase and handed it across the table. "It contains the amount we agreed on."

Logan pocketed it with a nod. Then Wu pulled two manila folders from the briefcase and slid them across the table to us.

"Inside are your proposed contracts. You'll find the offered salary is quite competitive."

I pulled the folder toward me with a finger, flipping it open and looking at the numbers. He was right, the salary was competitive.

Very competitive.

"Well, I assume that shatters any illusion of anonymity I had," I said bitterly.

Wu smiled apologetically. "When I saw you on the security feed at the gala, it wasn't that hard to make the logical jump. Go easy on yourself. I wasn't exactly playing fair."

I sighed, and Wu turned our attention back to the contracts in front of us.

"Of course, you'll notice…"

A faint, silvery chime accompanied by a slight vibration in my wine glass distracted me from what Wu was saying. The chime sounded familiar, and I looked around the restaurant. No one else seemed to have noticed it. At least, no one else was looking around like I was. That was strange, though, the noise sounded like—

The chime sounded again, somehow more insistent this time, and the wine glass vibrated once more, a soft buzzing against my fingertips. Confused, I peered into my wine glass.

And almost dropped it when I saw Lorelei peering back up at me from the surface of my white wine.

"Lorelei?" I hissed. "What are you doing?"

"I'm sorry," her voice was tinny and far away. "I wouldn't have bothered you, but I've been trying to contact you for a while and it's urgent."

"What? Why—"

Someone cleared their throat pointedly, and I looked up to see Logan, Wu, and Lucca all staring at me as if I'd grown three heads.

"Uh," I said lamely. "Will, ah, will you excuse me, please?" I pushed up from the table without waiting for an answer and, taking my wine glass and keeping my shoulders as square as possible, fled to the ladies' room.

I shut myself into a stall and gritted my teeth. I couldn't imagine how that must have looked to Lucca and Wu. Logan, at least, was getting used to my elvish shenanigans, but I doubted the other two had much experience with magic.

I kind of wanted to keep it that way.

"This better be important, Lorelei," I growled down at the glass, though I knew the Keeper wouldn't contact me without warning unless it was.

"The Oracles have begun to report visions."

I cursed quietly. "What did they say?"

"They all mentioned the typical portents of doom. Fire, death, that sort of thing. A door swinging open, an enemy among us. An old hate surfacing."

A chill shivered down my spine. A door opening. Just like Jeremiah had said.

I wish I knew what the hell was going on.

"The Order of the White Hart claim they don't know about the rings. They said—" She lifted her head, looking away from me, toward something outside the field of view offered by her scrying dish. "You. Why are you here? I told you before, I can't help you."

"Lorelei," I said, "what—"

"I have a favor to ask." The voice was low and silken, and I recognized it immediately.

"Tristan?"

Then Lorelei screamed as an explosion ripped through the scrying, and the wine glass in my hand shattered in a shower of glittering shards.

21

I stood frozen for the span of a few heartbeats, my eyes locked on the jagged pieces of glass scattered across the tile. Small puddles of expensive wine pooled on the floor and I wiped a few stray droplets from where they'd hit my cheeks.

Someone had attacked Arcadia.

No. Not someone. *Tristan.*

My face flushed with anger and shame. I knew I shouldn't have trusted him again. I knew it.

I slammed open the stall door and rushed back to my table.

"I'm sorry," I said as I grabbed my purse. "Mr. Ree—Wu, Mr. Lucca, it's been a nice dinner, but I have to go. Thank you for your offer, I'll think it over and get back to you." I turned before they could respond and walked as quickly as I could to the front door.

Once outside the restaurant, though, I realized I didn't have my motorcycle. I'd agreed to wear this stupid dress and taken a stupid cab, and now I was stuck here while who-knows-what was happening in Arcadia. I bit down on a scream of frustration and felt a hand on my shoulder.

I spun around and just barely kept myself from knocking Logan's teeth out.

"Whoa, easy there, Lys. Friend, remember?"

I scowled at him for a second, and then grabbed his good wrist. "How did you get here?"

"I…what?"

I repeated myself, slowly enunciating each word. *"How did you get here?* Did you take a cab?"

"Eyja drove me on my bike. She's at the bar across the street, to be my backup if anything went south."

"Smart. Tell her to catch a cab. I need to borrow your bike."

"Why, what's—"

"Don't argue with me, techie, it's an emergency!"

He pressed his lips in a tight line and then turned toward the valet standing at the booth by the front door. He pulled a ticket from inside his suit jacket and handed it to the man along with a twenty-dollar bill. "I need you to run."

"Yes, sir," the valet replied, taking off around the corner of the building at a sprint.

We stood in the cold for what seemed like forever but was probably less than a minute before the valet pulled the bike up to the front walk. I gathered up my skirts and hopped on the bike, and before I could get going, Logan jumped on behind me.

"I'm going with you," he said, wrapping his good arm around my waist.

"Logan—"

"It's my bike."

I grit my teeth. "Fine."

His laughter ticked my neck and I shivered as I pulled away from the curb.

We wove our way through the crowded Atlanta streets. The press of cars, the noise of engines, and the rising wails of fire trucks only served as fuel for my anger and frustration, and Logan's grip tightened on my waist as I wound dangerously through the traffic.

I didn't understand how Tristan could do this. I expected him to betray *me* again, sure. But to attack Lorelei? And Arcadia was as much his home as it was mine. It didn't make any sense. The smell of smoke and exhaust burrowed itself behind my eyes, where it settled into the beginnings of a headache.

Wait. Smoke?

I slowed the bike as we turned a corner. A black cloud billowed from what remained of The Grove.

Emergency vehicles were parked on the curb, and firefighters stood with a large hose, doing their best against the roaring blaze. The entire back half of the building had been blown away, and there were people laid out on the sidewalk, awaiting their turn for the medics in the ambulance.

"Oh, gods," I whispered.

Whatever explosion had happened here, it had not only destroyed The Grove and injured countless people, it had destroyed my only way into Arcadia. The archway here had been the only one in Atlanta. There were others in the state, but they would take far too long for me to get to. Who knows what damage Tristan would do while I was trying to find a way in? He could finish what he'd come to do and slip out another archway before I could even get there. By the time I found another entrance, he could be anywhere in the world.

Which, I guess, had been his intention all along.

"Alyssa!"

I jumped, and looked at Logan with wide eyes. He looked at me in a way that made me realize he must have been trying to get my attention for a while.

"What do we do?"

I looked back at the chaos, shaking my head. "I don't know. That was the only—" I froze as a realization came over me. "I'm such an idiot!"

"What?"

Seraphina had a gate.

She just needed a Weaver to activate it for her.

I whipped the bike around and gunned it between the rows of cars, earning curses and honks from angry drivers.

We wove through the city, but I slowed as the adrenaline ebbed and something started to nag at me. Maybe I wasn't thinking clearly about everything. There was no reason Tristan would attack Arcadia. Lorelei had said the Order didn't know about the rings. I had no idea if that meant they didn't know Seraphina had given rings to me and Tristan, or if they didn't know about them at all, but something wasn't adding up.

I didn't have the luxury of time to sort things out. I needed to get to Arcadia, and I needed to get there *now.*

As we pulled up in front of Azure Gateways, I yelled to Logan: "I might need you to back me up, techie."

"On what?"

The bike had barely stopped before I jumped off. Logan let out a yelp of surprise and I cursed as I almost twisted my ankle. High heels were not made for acrobatics.

"Where are you going?" Logan yelled after me as I regained my balance and took off for the door.

"Penthouse! Seraphina!" was the only answer I gave him, and then I was inside the building.

I slid to a halt in the entryway, startling the desk clerk.

"Alyssa D'Yaragen for Seraphina Dubhan," I gasped. "Please. I should be on the approved list."

The clerk gave me a long look and then tapped through the touchscreen, grunting in acknowledgment. "Go ahead, Ms. D'Yaragen."

"Thank you."

The doors slid open and I all but ran into the elevator. The thirty-second ride felt like an eternity.

I needed to get to Arcadia, and I needed to get there *now.* I had no idea what was happening. And the way Lorelei had screamed...

I closed my eyes, taking a deep breath and reigning in my impatience. I needed to calm down. To focus.

Patience had never been my strong suit.

The elevator doors opened and I dashed to Seraphina's door, ringing the door bell and pounding on the wood with my fist. An eternity passed before she finally opened the door, her expression confused.

She wore a gauzy white shirt over leather leggings and soft black boots. Her long, white-blond hair was pulled back in an intricate braid with long curls falling loose around her face, and her expression shifted when she saw me.

"Alyssa," she smiled, and reached out her hands to embrace me.

"I need your gate." I pushed past her and headed toward the conservatory.

There was a stunned silence, and then the scuff of her boots on the floor as she caught up with me. "What? Why?"

"Tristan. He…I don't know. Something's going on and there was an explosion at The Grove. The gate there is gone. The only way in now is yours."

"But it's not active. You know that. "

"I know." I turned to her, watching her face carefully. "I'm going to activate it."

She stopped mid-stride and stared at me with wide eyes. After a second of confusion, her eyes grew even wider and her mouth dropped open. "You…you're a Weaver."

I simply turned on my heel and pulled open the glass door to air so warm and humid it was tangible.

"Alyssa, wait!"

I didn't wait. I strode down the pathway with determination. Her boots made a soft counterpoint to the angry clacks of my high heels against the stone, and she all but ran to catch up with me.

"Why didn't you tell me?"

"Because I wasn't sure I could trust you." She stumbled as if she'd been slapped, but recovered quickly.

"And you can trust me now?" Her voice held an edge of bitterness, but I was too worried to care. I'd deal with relationship issues after I dealt with this.

My voice was barely a whisper. "I don't have a choice."

I came to a halt in front of the archway and looked it over. I'd never activated a gate before. They had all either been active long before I'd been born, or else when I was still very young. Even the one in The Grove had been activated before I'd come to Atlanta.

Seraphina stopped beside me. "Do you know what to do?"

"Um," I said, grimacing. "Not exactly."

"What?" Her voice was incredulous.

"I've never done this before. But how hard can it be?"

"If you blow up my apartment, I'm never talking to you again."

I laughed, then bowed my head and ran my hands through my hair. Right. I could do this. "No problem," I said. "Piece of cake." I stepped from the pathway to the neatly cut grass surrounding the arch. The heel of my shoe sunk into the soft earth, and I stopped and pulled them both from my feet.

The soft grass against my soles helped ground me immediately, and a bit of the tension seeped from my shoulders. I took slow steps toward the arch, pulling in what peace I could from my surroundings with deep lungfuls of air. I focused on the small sounds and sensations around me: the soft sigh of my skirts rustling together, occasional drips as the moisture in the air condensed on the foliage and fell to the conservatory floor, the aroma of exotic blooms, rich and heady, mixed with the pungent scent of soil and growing things.

I could do this.

The stone of the archway was rough under my hands, and I closed my eyes, reaching out to the Eldergloom. I pulled it into me, and with it I explored the arch. Right now it was nothing more than carefully worked stone, but I could feel the potential there, the pathways through the rock, ready and waiting for me to infuse them with magic. With life.

Everything around me hummed with that power. The grass beneath my feet, the trees and flowers surrounding us, Seraphina as she paced around the center of the atrium. I could even feel the fleeting sources that were other people, honeycombed in the steel and glass of the high-rise. And there, far below me, under the exhaust and pavement, was the earth.

I took a few more deep breaths, and with each one I pulled all that potential, that energy, up through the soles of my feet and in from the air around me. Then, in one long exhale, I sent it out through my fingers and into the stone.

With a burst, the glow of the Eldergloom shot through the pathways, tearing like lightning down the bare conduits laid out for it. The arch drank in my power, up through my feet and through my body with more speed and potency than I'd ever felt before. It flooded into the gate, filling every crack, every crevice. It wound its way through the delicately carved script, turning it from a simple string of words into an incantation.

I laughed aloud at the sheer exhilaration of it and opened my eyes to watch the veins in the rock glow silver. The plants around me swayed as if moved by wind, and my hair lifted and swirled around me.

Then the shining script shifted from silver to a purple so deep it was almost black. It still shone, but it hurt my eyes to look at, as if the glow was actually an absence of light. I watched in growing horror as that absence bled down to the rest of the arch, corrupting the Eldergloom and twisting its purpose.

I gasped as that absence reached my hands and plunged inside of me. It wrapped around my core, where I'd spooled the Eldergloom, and it pulled.

I screamed.

It was icy cold and empty, the antithesis of the power I used, and it fed on the life energy gathered within me. I tried to hold on, to pull back, but it simply slid over my defenses and took everything I had.

And once that was gone, it fed on *me*.

It tore another scream from my throat and I looked around desperately. My eyes landed on Seraphina. She stood on the other side of the arch with her hands laid on the stone, mirroring me. Her head was bowed and her shoulders rose and fell as she took in great gasps of air. The same purple glow reflected against her hair where it fell on either side of her face, and when she raised her head, her eyes were filled with it.

Then those glowing eyes met mine and she smiled.

There was another pull inside of me, and I fell to my knees with a strangled cry. I struggled to pull my hands from the stone, to interrupt the connection with the dark energy in the arch, but it was if the power had wrapped itself around my wrists and kept me pinned in place.

My vision blurred as the tendrils of ice drained me. It squeezed and stabbed into every crevice of my being, until I was nearly dry.

At the last second, as my heart stuttered, the power slithered out of me and released its hold on my wrists. I drew in a choking gasp and slumped to my side in the grass, fighting off a haze of darkness that threatened to drag me under.

"Thank you, Alyssa," Seraphina's voice sounded muffled and far away, though I could see through the fog in my vision that she still stood opposite the gate from me. "I could never have done this without you. *A'chara.*"

"No," I whispered.

Then she stepped through the gate and was gone.

22

"Alyssa. Alyssa! Wake up!"

Everything was shaking. Each new shake rattled my skull, and I groaned at the pain behind my eyes.

"Go 'way," I muttered, batting one hand at the voice. My cheek rested on something dry and scratchy, and the musty smell of earth was strong.

"Alyssa," the voice persisted, and the shaking renewed its strength.

"I said go away." I flailed my hand again, and this time it made contact.

"Ow!" The shaking stopped and I sighed in relief as the pain in my head ebbed.

There was a short moment of peace before I felt hands on my face, turning my head toward the light.

"Alyssa. You need to get up."

I heaved a sigh and cracked my eyes, peering up at Logan. His face was pinched with worry, his nice suit rumpled. I opened my mouth to ask him what was wrong, when I noticed the stone arch behind him, and I remembered.

Logan fell as I shoved myself to my feet, and I almost followed him to the ground as a wave of vertigo crashed over me. I put one hand on the arch to steady myself, then jerked my hand away and stumbled backwards. It felt...wrong. My knees were still too wobbly for my sudden movement, and I ended up on my butt in the dead grass.

"Lys, what's going on?"

I stared at the archway, then turned my gaze to Logan. "Seraphina," I hissed. "She's..." What was she? Her powers, like mine, only dark where mine were light—the inverse. "I think she's the Talmorin Weaver."

"What?"

"But that's impossible," I shook my head. "She'd have to be a dark elf. But she's not!" I pushed myself to my feet again, standing in front of the arch with my hands balled at my sides. "I don't understand!"

Logan stepped in front of me and placed his hand on my shoulder. "Lys, calm down, and tell me what the hell is going on here."

I met his eyes, and his image blurred as tears of frustration rose. "I can't explain right now, I just need to get to Arcadia."

He nodded. "What can I do?"

I shook my head and my eyes darted around the conservatory. "I don't—" I stopped, my breath catching as I saw the damage around me for the first time.

The grass under my feet was dead. So was every plant in a roughly ten-foot diameter around the arch.

"She killed everything," I whispered.

Logan's eyebrows pulled down as he surveyed the withered vegetation. "Yeah. I'm not going to pretend to know what that means."

"I need to go. She killed everything and I need to go. The Grove... Lorelei..." I took a deep breath to steady myself. "I don't know what you can do, Logan. This is elf business, and you can't come with me."

"Because of my tech," he said, and for the first time, his voice sounded bitter when he said it.

"It's not just that. But thanks, though." My smile was halfhearted, and he returned it with a crooked grin.

"Yeah. I'll just...wait here?"

"Better not. I don't know—" I broke off. "Wait, how'd you even get up here?"

His grin spread across his face. "Oh, c'mon, Alyssa. I'd be a piss-poor runner if I couldn't sneak past a doorman and into a mid-level security apartment."

I let myself laugh, just a little, then put my hand on his where it still sat on my shoulders. "Call Rose. Tell her where I went. Tell her..." My lips pressed together tightly. "Tell her it was Seraphina the whole time."

He nodded once and dropped his hands from my shoulders. He caught my fingers in his and gave them a small squeeze before stepping back.

I turned to the arch. I didn't know if this was going to work. She'd powered it with dark magic. Would my words work?

"One way to find out," I muttered to myself, before taking a deep breath and saying "A'chara."

The script flashed silver, then was overtaken by the deep purple glow before it faded away again. I pressed my lips together, took a deep breath, and stepped through the arch.

There was a heartbeat of cold, icy pain that was everywhere and nowhere all at once, but before I could scream I stumbled to my knees on the fresh, green grass of Arcadia.

I pulled in a deep, shaky breath, the air tinged with the acrid smell of smoke. A dark cloud billowed from one of the buildings. I pushed to my feet and ran to the source of the smoke, the damp grass cool against my bare feet.

The interior of the Arcanum was strangely deserted. The tall, arched hallways were filled with smoke, and I covered my mouth with a hand as I pounded down the hallway. My eyes watered, and I almost tripped over the door to the scrying chamber where it lay off its hinges.

I stumbled across it and into the smoke-filled, moonlit chamber. The stone scrying pool had been completely destroyed. Chunks of charred marble lay strewn across the tile floor. One of the smaller trees in the corner burned, black smoke rolling from its branches. I pulled on the Eldergloom and enveloped the tree in an orb of water.

A scrape and a moan from the far side of the room caught my

attention, and I rushed over to a figure covered in rubble. Tattered green slippers stuck out from under a branch, and I pushed the debris away to find Lorelei, singed and bloody. Her eyelids fluttered open as I pushed her pale sage hair back from her face.

"Lorelei," I said softly, looking her over for wounds. A small rivulet of blood trailed down from her hair line into her green dress, staining it an ugly scarlet-brown.

"Alyssa," she coughed, then grimaced and held a hand to her side.

"Don't move, I'll help you." Shifting her weight, I propped her against the wall behind her.

"I'm okay," she said with another grimace. "It's just a rib."

"What happened?"

"Tristan, he—" She broke off in another coughing fit, and then moaned.

"Nevermind, you rest."

I sat back on my heels and was startled by the sound of movement from the corner of the room. Rubble shifted, and I saw a familiar curly blond head among the dust.

"Tristan," I growled.

I leapt to my feet, fury filling my body. I clenched my hands and my eyes flashed silver, and then I was standing over him, the Elder-gloom seeping from fists in my rage.

His eyelids fluttered open and he took a few seconds to focus on me. There was a large gash across his left cheek, and most of his body was covered in dirt and dust and blood. And his hand…oh, his hand.

His left hand was nothing but a bloody stump, burnt and broken.

My fury left me in a rush, and I fell to my knees beside him, pulling the bits of marble and wood from him. His body hadn't fared much better than his hands; wounds peppered his stomach, and there was blood everywhere.

"Tristan—" My voice caught.

"Alyssa?"

"Yeah, it's me. Don't move."

He blinked up at me, his eyes going in and out of focus. His gaze finally caught mine, and he gave me a shadow of his crooked grin. "Hi."

I choked back a sob, tearing off the long layers of my skirt and pressing them to his stomach. He cried out, his body tensing in pain.

"I'm sorry," I whispered. "I don't know what to do. I'm not a Healer."

"No, you're a fighter," he smiled again, and closed his eyes with a sigh.

"Just..." I struggled to find the right words. I needed to find a Healer. Where was everyone?

"Alyssa?" He mumbled, his eyes still shut.

"I'm here."

"I'm sorry," his voice was thready, and he opened his eyes halfway to catch my gaze with his. "Seraphina...the ring. It just...something happened. I didn't know."

Tears blurred my vision, and I pushed a bloodsoaked curl back from his face. "Neither did I."

Footsteps from the hall behind me pulled at my attention, and I leapt to my feet. Finally, someone else. Maybe they could help. "Hurry," I gasped. "He needs—"

Seraphina stood in the doorway, watching me. She held a drawstring bag in one hand, and I recognized it from my dream with the Aisling, covered over with glowing runes.

"Well," she sighed. "Isn't that just so sweet. Maybe this will be the spark that brings you two back together." She peered past me to where Tristan lay, unconscious again. "That is, if he lives."

Without even a thought, I pulled on the Eldergloom and screamed wordlessly, flinging the red-hot power at her in a stream of fire.

A gout of flame sprayed from my fingertips to where Seraphina stood amongst the rubble.

She simply waved her hand in front of her. With a flash of darkness in her eyes, the air in front of her shimmered, and when my fire hit her barrier, it simply disappeared.

"Dark Weaver," I hissed.

"Light Weaver," she replied mockingly, bowing her head in acknowledgment.

"But...*how?* You're not Talmorin. You're—"

"Light? Like you?" She laughed and shrugged one elegant shoulder, leaning back against the charred door frame. "My mother was Arcadian. My father, Talmorin. I got my mother's complexion, but my father's gifts." She held up a hand and dark fire burned in her palm. "Convenient, isn't it?"

"A bastard born of light and darkness..." I whispered in realization. "You summoned the elementals."

"Each and every one."

"Why?"

"I needed to make sure you were really a Weaver. I was fairly sure by that point. The power that had flown between us that first night, when we danced..." Her eyelids fluttered as if in pleasure. "But I had to see for myself. You are a stubborn one, weren't you? But you finally gave in and used your powers. Thank you. It would have been too much of a risk to destroy the arch at The Grove without that confirmation, and the timing had to be *just right.*"

My face flushed and my heartbeat pound in my chest and at my temples. She was responsible for the destruction, both here and in Atlanta. I glanced back to where Lorelei and Tristan lay bleeding.

"Yes, yes, that was me, too. Poor Tristan," she sighed. "So easily taken in by a pretty face, especially one he thinks he has figured out. Too bad these rings are so easy to manipulate..." She raised her hand, showing me the golden Hart ring on her finger. "...just like him. And you." I looked down at the matching silver ring on my own hand, and ripped it from my finger, flinging it across the room.

"Why?" I growled through clenched teeth.

"Oh, please, I'm certainly not going to answer *that* one. Give me some credit."

I glared at her. "I don't understand."

"Of course you don't," she laughed. Then she turned on her heel and walked down the hall away from me.

"Oh, no you don't," I snarled. I lowered myself into a crouch and pressed my palms against the floor, then pushed power through the earth and sent it rushing toward her.

The ground in front of her exploded in a burst of stone and dirt as a wall of vines wove itself in front of her. Each vine was as thick as my wrist and adorned with thorns the size of my hand.

She stopped and regarded the wall of thorns for the span of a few heartbeats. Then she sighed, and turned to fix me with a flat stare before she reached out behind her to touch one of the vines with a single finger. Her eyes flashed dark, and decay spread from her fingertips and up through the greenery. The thorns blackened and fell from the vines, and the vines themselves curled and withered.

When the decay hit the roots, the vines crumpled in on themselves. She stepped daintily over the heap of compost and continued down the hallway.

I shrieked in frustration and slapped my hands down on the floor again. This time, trails of frost raced across the tile and snaked up her feet, wrapping her ankles in ice. She stopped with a jerk and looked down. A moment later the ice dissolved into steam, and she turned back to me again.

"Alyssa, stop."

"No." I pushed to my feet and flung out a hand, and the steam solidified into long shards of ice. The shards swirled around her once before diving at her chest. She raised both hands to the height of her head, palms outward, and the shards fell to the ground in a splash.

"We're opposites. No matter what you do, I can negate it. Just stop. I have no quarrel with you, and I'd like to keep it that way."

"Oh, but I have quarrel with you."

"You shouldn't take all of this personally. It was never about you."

"Don't take it *personally?*" New fury rose in my chest. "You *used me!* Led me on simply so you could gain my trust! You destroyed The Grove. Killed and hurt all of those people! And Lorelei. And *Tristan!*" My hands clenched into fists. "You're right, this isn't about me. But it sure as *hell* is personal." My hair whipped around me, stirred by the power of the Eldergloom and my raging emotions.

"Let it go, Alyssa. I'm older and stronger than you. You won't win this."

"No!" I yelled, stomping a foot with a burst of power and causing a large chunk of the already-cracked ceiling to fall toward her head. It bounced off her shield and tumbled to the floor, useless.

"Now you're just being childish."

"Nuh-uh," I replied, and twitched a hand. A gust of wind swirled down the hallway and enveloped her in a whirlwind of dust.

The whirlwind fell in a sheet of deep purple. When the dust cleared, Seraphina stepped forward, hands held out to her sides, her eyes glowing darkly. Black lightning flickered at her fingertips.

"Fine," she said. "If you want to fight so badly, I shall oblige you."

She flung her hands out toward me and black lightning followed. I flung up a shield, and when the lightening hit, cold emptiness followed behind it. Ozone filled the air, and just as the lightening dissolved into nothingness I realized it was only a distraction. One moment, Seraphina stood at the far end of the hallway. The next, the air in front of her shimmered and she disappeared.

I cursed, tensing and looking around frantically. Did she run? Or was she still here, somewhere?

I lowered myself into crouch and forced my breathing to slow, listening. My eyes still glowed silver with harnessed magic, and I slowly scanned the hallway in front of me.

There was a soft scuff to my left, and a pebble clicked as it shifted.

I swung a hand in that direction, but before I had a chance to unleash an attack, she reappeared in front of me and wrapped her hand around my wrist.

Pain tore through me and I screamed.

She pulled on my power, as she had earlier, draining my life through her fingertips and out of my body. Cold burned through my veins, leaving an aching emptiness.

"I let you live earlier out of gratitude, not out of mercy. Do not confuse the two." Her voice was quiet and calm, laced with just the slightest edge of irritation, though I could barely hear her past the sound of my own screams and the blood rushing in my ears. "Since you insist on continuing this ridiculous conflict, I have no choice but to finish it."

Her grip tightened and the pull increased. My vision blurred and my knees buckled, yet she held on even as I fell to the floor. I tried to yank my wrist free from her hand but could only manage pathetic tugs. The cold slowly filled my body, and I begin to slip away. I heard someone cry out my name, but it was far away, unimportant. I closed my eyes, drifting.

Opposites. She said we were opposites.

I was doing this all the wrong way.

I fumbled, searching for my limbs. My hands were there somewhere, I knew it. The one in her grasp still burned painfully, but there was another one...there. With effort, I forced my fingers to move, and I turned my hand palm down against the floor.

This time, instead of pushing Eldergloom into the floor and out, I pulled. I pulled all of that power up through the earth, the way I had when I'd activated the archway, except this time I pushed it all into Seraphina.

This time, it was she who screamed.

Her grip on my wrist relented and darkness took me.

23

The soft sound of water sloshing permeated my sleep. I began to drift off again as soon as it stopped, but something cool and damp touched my forehead, and I stirred.

I regretted it immediately.

Everything hurt. My entire body felt like one giant bruise, and even thinking about moving brought the ache back up to the surface. Even my *hair* hurt. My tongue was thick, my mouth dry and pasty. I groaned.

"Alyssa?" The voice was soft and feminine, and right by my ear.

"Lorelei?" I said. Or at least, that's what I tried to say. It came out more as "Lull-lull" as both my voice and tongue failed to function.

"Hold on, I'll get you some water."

Metal scraped against stone, and then Lorelei's hand was under my neck, helping me sit up. I opened my eyes just enough to see a goblet in front of my lips, and I tilted my head forward for a sip. After some coughing and sputtering, the cool water slid down my throat, a refreshing line of cold that spread all the way to my stomach.

She propped up some pillows for me and leaned me against them. I settled back and cleared my throat before finally opening my eyes the rest of the way.

I was lying in the healing ward, in a single bed with crisp white sheets. The beds I could see were empty, but I had the impression of other people in the room, and knew there were other alcoves on either side of mine.

"How are you feeling?" Lorelei smoothed my hair back from my face and regarded me with concern.

"I...don't know." I moved my body ever so slightly, searching out the aches and pains. "What happened?"

"I was going to ask you the same thing. When the others found you, you were unconscious in the hallway outside of the scrying chamber. I heard the sounds of fighting, but I couldn't make it."

I closed my eyes. "I tried to stop her. I couldn't."

Her voice was soft. "Who was she?"

"Seraphina," I said, bitterness coloring my voice. "She fooled me. She fooled us all, even—" My eyes flew open and I pushed up off of the cushions. "Tristan!" A wave of dizziness crashed over me and I laid back against the pillows with my eyes closed again, breathing deeply. "Where's Tristan? Is he okay?"

She didn't answer, and my heart plunged into my stomach. I opened my eyes to see her regarding me with something akin to sadness.

I forced the words past my lips, even though I didn't want the answer. "Is...is he..."

"He lives." She said, but her tone betrayed her.

"But?"

She pushed a strand of moss green hair back from her face. "He hasn't awoken yet. His injuries...I'm not sure how well he will recover from them. It was a close thing and there's only so much our Healers can do."

I fixed her with a hard stare. "I want to see him."

She nodded.

After she helped me up, I walked slowly to the bed in the alcove next to mine. Tristan lay amongst the white and sage-green sheets, his face drawn and pale, his eyes closed. A light blanket was drawn up to his shoulders, and if I hadn't known any better, I would have guessed he was simply sleeping.

His arms lay outside of the covers, resting at his sides. His left arm was bandaged from his elbows down, his hand wrapped in layers and layers of spidersilk gauze.

"Oh, Tristan," I said softly, and lowered myself into the carved white chair next to his bed. A white cloth sat in a silver bowl of water on the bedside table, and I dipped my fingers in the water for the cloth, wiping his forehead gently. "I'm so sorry."

This was all my fault. If I'd paid attention, if I'd figured things out sooner, none of this would have happened. I laid my cheek on the edge of his mattress, grief and guilt seeping weighing my head down.

"Why was there no help when the explosion happened?" My voice caught, but I ignored it. "Why was I the first to reach you both?"

"The Order had called a conclave. Nearly everyone from the Arcanum was at the Colloquiate."

"Why weren't you there?" I asked.

"I felt your situation was more important," she said with an air of dignity, then a hint of a smile appeared on her lips. "Besides, those meetings are dreadfully boring and usually concern minor policy changes. I sent Sibeal to take notes for me."

I nodded and let my eyes drift shut.

"Alyssa...we still do not know what happened, or why. The Order was hoping you would be able to fill in the gaps once you awoke."

"It was Seraphina," I whispered.

"So you said. Who was she?"

"Someone I thought was my friend. Turns out I was wrong. She's half Arcadian, half Talmorin."

Lorelei pulled in a sharp breath. "The Talmorin Weaver?"

I nodded without opening my eyes. "She was also the Emissary from the Order." I smiled wryly. "Though I suppose now we know why they denied it. They were telling the truth. She must have gotten a hold of Hart rings somehow and twisted the enchantment."

"Why?"

"To scry, probably. I'd wager she was able to cast through them, too. The explosion was from the ring on Tristan's hand."

"But to what *purpose?*"

"To gain access to me. And to Arcadia. I...I activated a gate for her, Lorelei. She hijacked my power halfway through, somehow, so she could pass through. I didn't know."

There was a shocked silence and I opened my eyes to see her hastily compose her features. "We will worry about that later. Though, I will have the Acolytes dismantle the Atlanta gate post haste."

I nodded and she crossed the room and spoke in hushed tones to a robed Acolyte at the far end of the hall. She returned and nodded at me.

"Well," she said, "if all she wished was destruction, she did a poor job of it."

I sat up with a start as I remembered something. "I think she took something from the Hall of Relics. An Aisling showed it to me in my dream the other night, or I wouldn't have even noticed it. It's in a small drawstring bag. White, with a glowing design I didn't recognize."

Her eyebrows pulled together in confusion.

"What? What was it?"

"That makes no sense. That relic holds no power anymore. It's a dead focus. An amulet worn by one of our warriors, long ago. It's kept more for historical preservation than anything else." She shook her head.

I sighed. "I don't know. That's what I saw, though."

"I'll check the Hall and crosscheck it with the archives, in case she took anything else."

I nodded.

"Will you be heading back to Atlanta now that you're awake?"

I looked at Tristan. "I...might stay for a while. Rest a bit more, see if...if he wakes up."

She nodded. "Of course. Take your time."

A thought struck me as she turned to leave. "Wait, Lorelei."

She paused and looked back at me.

"Seraphina said the timing of her attack needed to be just right. And she waited until everyone was at the conclave." I paused, letting my comment settle in the space between us. "How did she know?"

Her face paled. "I will question my Acolytes. If any of them have betrayed me, I shall handle them personally."

I knew she would, so I simply nodded and laid my cheek against the sheets once more.

I spent the afternoon by Tristan's side, watching him for any signs of recovery. The Healers offered me a small bowl of boiled grains with honey, and I ate it slowly, savoring the sweetness. The day dragged on, and I finally stopped an Acolyte as she hurried by.

"Could I get a change of clothes? I should go home."

She nodded and rushed of, returning a short time later with a golden shift dress and a pair of soft slippers. I shoved my bloody, stained dress from the night before into the waste basket by the bed.

I laid a kiss on Tristan's forehead, and turned to leave. I'd only gone a step when he groaned, and I turned back to him so quickly I made myself dizzy again.

"Tristan?" I sat down hard in the chair next to him, watching his face carefully.

He groaned again and opened his eyes. He focused on me for a moment before whispering, "Alyssa?"

"Hi," I said, my voice wavering.

"Hi." He reached his good hand up and brushed my hair away from my face. "You're hurt."

I put my fingers to a cut along my cheek that I hadn't even realized was there. "I'll live. How...how are you?"

He looked down at himself, pulling in a sharp breath when he saw his ruined hand. His eyes closed, and when he spoke, his voice was rough with suppressed emotions. "Incredibly stupid, apparently. I knew she was up to something. I *knew* it. *Damn it*," he spat. "I did exactly what she wanted, didn't I?"

Tears filled my eyes. "I did, too."

"I'm sorry. I knew something was off...I went to Seraphina to see if I could figure things out, and...I can only do things the way I know how." He avoided my gaze, staring at the bandages on his left arm. "It was never my intention to hurt you like that again. But I guess, when was it ever my intention, right?" He laughed, and it held an edge of desperation and self-loathing.

He went on. "I had a dream about you, you know. It's why I came looking for you. An Aisling showed you to me. You were in trouble. Shadows were closing in and buildings fell around you and you cowered in the rubble alone...so alone. I wanted to save you, to show you that you didn't have to do it alone. But...maybe..." He finally met my eyes, and his were bright with unshed tears. "Maybe the trouble was me."

I pulled in a breath to speak, but he shook his head.

"You should go home," he said softly. "Go home, be happy."

"But...what about you?"

"I'll live." His smile was bitter around the edges.

I nodded and did the only thing I could do.

I went home.

***

It was one in the morning when I dragged my way from the elevator to my apartment door. The Acolyte who'd escorted me from Arcadia had wanted to accompany me upstairs, but I'd told him just to go home. I was a big girl and perfectly capable of traveling up an elevator and walking down a hall on my own.

Apparently I was wrong, because I wound up leaning against my door frame, fighting to catch my breath. It seemed like I would be recovering from my fight with Seraphina for longer than I thought. I sighed, digging through my pockets, and then cursed when I realized I didn't have my keys. I'd dropped my purse somewhere between Deacon's and Seraphina's place. I leaned my forehead against the doorframe, took a deep breath, then knocked on my own front door.

"Please be home, Rose," I muttered.

The *click* of the lock disengaging pulled my head up. Then the door swung wide open and I was looking down the barrel of a gun.

"Uh," I said.

Then the gun was gone and Rose wrapped me in a bone-crushing hug.

"Alyssa, thank God."

"Ow," was all I could manage.

She released me and looked me over, ushering me into the apartment and closing the door behind us. "Where the hell have you been? It's been three days. I thought you were dead in a gutter somewhere. The Grove is a pile of rubble, Logan called and said Scraphina did something and you disappeared through an archway after her and I swear to *god* if that blond bitch hurt you I—"

"Whoa, Rose, I'm fine."

"Really?"

"Well," I winced in pain and hobbled to the couch. "Not really. But I'm alive."

She stowed the gun in the kitchen drawer and sat on the edge of the coffee table. "What do you need me to do?"

I shook my head. "Just...let me sleep? I can tell you all about it tomorrow. It was a long trip home. I had to take a cab all the way from Macon."

"Okay," she nodded, standing to gather a blanket and spread it across my legs. "Oh, you'd better call Logan. He's checked in with me no less than ten times a day."

I laughed softly. "I don't have my phone. Will you call him for me?" I yawned. "I know you'd just *hate* the opportunity to talk to him again."

"Oh, no, Alyssa, I'm pretty sure that ship has sailed."

I frowned at her, but she went on.

"Besides," she walked into the kitchen and grabbed something from the counter. "He stopped by and dropped your purse off." She tossed my phone in my lap and walked to her room, closing the door behind her.

I thumbed the screen to life, cuing up the dial pad before I stopped and stared at the top of the display. The tiny voicemail icon was still there, waiting patiently yet insistently.

Seraphina and Tristan's messages. I'd never checked them.

I stared at the icon for a few moments longer, then pushed a button.

Messages deleted.

Logan came by the next night to check on me, and I made him take me to Manny's for a desperately needed beer. I leaned on his arm as we walked into the pub, and led him straight to the back of the room where Jeremiah sat. He looked significantly better, the color back in his cheeks and the dark circles under his eyes fading. He noted my hand on Logan's arm, raised an eyebrow over his glasses, and gestured for us to join him.

"Alyssa. You're alive. Good for you." He blew out a cloud of smoke and waved at Manny to bring us drinks. "I see Blondie survived as well. Glad to see everyone in one piece."

Guilt and anger stabbed through me, and my face must have given something away, because he grimaced.

"Uh oh, what did I say wrong?"

"Tristan…he…" I glanced at Logan, catching and then dropping his gaze. "Tristan wasn't nearly as lucky as the rest of us. He's alive, but still in Arcadia. He'll be recovering for a while."

"Ah."

"I figured out your premonition, too. The fire and death is over with, so you should be fine for a while."

He frowned at me.

"It is over, right? The Grove exploded three days ago."

He shook his head. "I had another one this morning. Mild by comparison, but there. And the same. Fire. Smoke. Death. Doors."

I cursed. "Then if it wasn't Arcadia and The Grove you saw burning, what was it?"

"Your guess is as good as mine, sweetheart."

I chewed my lip.

"Oh, I see," Logan said, and I glanced up at him sharply. "He's allowed to call you 'sweetheart' but I'm not allowed to call you 'babe'?"

Jeremiah snorted and I sighed.

"It's Jeremiah," I said in explanation. "He's allowed to do a lot of things."

"Can he shoot magic from his fingers, too?"

Jer's eyebrows shot up at that, and he fixed me with a curiosity-laden gaze.

I waved a hand dismissively. "He knows."

"No, Blondie, I'm just a mere human like you, albeit an oracularly-gifted one."

"He's my other secret weapon," I said.

Jeremiah snorted again.

Manny set down two glasses of beer as he passed our table with a smile. I lifted mine in a toast.

"Well, people got hurt, the bad guy got away, and we have no idea what's coming next, but hey, we're alive."

"And," Logan added, lifting his own glass, "we have a whole hell of a lot of Americorp money to spend."

"Hell yeah," I said.

"To life and money," Jeremiah raised his glass.

"To life and money," Logan and I echoed, and downed our drinks.

The Grove began rebuilding. One thing I could say about the Arcadian community: it was resilient. Five people, three Arcadian and two human, died that night. Lots more had been hurt. The official cause of the explosion was anti-elf terrorism, but only the humans believed that.

The elves knew better, and whispers began to spread.

Seraphina hadn't resurfaced. I still didn't know why she'd attacked Arcadia and Lorelei, or what she'd stolen from the Hall of Relics. And, at least for the time being, Lorelei wasn't sharing any information with me. "Official Sanction from the Order," she said. I'd know if and when I needed to.

I hated being left out.

Plans for the Botanical Garden project were put on hold, and I wondered how pissed Lucca had been when he found out he'd been duped as part of Seraphina's elaborate plan. I still wasn't quite sure why she'd gone so far as to actually involve Thomas Lucca. As a cover for the Hart rings, I assumed, though the deceit would have been just as easy to pull off without involving an organization like Americorp. Maybe I'd find out some day. I sort of hoped I never had reason to.

For now, things were quiet. My store did decent business, and it was nice not to have to stress about money for a change. The elemental attacks never resumed. Seraphina had what she needed from them, after all.

The quiet was...strange. Nice, but strange.

Logan decided to take the corporate runner job at Americorp, enticed by the job security.

As for me, well...

"Well, Ms. D'Yaragen?" Wu's voice interrupted my thoughts. "As you can see, we've agreed to most of the terms in your counteroffer. The amount you see there is your monthly consulting fee regardless of jobs completed. Those will come with bonus pay. Full health coverage is included, providing you visit an Americorp clinic. You can take up to two weeks of unannounced personal leave every six months. I know you wanted a full month, but that's simply too far outside company policy." He leaned back in his chair across my desk from me.

I stared down at the screen in front of me, bouncing rubber tip of the stylus against the tabletop as I considered. A full month would have been nice, in case I needed to disappear for a bit to handle elf business, but two weeks was doable.

"Of course, you'll also be able to purchase any Americorp tech or mods at a significant discount, and the installation fees at Americorp clinics will be waved."

"If I quit, do I have to give them back?" I quipped, picturing absurd images of goons showing up to repossess a full limb mod.

"Only if the tech hasn't been released to the public."

I blinked at him, taken aback.

"We have to protect our intellectual property, you understand."

"Right. Thanks, I almost forgot I live in a dystopia," I muttered.

"Pardon?"

"That sounds reasonable," I answered back brightly, giving him a wide smile.

He frowned at me, obviously aware I'd said something different the first time but declining to push the matter. I wasn't sure if he didn't want to start an argument with a potential new employee, or if he'd decided my attitude was simply not worth his energy.

I looked down at the tablet again. This was as close to my outrageous terms I was going to get. To be fair, I was surprised they agreed to the consulting fee, but they wanted me, and I knew it. They'd seen what Logan and I could do together, and they weren't going to take half of that team when they could get the whole deal for what probably seemed like pennies more.

"The exclusivity clause has been removed?" I asked.

He sighed. "Yes. You may take freelance jobs on your own time as long as Americorp or any of its subsidiaries are not the target. If you are found selling or stealing Americorp tech or secrets…well. Let's just say, you don't want to do that."

"I get it." I had the feeling if I tried to play double-agent on them and got caught, contract termination would be the least of my worries. "So, I just sign on the dotted line?"

"Sign and date at the bottom, and initial pages three, four, six, and eleven."

I did, signing with a flourish, the stylus making a soft *hush* against the screen. I double checked that I'd made my mark in all the appropriate places, then handed the tablet back to Wu.

"Excellent." He stood and held out his hand. "Welcome to the Americorp family, Ms. D'Yaragen."

I stood and shook his hand. "Thank you. I look forward to a lucrative business relationship with you, Mr. Wu. Anything else?"

"Actually...there *is* one more thing, if you'd satisfy my bit of curiosity."

I raised my eyebrows.

"How did you cause the implosion of the floor under our security guards? We've been unable to find any traces of explosives or evidence of any debris from any tech."

I let a smile slowly spread across my face, drawing out the silence.

He chuckled. "You're not going to tell me, are you?"

"Sorry," I answered. "Trade secret."

"As long as you're leveraging those trade secrets for the benefit of Americorp, I think this will be quite a lucrative business relationship indeed."

I nodded with a grin and walked him out.

I might not be able to see the future, but I could at least make sure mine was well-funded.

ACKNOWLEDGEMENTS

First of all, thank you to my local Starbucks baristas, for without their delicious Pumpkin Spice Lattes and convenient wall outlets, this book would never have been completed. Thanks to the very best friends: Gabriel, Esther, and Christi, for dozens of writers retreats and many boozy drinks in hot tubs (which we all know are the best inspiration), and Cassandra, Becca, and my sister Meredith, who don't write but who give great feedback. Thanks to my Pitch Wars class of 2015, for being a great support group and resource. More thanks than I can ever give to K.T. Hanna, my wonderful Pitch Wars mentor, who helped shape this book into its final form. And thank you to my family, especially my two wonderful sons and my long-suffering husband Tim, who has always been there and who never doubted me for a second. I hope you all enjoy my story.

ABOUT THE AUTHOR

Sarah Madsen is an Atlanta-area author and freelance TTRPG writer. A few of her favorite things are gin cocktails, expensive lattes, and romanceable NPCs. When she's not at Starbucks, you can find her on Twitter (@UnfetteredMuse), Facebook (facebook.com/SarahMadsen-Author) or WordPress (unfetteredmuse.com). *Weaver's Folly* is her first novel.

FRIENDS OF FALSTAFF

Thank You to All our Falstaff Books Patrons, who get extra digital content each month! To be featured here and see what other great rewards we offer, go to www.patreon.com/falstaffbooks.

PATRONS

Dino Hicks
John Hooks
John Kilgallon
Larissa Lichty
Travis & Casey Schilling
Staci-Leigh Santore
Sheryl R. Hayes
Scott Norris
Samuel Montgomery-Blinn
Junkle

Made in the USA
Columbia, SC
12 February 2021